MORE PRAISE FOR *KINSHIP OF CLOVER*

"Midway through this wonderful novel, you will find a woman dancing in her wheelchair. That scene is one of many memorable moments in a story about young people organizing for a sustainable future, even as their once-radical elders try to hold on to a gradually disappearing past. This is a book about time and love, politics and family, and it is sharply observant and deeply compassionate."
—CHARLES BAXTER, author of *The Feast of Love*

"Ellen Meeropol brings her keen political sense and psychological understanding to this story of family secrets and family trauma. *Kinship of Clover* is compelling and the characters stay with you long after you've finished the book."
—NANCY FELTON, Broadside Bookshop

"*Kinship of Clover* counters our culture's typically insular fiction. From a teenage girl in a wheelchair experiencing her first romantic relationship, to an older activist suffering from Alzheimer's, to a father adjusting after years in prison, to a young man affected by childhood trauma, to environmentalists worried about global destruction, to biracial characters accepting their heritage, *Kinship of Clover* depicts our diversity. Meeropol's social concerns drive issues that surround these sensitively drawn characters. But the novel's subjects are secondary to the story, one as elaborate and engaging as its ideological undercurrent."
—NAN CUBA, author of *Body and Bread*

"Ellen Meeropol's new novel, *Kinship of Clover*, is a stunning kaleidoscope of humanity, with characters so real and complicated and full of life that you'll want to linger with them over coffee long after the last page is turned. She treats them all with tremendous generosity, but it's her creation of Flo, the feisty revolutionary whose mind is devoured a little more each day by Alzheimer's, who won my heart through and through."
—EMILY CROWE, Odyssey Bookshop

"Ellen Meeropol, writing with heartbreaking truth, clarity, and empathy, illustrates how deeply entwined are the search for justice, the cost society imposes on political beliefs, and the price children can pay for their parents' convictions. *Kinship of Clover* weaves strands of family and friends who go back decades, in connections and beliefs, until you are desperate to see the final fabric. Meeropol had me turning pages deep into the night, forcing me to think, making me cry, and, finally, having me believe in the possibility of a better world. I loved this book."

—RANDY SUSAN MEYERS, author of *Accidents of Marriage*

"This smart, lyrical novel cooks up a cast of quirky characters dealing as best they can with a host of twenty-first–century issues: climate change and biodiversity loss, physical and mental illness, personal tragedy, alternative lifestyles and the enduring love among friends and family. Ellen Meeropol's deep knowledge of the environment, health care, progressive politics and the human heart shines through on every page. A thought-provoking delight to read; I couldn't put it down!"

—JENNIFER BROWDY, PhD, author of *What I Forgot . . . And Why I Remembered: A Journey to Awareness and Activism Through Purposeful Memoir*

"Ellen Meeropol writes with courage and tenderness about characters who are under overwhelming threat. The dangers include a trauma too difficult for a young man to integrate, an activist's fine brain under assault by Alzheimer's, and the destruction of our precious eco-system. Yet even when defeat and disaster seem inevitable, Meeropol weaves a tale full of heart and hope."

—JACQUELINE SHEEHAN, author of *The Center of the World*

kinship of clover

A NOVEL BY

Ellen Meeropol

 Red Hen Press | *Pasadena, CA*

Book design & layout by Selena Trager & Cassidy Trier
Cover leaf icon by Joey Chen from the Noun Project

Library of Congress Cataloging-in-Publication Data

Names: Meeropol, Ellen, author.
Title: Kinship of clover : a novel / Ellen Meeropol.
Description: Pasadena, CA : Red Hen Press, [2017]
Identifiers: LCCN 2016033103 (print) | LCCN 2016054025 (ebook) | ISBN
    9781597093811 (softcover : acd-free paper) | ISBN 9781597095884 (Ebook)
Subjects: LCSH: Botanists—Fiction. | Survival—Fiction. | GSAFD: Science fiction.
Classification: LCC PS3613.E375 K55 2016 (print) | LCC PS3613.E375 (ebook)
    | DDC 813/.6—dc23
LC record available at https://lccn.loc.gov/2016033103

The National Endowment for the Arts, the Los Angeles County Arts Commission, the Dwight Stuart Youth Fund, the Max Factor Family Foundation, the Pasadena Tournament of Roses Foundation, the Pasadena Arts & Culture Commission and the City of Pasadena Cultural Affairs Division, the City of Los Angeles Department of Cultural Affairs, the Audrey & Sydney Irmas Charitable Foundation, Sony Pictures Entertainment, Amazon Literary Partnership, and the Sherwood Foundation partially support Red Hen Press.

First Edition
Published by Red Hen Press
www.redhen.org

ACKNOWLEDGMENTS

I am grateful to the friends and writers who have generously offered their feedback on this book. The women in my manuscript group—Marianne Banks, Kris Holloway-Bidwell, Celia Jeffries, Lydia Kann, Kari Ridge, Patricia Riggs, and Jacqueline Sheehan—read and reread these pages with insight and support. Writer and reader friends offered their knowledge and suggestions; thank you, Liz Goldman, Jane Miller, Nancy Garruba, Kathy Briccetti, and Jane Hill.

Several people lent their expertise in my research about plants. I'm grateful to members of the University of Massachusetts community—Lilly Israel at the Permaculture Garden, Professor of Plant Pathology Daniel Cooley, and science librarian Maxine Schmidt.

I feel incredibly lucky to work again with my publicist Mary Bisbee-Beek, and the talented and passionate team at Red Hen Press, particularly Kate Gale, Mark Cull, Keaton Maddox, and the Trager sisters.

Part of the journey of this book was learning about the science and politics of global warming. I'm grateful to my climate change study group for our readings and discussions. Thank you, Marty Nathan, Robby Meeropol, Elliot Fratkin, Susan Theberge, Rene Theberge, Andrea Ayvazian, and Joel Dansky.

A portion of the book was published in *Writing Fire: An Anthology Celebrating the Power of Women's Words* called "The Girls' Club" (Green Fire Press, Housatonic, Massachusetts, 2015).

As with every book, I am deeply indebted to my family. Robby, Jenn, and Rachel read multiple drafts, offering critical feedback and ongoing encouragement.

for Josie and Abel, in the hope that we can figure out a way to fix this mess and leave a healthy planet to the children of the world

Kinship of Clover

Chapter One

The first time Jeremy saw the plants go crazy was at the cat's funeral, held in the family greenhouse crowded with teas and herbs and medicine-plants growing in pots and flats, their vines spiraling up wooden stakes against the walls. The air was earthy and moist and candles—dozens of them, hundreds maybe—shimmered and the plants danced in the flickering.

Sure, it was weird to have a funeral for a cat, even a cat named after a deity, but Jeremy understood there were many strange things about his family. Like that someone killed Bast and left his body in a carton on the front porch because some people didn't like cults and thought his family was one. Like that there were a bunch of adults and kids in the Pioneer Street house but they weren't organized into families like in library books. He knew that Tim was his twin brother and Francie was his mother and Tian was his dad, but his parents had other kids with other grown-ups and it rarely seemed to matter much who went with who.

What mattered was that things weren't going well for his family.

Even at nine, Jeremy realized that they were mourning more than Bast. The candles and chants were also for his little brother and sister who froze to death the year before in Forest Park. That was another thing about his family: they didn't believe in dwelling on unhappy things. That—and because the small bodies weren't found until summertime and then the cops put his father and Murphy in jail and Pippa had to wear an ankle monitor that didn't let her leave the house—meant that Abby and Terrance never got a proper funeral all their own. So the family members who still lived on Pioneer Street gathered in the greenhouse. They sat on cushions in a circle on the floor, chanting and singing for Bast and their lost babies.

Jeremy leaned back against the leg of the potting table and stared at the candles and the plants. He loved how the leaves in their many perfect shapes and shades of green quivered in the light of the dancing flames. Then the leaves were moving too, undulating and twisting in time to the chanting and the music.

Jeremy poked his twin brother's shoulder and pointed at the dancing vines. Tim shook his head and swatted Jeremy's hand away. Recently Tim had been extra mean. He didn't want to be a twin any more, he said, and he wouldn't talk about it. He refused the identical clothes Francie brought home. Jeremy loved the tangible connections to Tim, so he wore undershirts or socks that matched Tim's, items that didn't show.

No way would Tim want to talk about plants that moved impossibly all on their own.

Jeremy watched the plants swing and sway and spin for several minutes before the next thing happened. When the stems and branches and leaves reached out to him, he was halfway expecting it. Green vines circled his arms and slid under his shirt and skimmed along his back. Soft stems tickled his neck with their delicate suckers. He thought he heard a broad, red-veined leaf whisper in his ear. "We have names," it sounded like, but he knew plants couldn't talk. Soon they were burrowing under his skin and inside his body and as he patted the cardboard box with Bast buried in it, his hands left fern-prints in the moist dirt.

Jeremy was surprised but not afraid. The plants felt familiar, comforting even, and they connected him to all the plants and animals growing on the earth, then and forever, and he liked it. He thought maybe he'd like to learn their names, for when the plants visited again.

They didn't return for eleven years.

~~~

Eleven years later, Jeremy carried the news clipping about his father's release tucked in his wallet between his UMass student ID and a creased photo of his little brother and sister. The article was three weeks old, from the Springfield newspaper's Friends and Neighbors section, which was pretty ironic since their neighbors said a loud chorus of good riddance when Tian Williams was sentenced to prison.

Nobody on campus asked Jeremy if he was related to the Francine Beaujolais mentioned in the article. Few people knew his last name and they were unlikely to connect the quasi-nerdy botany major with an ex-convict cult leader. Tian was released just before February break and Jeremy spent a few days in his parents' apartment. His father was so different and his presence after ten years so unreal that Jeremy checked the article at least once a day for confirmation.

Like tonight, walking across campus to the radio station in the middle of the night. He tried to picture his parents in their apartment twenty-seven miles to the south, but no images came. He paused in the well-lit protection of a campus bus stop to open the fragile folds of newsprint, and read the short paragraph yet again.

> After serving almost ten years at the State Correctional Institution at Cedar Junction, city resident Sebastian Williams was released on parole. Williams was convicted in June 2005 of multiple charges, including criminal negligence in the deaths of his daughter and a male child associated with a cult located on Pioneer Street in the Forest Park neighborhood. Neither Williams nor his common law wife Francine Beaujolais was available for comment.

~~~

Even with the stop, Jeremy was right on time for his program and the DJ on the board was running predictably late. He glared at her through the glass and pointed at the wall clock; she held up her index finger, signaling him to chill. Sure, it was only a college radio station in the middle of the night—probably six students listening out there and five of them sucking on a hookah—but even so, people should take pride in their work and stick to the schedule.

Why should he care so much? His radio show started as a six-week community education project about endangered species for his fall semester biodiversity class. He aced the course, but when it ended he didn't want to stop. The station manager said no one else wanted that time slot, so he trekked to the dingy studio at the edge of campus at 2:00 a.m. every Wednesday morning to broadcast a half hour of lament into the empty winter sky.

The DJ finally finished. Jeremy sat at the control board, switched on the mic, and started the Missa Luba CD. Each week he chose different music to play softly in the background, ranging from Erik Satie to Billy Bragg. His dad had played Missa Luba a lot when he and Tim were little, before their family fell apart. The combination of joy and despair in the Congolese rhythms matched his mood these days.

He took a deep breath and launched into his introductory remarks.

"You're listening to Plants in Peril," he began. "There are three stages of peril: Threatened means that the species is vulnerable, declining in numbers. Endangered means that the numbers are critically low, and if nothing is done, the species will soon be extinct. Extinct species . . ." He paused to swallow, to soothe the sharp ache in his throat. "Extinct species have completely disappeared from the earth, with no hope of recovery."

Each week he varied the approach, listing plants alphabetically or by continent, by when they were last observed in nature, occasionally showcasing a favorite Order or Family. Tonight was special; he had researched background details about the extinct instead of just a list of names to read.

Jeremy knew the show was peculiar even before his brother visited and listened to a broadcast, stretched out half-asleep on the sagging studio sofa. "That was truly weird," Tim said as they walked back to the dorm. "Why would anyone listen to you read the names of plants they've never heard of and will never see?"

"That's the point," Jeremy said. "If I don't say their names, no one will remember them."

"That's creepy," Tim said.

Jeremy shrugged. I don't want them to die alone, he thought but didn't say.

"You're pathetic," Tim added. That was a brother for you and besides, Tim was a business major, so you couldn't expect him to care about the universe of vanishing vegetable matter.

"*Begonia eiromischa,*" Jeremy continued, "was discovered in 1886 in Palau. But its forest habitat was cleared for agricultural cultivation and no sightings have been reported in over a century."

Even after six months, he was amazed by the way his voice was transformed by its journey from microphone to soundboard, altered by radio waves and electronics and headphones, and returned to his ears exposed and new. The first week of the program he had been astonished to hear alien emotions threaded through his words—sentiments that he hadn't known he felt and barely recognized. Now he listened to discover his feelings and in the past three weeks, since his father's release, his voice sounded poised at the edge of tears.

Tonight, the tears threatened to spill over.

"Bigleaf scurfpea, or *Orbexilum macrophyllum,* was formerly found in Indiana and Kentucky." He savored how the Latin names balanced on his tongue, draped across his teeth, and fell from his lips. He didn't speak the language, but he was fluent in its elegies.

"Next we have *Thismia americana* from Illinois. Last seen in 1916 and declared extinct in 1995." He felt a particular kinship with this plant and his voice thickened with sorrow. *Thismia* was declared extinct the year he and Tim were born, delivered by midwife into a greenhouse filled with his family and growing plants. He grew up playing in the foliage, digging in the soil while the women of the family watered and harvested the plants and dried the leaves for tea. His drawings of spearmint and raspberry leaves, of *Camellia sinensis sinensis* and *Camellia sinensis assamica*, had decorated the walls of their house and of the nearby Tea Room. Studying the plants came much later, a concession to his mother's demand for a major that could lead to a job.

"*Vanvoorstia bennettiana*, a.k.a. Bennett's Seaweed." He paused to blow his nose on the bandanna stuffed in his jeans pocket. "First collected in 1855 in Sydney Harbor, Australia. Declared extinct in 2003 due to habitat loss secondary to trawling. Dredging. Infrastructure development." His voice rose with each assault of civilization and broke on the last word. "Settlement. Tourism. Recreation. Fisheries. Agriculture. Sewage."

He rummaged through the sketchbooks in his backpack. Somewhere he had a pen and ink drawing of Bennett's, one of the first assignments in his Botanical Drawing course. He could picture the algae: rusty reddish and lacy, the deep veins so heartbreakingly delicate, so vulnerable. The Kyrie ended and the on-air silence surprised him. He quickly located the dog-eared page in the IUCN Red List and read aloud from their comments on the vanquished *Vanvoorstia*: "There is no reasonable doubt that the last individual of this species has died."

He couldn't help how his voice turned the last word into a keening. Or how the wail in his mouth vibrated with the vines that sprouted without warning from the control board, from his backpack, from the stack of CDs on the table, from his own fingertips. The vines weren't real—he knew that—they couldn't really be *Vanvoorstia bennettiana* or *Rafflesia borneensis*—but they were perfectly accurate and they looked real. They felt real too, as they curled around his wrists, tucked shiny leaves into the crook of his elbows, pushed small sucker mouths into the skin of his upper arms. One thick shoot sprouting lacy algae leaves slithered up his arms and looped twice around his neck, snug but not tight.

The studio door opened a few inches, startling Jeremy. His time couldn't be up already. The manager was rarely in the studio this late, but there she was, hair sticking out as if she'd been rousted out of bed. Did she sleep at the station? She spread her arms in a what's-going-on gesture. Jeremy smiled and gave her a thumbs up, it's-all-right response before returning to his notebooks. Somewhere he had an image of the Saint Helena Olive flower—miniature white trumpets with fuchsia gullets—that he drew from a photograph of the precious last living specimen. There it was!

"*Nesiota elliptica* was a small tree endemic to the island of Saint Helena in the southern Atlantic." His voice deepened and his words became a requiem. "Threatened by timbering, plantation development, and the introduction of goats into their habitat, the last wild specimen died in 1994. A few cuttings survived in cultivation."

The ruby-throated white trumpets budded and their annihilated blossoms flowered from the bones of his knuckles. He cleared his throat and pushed the words through, one by one. "Despite extensive efforts to rejuvenate the species, the last surviving St. Helena Olive seedling succumbed to a fungal infection in December 2003 and the St. Helena Olive Tree was declared extinct."

The door opened again and this time a security guard followed the station manager into the studio. The manager's face and her wrap-it-up gesture left no room for discussion: the program was over. He stumbled over the station identification, then punched in the underwriting message and two PSAs before switching off the mic.

Exhaustion and something else—relief maybe, mixed with sorrow—flooded over him. He stood and rubbed his eyes with both hands, surprised to find his cheeks wet. The station manager took the headset.

"That's enough for tonight," she said, her voice kind. "This program is over."

"Were you listening?" he asked.

"No." She took his seat at the control board. "The night shift security guard at the University Ave post called me. He was worried about you."

Jeremy glanced at the guard. It was strange, given the circumstances, but he was pleased that someone listened, even if the guard was only moved to rat him out.

The security guard gripped Jeremy's upper arm and led him outside. "Sorry, man," the guard said, "but your roll call of extinction was majorly scary."

"It's okay." Jeremy tried to twist away. "I'm fine now."

"Sure. But I'm taking you over to Health Services. They'll check you out."

"Not necessary. I'm fine." And he was. The vines were gone, and the tiny white trumpet flowers.

The security guard looked dubious.

"Really," Jeremy said, giving the guard his best smile and a fist bump. "I'm cool."

The guard tightened his grip on Jeremy's arm. "Okay, you're cool, but you're still going to Health Services. We got liability, you know?"

The nurse practitioner had hoped to devote the last three hours of her shift to her backlog of paperwork. Shaking off fatigue, she waved the guard out of the exam room and hesitated in the doorway. Wondering how her new patient came to have *café con leche* skin with such blond curls, she smiled and introduced herself as Patty.

Jeremy liked that she used her first name, and that she didn't wear a white coat, just a mustard-colored sweater the exact shade of a cat his family had when he was little. He liked that they sat next to each other on chairs instead of him perching on the crinkly paper on the exam table. She asked questions, her voice all silk-spoken and cushioned with concern like his mom's, before everything went sour. Patty was about his mom's age too, and just as pretty.

"Why am I here?" he asked.

"Because people are concerned. Something happened during your radio program?"

He was too surprised to answer. Could other people see the vines too?

"Your program? It's about plants?"

"All these species are disappearing and people don't seem to care." Jeremy shrugged. "I can't stop thinking about it."

"You're a biology major?"

"Botany. Plants and flowers. Trees, too. They're so intricate when you really look at them. Amazing and so perfectly designed—whorls and ferns, branching and spirals—expressing Fibonacci numbers." His voice trailed into silence as he recognized the blank look on the nurse practitioner's face. Didn't medical people study science?

"How do you hope people will feel when they listen to your program?"

Jeremy snorted. "I doubt if anyone listens, unless it's just background noise to studying or getting laid. Nobody gives a hoot about the plants and that really bothers me."

"What would you like your radio program to accomplish?"

"I don't know exactly. The security guy called it a roll call of extinction and I like that. I want people to acknowledge what's happening and to feel something."

"What do you feel?"

"Sad," he said. "Respectful. See, it's like a vigil, a deathbed."

"Can you tell me what happened tonight?"

No way. They'd never let him out. "It's hard to explain. I felt incredibly connected to the extinct plants I was describing. That's all. It's no big deal. I just got carried away."

"Has anything like this happened before?"

He shook his head. Not for many years, anyway, and that was none of her business.

"You seem to care very deeply. I'm wondering if you use alcohol or other substances to help you handle your feelings."

"Nah. A beer every once in a while. For fun, not to handle anything."

"Anything else you'd like to tell me?"

She wasn't so bad and for a split-second he wanted to describe the vines, how they'd wrapped around him, hugged him so close, burrowed into him. Nope, not a good idea. Then she'd really think he was pathetic, or nuts. *Was* he nuts?

"Nothing else," he said.

She paused, then asked softly. "Do you feel sad enough, angry enough, to hurt yourself?"

"It's not like that. I don't think so, anyway." It was his turn to hesitate. Sometimes he pictured molecules from all the dead plants of the planet circulating through his arteries and veins, red blood cells mirroring the whorls and spirals of once-vital blooms. He imagined himself hemorrhaging their extinctions.

"Do you sometimes think about hurting yourself?" she asked again.

He didn't have to. The dead plants were exsanguinating him.

"No," he said. "What I think about is how do you stand it when you care about something so much and you can't make it better. I mean, what do you do?"

"What would you like to do?"

"Wave a magic wand and make it better." He grinned. "That's crazy, isn't it?"

She smiled too. "Not crazy. Wouldn't it be great if we could do that? But we can't, and this seems to make you very unhappy. I'm wondering how I can help you."

"I don't need help. I'm fine. Just let me go home and I promise, no more radio program."

"Fair enough. How about we call your roommate, so you're not alone tonight?"

"I have a single." He twirled a long strand of curl around his finger. He needed a haircut, one of the many things he'd let slide this semester.

"What about your parents?"

Right, Jeremy thought. Calling Francie and Tian at 3:00 a.m. would make a bewildering situation so much worse. His mom would be at work, in the middle of her night shift on the medical center switchboard. His dad would be wandering the four-room flat, snapping rubber bands against his wrist and unable to fall asleep until Francie got home. No way Tian would be able to keep his cool with Health Services, with any bureaucracy.

So he lied. "They live in Springfield, but I can't reach them. They're in Europe."

"I'd feel better knowing you're with a family member. Grandparent? Brother or sister?"

He shook his head.

"How about a girlfriend, a buddy?"

There was no one. Not even a cat. He was pathetic. Especially when you think what a big and glorious family he had before his dad went to prison and their commune fell apart.

"There's my twin brother," he said. "But he lives four hours away."

He and Tim Skyped every Sunday. Jeremy always felt better watching the image of Tim's dumbo ears sticking out from the tight blond curls they both inherited from their parents' racial mix, except that Tim was a business major and cut his hair so short the curls were irrelevant. The warm twin feeling rarely lasted through the week. Besides, Tim had moved to Brooklyn to get away from them all. The thought of Patty calling his brother made Jeremy's chest feel squirrelly with shame. Tim already thought he was a loser.

"Do I have your permission to talk to your brother?" she asked. "I don't think you should be alone right now. And I think you could benefit from talking to someone, a counselor. Perhaps even some medication. May I give you a referral?"

Jeremy stood up. "No, no, and no," he said. "Thanks for everything, but I'm fine. I just want to go back to my dorm. I have a lot of stuff to do."

"What is more important than taking care of yourself?" Patty asked.

"Our planet is dying, a holocaust of plant species. Isn't that pretty important?"

Patty nodded. "Yes, it is. But right now, I think that your mental health has to take priority over politics."

"You don't get it," Jeremy said. "This isn't political. I'm just sad about the plants."

"I think I understand how strongly you feel about the plants and I'm concerned that you're so upset tonight. I'd really like to contact your brother." She handed him a clipboard with a release form, and then a business card. "You can call me any time, if you need to talk."

Jeremy sighed. "Okay, okay. Call Tim. But he won't be able to come. And it's no big deal. I just get upset sometimes."

Patty was quiet for a few seconds, then spoke in a soft voice. "Is that why you're crying?"

Jeremy touched his cheek and looked at the glistening wet on his finger.

~~~

When the phone rang, Tim was dreaming about the long-necked girl who sat in front of him in macroeconomics class. The phone display read 3:13 a.m., which meant it had to be bad news. Probably about his dad, whose transition from prison to home had been rough. His mom was chronically stressed trying to buy food and pay rent and two college tuitions and now deal with Tian too.

"Is this Timothy Beaujolais?" asked a woman's voice.

"Yeah. Who're you? What's wrong?"

"My name is Patty Longwood. I'm a nurse practitioner at Health Services at UMass. Your brother Jeremy was brought in this evening. He's emotionally distraught and I don't think he should be alone."

"Distraught? What's wrong with him?"

"He became agitated during a radio broadcast."

"The dead plants thing, right? Jeremy is totally obsessed with that shit."

"Yes, he's talking about extinct plants, but I wonder if there are other issues. He's vague about whether or not he might hurt himself." She paused. "Jeremy says your parents are out of the country and you're his only other relative."

Out of the country? Their parents might be out of touch, but as far as Tim knew they were in their second floor apartment on Sumner Avenue.

Francie was likely at work, but he doubted that Tian had left the apartment in three weeks except to check in with his parole officer.

And no way was Jeremy suicidal. A little too sensitive, that's what their mom always said. Jeremy was two minutes older but Tim was the practical one. Jeremy's problem was that stupid radio program. One night when Tim was home for winter break, Jeremy dragged him down to the station. Reading those long Latin names, Jeremy acted like he was transported to a scene of carnage someplace far away, like Rwanda or Syria or Tiananmen Square.

"So, can you come get him?" the nurse practitioner asked. "He shouldn't be alone."

"You mean tonight? I'm in Brooklyn. I have classes tomorrow," Tim said. "There's no train until morning."

The nurse practitioner's sigh slid into silence. Tim tried to banish the mental image of Jeremy in the locked ward of some hospital, medicated up the wazoo, rocking back and forth and wondering why Tim broke their pledge.

They made the pledge the summer they were ten, the first time Francie took them to visit their dad in prison. Sitting in the family visiting room, Tian had been so remote he could have been carved of ebony, and tears wandered down Francie's cheeks to darken her T-shirt. The twins sat close together at the scarred visiting room table, whispering about X-Men characters until Francie told them to cut it out, didn't they want to talk with their dad?

By then, most members of the commune had deserted the big house on Pioneer Street. In the back seat of the old van driving home to Springfield from the prison, Jeremy and he promised each other that no matter how weird their parents were, no matter what the other adults in the commune did, the two of them would always be strong for each other. No matter what.

"Okay," he told the nurse practitioner. "I'll catch the morning train."

Chapter Two

This could be called a tale of two families, two oddly configured groupings of quasi-kin still living in the old city neighborhood bordering Forest
Park, in the shadow of the life-altering events that bound them together
eleven years earlier. After all they went through, you might think that the
two families would have stayed close, but it didn't work out that way. Every once in a while they would catch a glimpse of each other at the farmers market at the X, but they fingered the kale or sniffed the cantaloupe
and pretended not to notice.

Jeremy and Tim were nine when their world imploded. After the
deaths and the trial, their father went to prison and their mother had to
move them from their big house on Pioneer Street to a small apartment
on Sumner. The other commune members scattered except for Pippa
and Jeremy's mom pretty much blamed Pippa for the whole mess. She
said that Pippa crossed over to the other side when she took her baby and
moved in with Zoe's family, the other family. Jeremy imagined a wide
river with rapids raging between the two homes, instead of four lanes of
traffic on Sumner Avenue.

Zoe was five when her parents and cousin got involved with the twins'
commune and the wrong end of the law. Now, at sixteen, she didn't re-

member much about the upheavals, but she knew the bones of the story and occasionally wondered about it.

"Get on with your lives." That's what all the adults told them and that's what the children tried to do.

~~~

Zoe followed her grandmother's patchwork jacket down the frozen food aisle, which didn't take long because Flo scorned processed food of all varieties.

"You know they freeze out all the vitamins," Flo said every single week. "And canned is no better. Veggies got to be fresh. You remember that." Flo pointed her cane at Zoe to emphasize her point. Then she jabbed it at the golden mane of a lion on the cardboard cover of a frozen dinner, something about king-of-the-jungle sized portions.

"Lions' noses darken as they age," Flo said. "Like old people turning gray."

That didn't quite follow, but Zoe nodded, glancing at Flo's hair, fly-away wild and iron-gray. "Not silver," Flo liked to say. "It's the color of steel and just as strong." Flo liked to watch nature shows and often shared random snippets of information like changes in elderly lions' noses. Interesting, even if not always relevant to the conversation. Flo was smart and funny and blunt, and if her outspoken opinions sometimes got her in trouble, well, then Zoe knew where her own big mouth came from. When her dad offered her an after-school job to help her grandmother, she jumped at the chance to earn some money. "It might not be all fun and games," Sam had warned. "Ma can be a . . . handful."

Three days a week, Zoe took the city bus from the high school to Flo's apartment. Mondays she did Flo's laundry, laying out matching outfits on the dresser top, labeled with post-it notes for the day of the week, and made sure Flo got to the Y for yoga. After practice on Fridays, she met Flo and Sam for an early dinner, then helped Flo vacuum the apartment.

Wednesdays she took Flo grocery shopping. Or, Flo took her, Zoe thought as she steered her wheelchair behind her grandmother's cart in her never-varying path through the store. The demented leading the disabled—that was how Zoe liked to describe grocery shopping with Flo to her friends. The produce section was always last, so Flo's fruits and veggies didn't get squished. That's where they spent most of their time, Flo squeezing avocados for perfect ripeness.

That Wednesday was no different. The avocados were all either petrified or mush and Flo abandoned them, glaring at the woman restocking the produce shelves. Moving on to the lettuce, Flo held a bunch of red leaf in each hand, examining them for who-knows-what and comparing who-cares-what. Chill, Zoe told herself, wondering what her best friend Xander was doing at that moment. They'd been tight since kindergarten when the teacher assigned seats alphabetically by first name, and the two of them shared the back table with Vanessa, while Ashley and Brianna and Dylan got all the attention. Xander was at the library working on their group project for civics class and she wished she were there too.

Finally one lettuce ended up in the cart, the other tossed back on the slanting pile. "You think she's eating a balanced diet?" her father frequently asked. Zoe always nodded, but really she had no idea what Flo did with the bok choy and beets and speckled radishes. Like, what did Flo eat for breakfast or lunch? She never bought cereal or bread for sandwiches.

But that was Flo's business, right? She seemed pretty healthy for an old woman. "Your grandma's not that old," Sam liked to remind Zoe, but Flo seemed ancient to her. Anyway, Zoe hated having people in *her* face, nagging about what she ate, watching her weight, the dangers of fried foods and trans fats. Flo made it this far. Hadn't she earned the right to run her own life?

At the extra-wide checkout line, Zoe hung back while Flo arranged her prizes on the moving belt, lining them up from heaviest to lightest, from indestructible to most fragile. She handed the cashier her colorful collection of cotton bags with the logos from every nonprofit she supported, from public radio to the survival center, civil liberties to Occupy Wall Street.

"What's he doing?" Flo asked Zoe.

"Who?"

"That young man who is supposed to be bagging my food."

"He's texting."

"Why isn't he doing his job?"

"He will. Be patient." Pretty funny, Zoe thought, *her* telling someone to be patient.

Zoe handed the reward card to the cashier and sent an urgent mental message to the bagger. He looked vaguely familiar. Maybe he went to her school? If he knew what was good for him, he'd stop texting and pack Flo's food. Very carefully.

"Young man." Flo wasn't waiting for the completion of his text or receipt of Zoe's mind memo. "Stop that foolishness and do your job."

Zoe maneuvered her wheelchair around Flo and opened the NPR bag for the Fuji apples. The bagger glanced up, frowned, and returned to his phone. Zoe couldn't decide between broccoli and unripe pears—which was more fragile? Finally the bagger slipped his phone into the shirt pocket with Kenny stitched in purple and took the decision from her hands. He packed the broccoli and pears on top of the apples and then slipped Flo's perfect lettuce into the Occupy bag.

The bagger's phone buzzed. One-handed, he took it from his pocket and punched an icon. Eyes on the small screen, he added bananas to the bag and reached for three large sweet onions.

Zoe slid the credit card through the slot while transmitting another message to Kenny's brain: No, you don't want to do that. Please. Why didn't the cashier stop him?

"Young man!" Flo's voice was loud. "You just put my lettuce on the bottom of the bag. Didn't anyone teach you how to pack food properly? Your mother, doesn't she make salads? Shmushed lettuce is no goddamn good!"

Flo was working up to a fury.

Kenny the bagger threw her a look more mocking than contrite. He didn't rescue the lettuce from the assault of the onions. Eyes still on his phone, he held up his other hand and backed up two steps. Which was clearly more than Flo could bear, because she reached across the counter, grabbed an onion, and threw it hard at Kenny.

He ducked.

Someone—the dementia surveillance team?—must have been watching through the one-way glass upstairs. Within seconds a manager, a security guard, and three other adolescent baggers crowded around their station. By then, Flo had the second onion poised and ready to fly. The security guard gripped Flo's arm and moved her out of the aisle. The other baggers elbowed Kenny and made jokes. The manager gathered their bags and pushed Zoe's wheelchair to follow Flo and the guard.

"Get your cotton-picking hands off my chair," Zoe said, then mentally slapped herself. She'd picked up the phrase from her mom and it materialized on her tongue whenever she was furious, even though Flo insisted it was racist. But the manager was white, so it was okay this time, wasn't it?

In a small office tucked behind the Employee of the Month display board, the security guard escorted Flo to a chair in the corner, across from the manager's desk. Zoe maneuvered her wheelchair next to her grandmother. The guard stood at the door, arms crossed over her chest. The manager sat at his desk. He looked from Flo to Zoe and back.

"Would you like to tell me what happened out there?" he asked Flo.

"He was doing that thing with his phone . . ."

"Texting," Zoe added.

". . . instead of doing his job." Flo flashed Zoe a look that clearly said *Keep out of this.* "Then he shmushed my lettuce." She leaned back, having made her case.

"I'll deal with Kenny," the manager said. "He shouldn't have been texting. However, violence against our employees—for any reason—will not be tolerated. Besides," the manager added, pointing at Flo, "I remember you. This is not the first time you've been abusive to one of my staff."

Not the first time? Zoe looked at Flo. Maybe Sam was right about Flo starting to lose her marbles.

The manager turned to Zoe. "Who is responsible for this woman?"

"I'm not a child." Flo was yelling again. "I'm in charge of myself."

"I'm sorry," the manager said, standing up. "Either a responsible adult comes to deal with this woman or I notify the police."

"Call the pigs." Flo crossed her arms. "I'm not scared of them."

"Please don't do that," Zoe said, pulling her phone from her pocket. "I'll call my dad."

～～～

Elbows planted on the windowsill, chin resting on both hands, Sam stared out the second floor window toward the street. When Zoe was little, he waited in this position every afternoon for the Special Ed bus to pull up at the curb. If the driver had to honk twice, if Zoe's mother Anna or cousin Emily didn't quickly appear on the sidewalk, he would fly down the outside stairs and score some extra time with his daughter.

His phone chimed Zoe's song and her photo flashed on the screen. Sam grinned. It was the oddest thing how Zoe always seemed to know when he was thinking about her and chose that moment to call. Usually she needed a ride or extension of her curfew, but still.

"Zey, Hoey," he said. "At's whup?"

Spoonerisms were the way he first connected with his daughter outside of Anna's maternal realm. For years the silly switching of the first letters of words was their secret language. Now that Zoe lived with him, he longed for the simple bond of those days when Anna did all the real parenting—the limit-setting and three-meals-a-day and doctors' appointments. In those days, he was the fun parent.

Zoe ignored the spoonerism game. "Come quick. Grandma's in big trouble."

It was Zoe he was used to worrying about. Her bones were fragile— would she fall and break something? Or get an infection that could destroy her kidneys? Or—worst of all—would her shunt fail? He tiptoed through fatherhood, atoning for his initial inability to parent a baby born with a glistening red sack of spinal cord and nerves on her back, a baby who was whisked off to surgery before he got a chance to count her toes or kiss her downy head.

A baby he had initially wanted Anna to abort.

But after the first ruined year—even his ex-wife had to admit it—his parenting made up for lost time. So when Zoe was twelve and fighting constantly with her mother amid the chaos of the overcrowded downstairs apartment, his girl moved in with him, claiming the bedroom he had always kept ready for her overnight visits.

Now he worried even more. Zoe had rejected the crutches in favor of a wheelchair so he had fewer worries about falls. There were still so many other medical perils and he had to be vigilant about all the potential adolescent dangers lurking out there to hurt or tempt his beautiful girl.

Driving to the grocery store, Sam tried to identify the stew of emotions he'd heard in Zoe's voice. Her words crackled at the edge of tears, heavy with worry and fury, guilt mixed with I-can't-do-this-any-more. Or was he projecting his own feelings on Zoe? For months he'd been monitoring his mother's falterings, recording the memory lapses, cataloging the blank-faced moments of drifting someplace else, listing the incidents of objects placed in the very wrong place—reading glasses in the freezer, a magazine balanced on the rim of the open toilet, a half-empty glass of water in the oven. Most likely it's Alzheimer's, her doctor suggested. With his dad long gone, his ex-wife busy with her own life, and no siblings, Sam had no one to share the worries. Except Zoe.

Turning into the parking lot, Sam parked in a handicapped spot and jogged into the store. He knew exactly where the security office was located. Knocking on that door, his face flushed with the heat of shame. In sixth grade, he and a buddy got caught stealing comic books at this store. That time, Flo bailed him out and agreed not to tell his dad. This time, *she* sat in the hot seat across from the manager, hugging herself, her gray hair a chaotic halo. This time he was the responsible adult.

"Sam Tobin." He introduced himself to the manager, then turned to his family. "Are you guys okay? Zoe, Ma?"

"They're fine," the store manager said. "Kenny is the one who was assaulted."

"He's fine too," Zoe said. "Flo threw an onion at him, but she missed."

"He deserved it," Flo said. "He shmushed my lettuce."

Sam arranged a suitably stern expression on his face, then turned to the manager. "I'm very sorry for the trouble. May I take my mother home?"

"Certainly. If she apologizes to the employee and promises it won't happen again."

"Ma?" he asked, wondering what happened to the customer is always right.

Flo's face could no longer camouflage her emotions. She was tickled pink with herself. She'd been pleased with Sam that day with the comic books too. "Stealing is wrong," she lectured him on the way home. "But toeing other people's lines your whole life is worse." That's when he figured out—at age eleven—that he wasn't being raised to have a regular, nine-to-five life. Flo certainly never lived that life. She was her own boss, recording narration for progressive television programs and left-wing videos and indie documentaries. Until the year before when one of her long-term clients called with concerns about her mental status, and Sam had to close the business.

The store manager tapped his finger on the desk but Flo didn't offer an apology. Sam gestured to the manager to follow him into the hallway.

"I apologize for my mother," Sam said. "She probably doesn't remember that she threw the onion. She has Alzheimer's." The words stung and burned. He hadn't yet shared the medical diagnosis with Zoe or Anna; this was the first time he said them out loud.

The manager's face softened. "I'm sorry to hear that, but—"

"I know. I'll make sure nothing like this happens again."

Walking out of the store a few minutes later behind Zoe's chair, Flo striding ahead with her cane, Sam had no idea how he could keep that promise. They could shop at a different grocery, but the competition's baggers were not likely to be more respectful of lettuce.

Face facts, he told himself. Flo was only seventy-three, awfully young for dementia, but the symptoms were getting worse, and quickly. He had to consider moving her someplace where she could get the care and supervision she needed. Even if she agreed, it wouldn't be easy to find a place where she would fit in, with her big mouth and her Stalinist politics. With Flo, the dementia might be the easy part.

Chapter Three

Tim and Jeremy dozed during most of the trip to Manhattan. More accurately, they each faked sleeping so they wouldn't have to talk. There's something about traveling on a train, the rocking motion maybe, that makes a person feel invisible and outside of time. It invites introspection, and so each brother, wrapped in his cloak of pseudo-slumber, privately dissected the events of the last fourteen hours. Neither shared their suspicion that the plan of bringing Jeremy to Brooklyn was unwise, that maybe they should have called their parents. No, that felt like a last resort and they weren't there yet. The train arrived at Penn Station during evening rush hour.

Trying to follow Tim's zigzag path through the crowd, Jeremy felt minuscule and utterly insignificant in the crowded space. Staring at the circles of lights on the ceiling, he bumped into a spiky-haired woman standing in the middle of the concourse yelling into her phone.

"Sorry," he mumbled, hurrying to catch up with his brother.

"You *got* to keep up," Tim said. "I have a class tonight." He grabbed for Jeremy's duffle bag, but Jeremy pulled it back.

They ran down the stairs to the subway. Tim swiped his Metro card for Jeremy, who held his duffle high above his head, and they pushed through the turnstile just in time to slip through the closing doors. ℕ seats were available on the Shuttle or on the Brooklyn-bound 5. Jeremy grasped the pole with one hand and hugged his duffle with the other. He closed his eyes. Once his body found the rhythm, it was soothing to stand jammed in so tight with these strangers, swaying back and forth to the clacking pulse of the train. He could imagine falling asleep with the rocking and the singsong phrases from the speakers and the gently blinking colors of the stations lit up in a line on the wall.

Except that the lit-up station names didn't correspond to the static-blurred PA system announcements.

"What's with that?" He nudged Tim, pressed against his right shoulder, and pointed to the display.

"That's for the 2 train," Tim said. "To the Bronx."

"But how would you know where to get off, if you were a stranger?"

Tim grinned. "If you were a stranger, you'd be fucked."

In Brooklyn the crowd thinned and they found seats. A woman on the opposite bench was reading a paperback novel, the slim fancy kind English majors carried. Jeremy couldn't see the title but the author photo on the back cover was a match for the woman reading the book. An artsy black-and-white pose, but clearly her. He considered pointing it out to Tim, the author reading her own book, sharing a brotherly moment of scorn at her expense. But he didn't. If he ever accomplished something like that, wrote a book or had a show of his drawings or saved some plant species, he'd want to show it off too. At the moment achieving anything of importance seemed increasingly unlikely. If he blew this semester, he might never even graduate.

"Tim," he said. "I really appreciate you coming to the rescue, but what about my classes?" He already missed botany lab, Professor Clarke's eloquent lectures about biodiversity loss, his single room dusty with drying plants and sketchbooks, the radio station hush in the wee hours. "What am I supposed to do in Brooklyn?"

Tim looked down at his lap. "I don't know. Homework, maybe? Drawing? Or just take a leave of absence and chill."

Leave of absence? How many species would disappear while he chilled in Brooklyn? A white-capped wave of anxiety broke against Jeremy's chest. "*Orbexilum macrophyllum,*" he murmured. "*Nesiota elliptica. Begonia eiromischa. Camellia sinensis.*"

Tim gave him a nervous look and stood up. "Next stop is ours."

Tim hated it when Jeremy started chanting his pathetic dirge of dead plants. He couldn't remember when it started. Sometime in high school, Tim thought. What if his bro freaked out again, like whatever happened last night that landed him in Health Services? Would this be like the months of not-eating and barely-talking that their mom went through when Tian first went to prison? Or like Tian's creepy post-prison habit of wearing a mess of rubber bands on his wrist and snapping them all day? This freak-out stuff must be genetic, so how long would Tim be safe? Like Jeremy, he inherited the same peculiar mix of Tian's dark skin and Francie's blond hair, but so far—knock on wood—he had avoided the nutty genes.

Still, Tim didn't get why Jeremy went all convulsive about dying flowers. If he cared so much about the health of the planet, he should major in something useful, like business or even medicine. Tim's economics professor said that global warming wasn't even real, just a commie plot to destabilize the fossil fuel companies.

Why on Earth had he invited Jeremy home with him?

Not only that, but Jeremy had asked a damn good question on the train, Tim thought as they trudged up the stone stairs at Borough Hall. What *was* Jeremy going to do with himself? Tim hadn't thought beyond the fact that his apartment-mate got a last-minute opportunity to study in Spain for the semester, so the second bedroom was empty and paid for. Maybe Jeremy just needed a few weeks away from all those science labs and his dying species obsession. Spring was coming. He could sit bare-chested in the Japanese garden at the Botanical Gardens, commune with nature and contemplate his navel until he was ready to resume real life. The image made Tim laugh out loud.

"What's so funny?" Jeremy asked.

Tim guided them around the corner onto Court Street. Jeremy probably wouldn't be amused by his fantasy. "I was just thinking that Brooklyn has these awesome Botanical Gardens. You could hang out there. And you could, maybe, you know, get some plants for the apartment. Make it look nice."

Jeremy's reaction was visceral and unmistakable. Tim held up his hand, acknowledging his mistake, but Jeremy said it anyway. "It's not about prettying up the house like, what's-her-name, Martha Stewart. It's about whole species of living organisms disappearing from the Earth forever. That's huge, you know?"

"I know," Tim said. "Sorry." He brushed his hand over his close-cropped hair. "We've got barber shops too. You could get a haircut."

Ten blocks later, Tim unlocked the apartment door and kicked his backpack out of the way so they could enter. He had lucked into this primo rental because the owner desperately needed help keeping the accounts of the bookstore downstairs. It was a sweet deal—for eight hours of work each week, he got a two-bedroom apartment. His roommate's rent paid most of his other expenses. Tim could afford to help his brother.

"That's your room to the left." Tim pointed down the hallway and scooped up his backpack. "Got to run. My macro professor actually takes attendance. Help yourself to food—there's cereal, milk, potato chips, maybe some peanut butter. Take-out menus on the TV. Or you can wait for me to get home and we'll go out."

Tim hesitated in the doorway. Jeremy looked shell-shocked, still hugging his duffle like a drunken girlfriend who couldn't stand up on her own. Tim wondered if Jeremy had ever had a girlfriend, or if he just loved the female parts of flowers. The pistil, wasn't it? Or the stigma? He blanked on the textbook diagram in his required freshman biology course.

He pointed to Jeremy's duffle. "You can put that thing down. Unpack. Or just sleep. Or go out. Make yourself at home." He tossed the extra set of keys at Jeremy. "Nice catch, bro," Tim said, turning away.

He was late, and he had to get away from Jeremy's dead face. He pulled the apartment door closed behind him with a heavy clunk. He took the stairs two at a time and jogged to the subway. He loved his brother, and there was the pledge and all, but still. What the fuck had he gotten himself into?

꩜

Once he was alone, Jeremy let his duffle thud onto the oak floor and looked around. The apartment was small, but it was neater than he would have expected of Tim. No crushed beer cans or empty pizza boxes like the few off-campus apartments he'd visited at UMass. And it was quiet, no music seeping through thin dorm walls or the thumping of footsteps down the hallway. He missed all that. He wished he were back in his dorm. Or even sitting with Patty and her mustard sweater in the exam room. He dug in his pocket for the business card she'd given him. Maybe he could call. Because, really, what difference did a change of place make? Why should being in Brooklyn slow down the parade of ecological horribles marching across his brain? Why should a different city banish the funeral march of dead plants?

Jeremy knew what his twin was thinking. He could read in the set of Tim's jaw that he was already regretting his invitation. He bet that Tim was thinking about their father, worrying that Jeremy would go all soft too. Tian still looked dangerous, with his grim expression and prison tats, but inside he was boneless, diminished. Jeremy wished he could have inherited his dad's tough looks and his mom's tough insides, but he got only Francie's blond genes and Tian's mush.

Chapter Four

At the toot of the car horn, Flo buttoned her jacket and gathered her pocketbook and cane. She checked the list taped to the apartment door—coffeepot unplugged, cat fed, stove burners off, keys in hand—and let herself out. Damn good thing Mimi still had fully functional gray matter and a driver's license, Flo thought as she maneuvered into the passenger seat, because their Thursday morning group was a lifesaver.

"Quite a brouhaha at Food Castle yesterday," she announced to Mimi.

Flo couldn't wait to tell her friend about the adventure, except that the story kept floating out of reach, like those gently drifting black spots hovering behind her eyeballs. Something about Zoe. There was an onion, and comic books.

"Wait and tell us all at once?" Mimi asked, turning onto Route 5. It was a little longer to the mall this way, but she refused to drive on the highway.

The three other women had claimed their regular places on the blue Coffee Hut sofas, facing each other across a fake-spool coffee table. Fanny and Marlene had their skinny decaf lattés and Claire was sipping her green tea.

"We have to talk about the name of our group," Fanny announced, as she did every week.

"I like the Old Hags' Club," Mimi teased. Flo grinned.

"You ladies may be hags, but I'm not," Claire said.

"We need our drinks before you start," Mimi said. "The regular, Flo?"

Flo nodded and sat down across from Marlene. These women were her best friends in the world. Seven of them met in a consciousness-raising group in 1970. She had just moved to Springfield and was pregnant with Sam. Together they counseled rape victims, protested wars and male privilege, and raised their children—except for Fanny who called herself child-free. They met every Sunday night.

Now in their seventies, after losing two members of their group and several partners, they organized food brigades after a hospital discharge as efficiently as they once planned sit-ins. Their meeting changed to Thursday mornings when several members admitted that they didn't see so well at night. Recently, several of them had lost the leadership of organizations they created. Just last month they listened to Mimi describe how the Board of Directors of the food pantry that she started in her living room four decades earlier had maneuvered her out of her job.

"That's exactly what the women's shelter trustees did to me," Marlene had sloshed her latte with the force of her response. "Can you believe it? After I created the project out of my own broken ribs. Look around the room. We've all been deposed from positions of power in organizations we started."

"Not me," Flo had said.

Mimi leaned over and whispered. "You were kicked out of the Party, remember?"

"That's different," Flo had said.

"Yeah, you didn't *start* the CP."

Now, Mimi handed Flo her Mocha Delight and sat next to her. "Flo has a story to share," she prompted. "About something funny that happened yesterday."

"What about our name?" Fanny said.

Mimi rolled her eyes.

Flo rubbed her chin. Touching a stiff hair, her fingers flew back in time to remember the feel of a stubbly cheek, black hairs that scratched her skin raw. Another lifetime.

Mimi touched her arm. "Flo? About Food Castle?"

Flo shook her head slowly, trying to remember. Did she go to Food Castle? She had to shave those few bristly hairs. Maybe she should add "Shave chin" to the list on her front door, except she would hate for Sam or Zoe to see it.

"Really, we need a name for our group," Fanny insisted. "Something that expresses how much we love each other. You know, and how long we've been together."

"Longer than most marriages," Marlene said.

"It's not only that. It's all we've been through, the losses we've suffered. Our dear husbands." Fanny glanced at Mimi. "Partners, I mean."

Mimi's beloved Joanna had been the most recent death.

"Claire probably wants to call us the Deposed Despots Club." Fanny's voice dripped sarcasm. She still hadn't forgiven Claire's unkind comment about her management style, made just one week after Fanny's previously beloved nephews wrested control of the family law firm.

"Hey," Claire said. "Some of us still work for a living?" Claire worked weekends supervising night shift nurses at a community hospital. She hadn't shared with her friends that the administration had pretty much demolished her benefits when they decreased her hours the year before. "And not all of us are tyrants on the job?"

Flo looked down at her lap. She knew these women so well—how Fanny could be harsh, how Claire's voice climbed into a question at the end of every sentence, making Flo long to chop off the final clause—but in the last few months, Flo often had no clue what they were talking about. That's what she should add to her list: pay closer attention.

"Earth to Flo," Marlene said.

"Never mind," Mimi said. "You can tell us about Food Castle later. You know what I was thinking about last night, when I couldn't sleep?"

"Hey. I saw you on Facebook at 3:24 a.m.," Fanny said.

Mimi ignored the interruption. "How about we organize a rally for International Women's Day next month? Talk about the war and feminism. Like we did two, three, years ago."

"More like ten years ago?" Claire said.

"Whatever." Mimi shrugged. "There's still a war and still plenty of male chauvinism, right? I was thinking about the speech you gave in Yellow Springs, Flo, about child care and the feminist movement. Remember that?"

"Yellow Springs?" Fanny asked.

That, Flo remembered: the feminist-socialist women's conference on the Antioch College campus. "Uh-huh. I was nursing Sam and the conference food collective wouldn't let me have milk with meals. They insisted that milk was just for coffee. Remember that part?"

Mimi laughed. "Do I ever. You got up on stage shirtless, Sammy hanging on your tit, and let them have it about the rights of women to have kids if they wanted to. How children had to be part of our revolution."

"Even the boys." Flo laughed. "What a hoot that was."

That was just one of the reasons Flo loved Mimi so much. Nobody else, not even Sam or Zoe, could remind Flo who she was, beyond the memory lapses and chin hairs. No one else remembered all the demonstrations, all the political meetings, the endless arguments about the primary contradiction and was feminism a bourgeois sidetrack. Being known like that was priceless, like they said on TV. Flo might not remember much these days, but she knew that.

"That's exactly my point." Fanny smacked her hand against the coffee table. "We need a new name for our group, to reflect who we really are."

Who exactly were they? Flo wondered. Who was she?

Chapter Five

Spring came early that year.

Not isn't-this-wonderful early. More like this-isn't-right early. By the spring equinox, the daffodils and hyacinths were in full bloom and the forsythia was almost there. Weather pundits nattered away about the surreal string of ninety-degree days in the Midwest, early mosquito swarms bringing bizarre tropical diseases and invasive crop-destroying insects in the South, and sky-high levels of yellow pine pollen coating cities and lungs nationwide. It was the warmest winter ever recorded, beating every record by several degrees. Researchers blamed solar flares or La Niña.

Zoe loved the unnatural warmth and she didn't care about the cause. Spring liberated her from snow piles blocking curb cuts and icy sidewalks and bulky coats. Maneuvering her wheelchair with ease over the minimal threshold of the diner, she was as mobile as a normal teenager. Not that her life mirrored her friends' that much, especially since she took the Monday-Wednesday-Friday job helping her grandmother. At least there'd been no further episodes of target practice with onions at the new store.

Every Friday Zoe met her father and grandmother at the diner on the corner for an early dinner. This week, Flo and Sam were already seated side by side at the half-booth, half-table in the back of the diner, under a poster of giant ice cream cones masquerading as a mountain range with peaks of pistachio and blackberry and double chocolate. Negotiating the narrow path between tables, Zoe marveled at the bizarre permutations of genetics, more interesting when it was attached to people than in diagrams in her biology textbook. Flo was pale with wild, steel-gray hair. Sam's springy curls were sandy-brown and his skin was the color of the half-milk coffee Zoe's mom used to make on special occasions. Zoe looked down at her own hands, already deeply tanned in early spring.

"Zoe," Sam called out. "Prow was hactice?"

Her father's spoonerisms got old years ago, but Zoe didn't want to hurt his feelings. He seemed to get such a kick from the stupid sounds. But she didn't want to encourage him either.

"Wet," she answered, parking her chair in the empty space across from them. She missed sitting on the cracked leather seat. Sam offered to fold the chair and stow it out of the way in the back hallway so they could take a regular booth. It wasn't worth the effort but it still made her sad. So let's go someplace else, he suggested, but she didn't want that either. She'd grown up eating at this place, even though the vegetarian options were limited. When she was little and mourning that she wasn't allowed to be near balloons because of her latex allergy, the owners Madge and Owen promised their diner would always be a balloon-free zone. They'd kept that promise and she was loyal too.

Madge called from the kitchen through-window. "What'll you have?"

"The usual," Flo said.

Zoe rolled her eyes. Her grandmother, so fanatic about healthy food on their weekly grocery shopping, always ordered a medium-rare burger, extra pickles, and onion rings on Fridays. "How could she be so phony?" Zoe ranted at her dad. "Consistency is for small minds," Sam liked to quote in response.

"Southwestern tofu wrap for me, please," Zoe said.

"Make that two," Sam added. "And a coffee."

Sam placed his silverware packet, tightly wrapped in a napkin with a green band, perfectly perpendicular to the table edge. "Listen," he said. "I've got something important to discuss with you two."

Uh-oh, Zoe thought. In her experience, important equaled bad news.

Sam tended to procrastinate making big decisions, but by the first Friday of spring, he knew that Flo had to move into Assisted Living or a Memory Unit, or whatever other euphemistic names they came up with. He had researched every facility within a twenty-five mile radius—deeply researched, hacking into password-protected accreditation association chat rooms and archives. He read ten years worth of consumer complaints, health and safety regulation violations, and employee grievance records. In the six years since he transformed his not-quite-kosher online inquiry business into website design, Sam hadn't lost his investigative touch. Of all the potential new homes for Flo, only one seemed worth a visit.

Madge brought three glasses of ice water and Sam's coffee. "You guys doing okay?" When they all nodded and smiled, she squeezed Zoe's shoulder before leaving. Sam sipped his coffee, wondering if Zoe liked the touch, or it made her feel like a little kid. It was hard to know what a teenager wanted.

When he was Zoe's age, he played ball in Forest Park every warm evening until the game disappeared into dusk. His strongest memory was that his mother—who hated organized sports—watched every game and his dad never came. Baseball won't get you into college. Baseball won't get you a job. Dad had a hoarse voice, thick with smoke. "Lung cancer will get you," Flo used to warn him. But she was wrong. His heart gave out when Sam was in eighth grade. Sam's most profound connection with his dad had been listening to the Grateful Dead while they washed dishes every evening after dinner. Sam couldn't listen to the Dead after his father died. Until freshman year in college when he walked by Anna, sitting alone on the grass outside the library listening to the lyrics about the highway between dawn and the dark of night. The song gave him courage to talk to her. And now they were all gone: his dad was long dead, Anna didn't love him any more, and his mother was losing her marbles.

"So, Ma. Zoe." He made himself look at them both. "I'm not sure how to say this, because it's not an easy situation." He hesitated, took another sip of coffee. Zoe twirled her silverware packet through her fingers like a mini-baton.

"Spit it out, Sam," Flo said. "You want to dump me in a nursing home, don't you?"

Zoe's utensil baton clattered onto the table. Sam choked on his half-swallowed mouthful.

"Dad?" Zoe said. "Is that true?"

"Not a nursing home. Assisted Living, probably a Memory Unit. There's a big difference."

There *was* a big difference. Sam had been charmed by the small non-profit facility halfway up the mountain in Holyoke. He wasn't crazy about the symbolism of the location, with the affiliated nursing home and hospice center at the top of the hill. "Closer to heaven," the director said with a practiced laugh.

Sam reached across the table and took Flo's hand. "I think it's time for you to live someplace where you can get some help."

"I don't need help," Flo said.

"You'll like this place," Sam said. "It's convenient—fifteen minutes from Zoe and me. Closer to the mall."

"So you won't have to miss your Thursday morning meetings," Zoe said.

Flo flashed her a look. Whose side are you on?

"There'll be people there to make sure you don't hurt yourself," Sam said. "Or anyone else."

"I'm fine," Flo said.

"You'll love it," Sam insisted. "When I visited, there were these two women sitting side by side on the piano bench playing Mozart. They were good and I stopped to listen. I noticed each woman played with one hand. The director told me that one woman had been a concert pianist until her stroke and then she couldn't use her right hand. The other musician had bad arthritis in her left hand. Together they sounded great."

"Heartwarming," Flo said.

Okay, so maybe that was a bizarre reason to choose a facility, but it made sense to Sam. Hillside Village seemed like an accepting sort of place and Flo's outspoken opinions would challenge most institutions. Over the years, his teachers had rolled their eyes more than once at her contributions to Parents' Night and Sam learned to balance his pride and his embarrassment. In grade school he hated that Flo never took his dad's name. Anna never took his name either, but by then it was pretty common. Besides, maybe she already knew something he didn't, back then when they got married.

"It *was* heartwarming," Sam said. "It's a good place."

"Maybe it is but I'm fine. If I go to some old people's prison, how can I continue my work, my organizing? I can't, that's how!"

"Come on, Ma. You haven't been active in politics for years."

"Of course I have," Flo shouted. "What do you know? I go to meetings and I leaflet and talk to people about important issues like workers' rights."

"Like at Food Castle?" he said, under his breath.

"I heard that," Flo said, slapping his hand. "Besides, those places cost a mint. I don't have that kind of money."

Sam swabbed the last drips of salsa from his plate with his finger. He couldn't look at Flo. She would hate this. "They'll help with the Medicaid application. You'll qualify, no problem."

His mother seemed to deflate, like the energy whooshed out of her body. "If I go there," she said, "it's like giving up. Who will I be if I stop fighting?"

"You'll be my mother." Sam took her hand, now limp on the table. "Zoe's grandma. Isn't that enough?" He didn't wait for her answer. "In any case, I'd like to take you there to visit. To see what you think."

"No. *No* is what I think."

Flo pulled her hand away and grabbed the ketchup bottle. Turning it upside down, she squeezed a squiggly red stripe across the table, dividing her space from Sam's before returning the bottle to its place in the plastic condiment caddy. In one smooth gesture, her index finger swooped from the ketchup line onto her tongue.

Chapter Six

Every spring Gabe's birthday brought his two estranged families together for a few hours of awkward celebration. Mid-April weather was risky for a backyard cookout, making the choice of a party venue tricky. With Tian in prison, it had been Francie's job to represent his side of the family. Francie and Pippa usually managed to negotiate a place that was mutually acceptable: fast food or roller-skating or a 3-D action movie. One year they splurged on a pint-sized basketball court with shooting lessons and a dribbling contest and discount sneaker coupons for party favors.

This year Gabe turned eleven, and two things were different: his father was out of prison, and his friends were having boy-girl parties in darkened basement rec rooms, with lava lamps excavated from their grandparents' attics, a high-school DJ, and parents banned from sight.

Tian shook his head at the request. "You see a basement in this apartment?"

Gabe's mother was more equivocal. "I don't know," Pippa said. "I'll have to ask Anna. It's her house. I suppose we could push back furniture in the living room to make room for dancing, but I'm not comfortable with the no-parents part."

Gabe had anticipated that objection and had his response ready. "How about if my big brothers keep an eye on us," he suggested. "You trust Jeremy and Tim, don't you? And Zoe could help."

"Run it by your father and Francie," Pippa said. "If they agree, I'll talk to Anna and you can ask the twins and Zoe."

⁂

By early April, Jeremy had been hanging out in Tim's apartment for three very long weeks.

"This is driving me batty," he told Tim.

"You were already batty when you got here," Tim reminded him.

Fair enough, but he certainly wasn't getting any better. He had plenty of time to surf the web and read obsessively about climate change. He spent all afternoon poring through the online news and bloggers, but no one seemed to care about the role of global warming in killing off vulnerable plant species.

He was so frustrated and so bored that when Tim suggested the lecture, his defenses were weak.

"You doing anything tonight?" Tim had asked, appearing to concentrate on balancing his coffee cup while slipping his arms into his backpack.

Jeremy glanced up from his laptop without answering. He never did anything in the evenings. Or in the days, for that matter, except to walk the Brooklyn neighborhoods to the defeated cadences of *Gomidesia cambessedeana* and *Euphrasia mendoncae* chanted under his breath. He walked until the Latin syllables emptied him of everything except the pavement and his feet.

Oh yeah—and he had the coffee shop project. He sat in them for hours, watching people heading to work or home or sometimes with nowhere to go. Like him. He was just noticing, marking time. Still, there were rules to the game. The coffee shops couldn't be chain stores, and they had to have big windows facing the street and he could never return to the same one twice.

Still, neither walking in requiem nor sitting in coffee shops constituted plans.

"No plans," Jeremy had admitted, trying not to sound facetious or ungrateful.

Tim glugged the rest of his coffee. "Great. Then meet me at the campus center auditorium at 7:30. There's a speaker right up your alley, a climate change activist."

"I thought you didn't believe climate change was real."

"I don't, but you do. Come on. I want you to meet some people. I'll even treat you to a burrito after." Tim was out the door and clumping down the stairs before Jeremy could think of an excuse.

That evening, Gabe's email request came through right before Jeremy lost cell service in the subway, so he couldn't answer Gabe even if he wanted to, even if he knew what to say. If he weren't already on the train, he told himself, he'd turn around and go back to Tim's place and skip this lecture.

Emerging from the station at Flatbush, Jeremy reread Gabe's email. He didn't know Gabe all that well, even though they shared a father. Tian had once reigned over the big house on Pioneer Street, but when he was sent to the Federal Corrections Institution up in Berlin, Francie moved the twins to the two bedroom flat on Sumner and Gabe's mother Pippa spent the second half of her pregnancy in a women's shelter, supervised by the court. When Gabe was born, the judge allowed Pippa to move with her baby into the two-family house a few blocks away, where Zoe's parents lived, but not together. The whole situation was a complicated mess. Sometimes Jeremy was glad he didn't have friends who might ask embarrassing questions about his family.

Gabe was the sole connection between the two households. Not that there was much contact beyond occasional self-conscious play dates at the playground in Forest Park so the brothers could get to know each other. Tim tried to teach Gabe to keep the bat level when he swung at the ball, but Gabe never liked baseball much. Jeremy and Tim might not know him that well, but Gabe was their half-brother and he was begging for their help with his birthday party.

Pushing through the crowd of students into the auditorium, Jeremy told himself to chill. This place wasn't that different from UMass. He stood at the back of the amphitheater looking for Tim. The hall was a study in gray—rug, walls, metal tubing connecting gunmetal chairs to slate desks. The muted colors were soothing, but the steep pitch of the room played havoc with his balance, pulling him forward until he was poised to fall into the drab empty space. His body swayed and he grabbed onto the back of a chair in the last row. As the lights dimmed, he saw his brother's windmilling arms and made his way to the seat Tim had saved. A woman stepped up to the podium and introduced herself as Greenhope, a senior in the Sustainability Studies department. Tim elbowed Jeremy and grinned, probably at her hot pink hair and matching high-top sneakers.

"Global warming is real and it's frightening," the pink woman began. "But we must follow the facts in front of our faces, even when they're harsh and ugly."

Tim leaned over and whispered, "Just what you need. More harsh and ugly. That nurse practitioner of yours wouldn't approve."

Jeremy wasn't sure what he needed, but the main speaker was neither harsh nor ugly and she captivated him with her first sentence. Dressed in a skirt and blouse, she looked more like an elementary education major than an activist type. "My name is Mary," she said. "They call me an eco-terrorist."

Whoa. Jeremy leaned forward in his seat.

"Civilization is a serial killer." She sounded both regretful and determined. "Carbon dioxide levels are rising fast and methane is thawing—methane is a time bomb, much more destructive than CO_2. Scientists estimate that over two hundred species a day are becoming extinct. Now. As we speak. Is this how we treat our distant cousins?"

Exactly, Jeremy thought. He looked at Tim, hoping his brother was excited by these ideas too, but Tim was reading a text.

"These species," Mary continued, "the insects and plants and animals, are our kin."

Yes, Jeremy thought. This was personal. Take *Thismia americana*, dying the year he was born. That connected them. *Thismia* could be a distant cousin, a long-lost great-uncle.

"Sometimes nature fights back, like the elephants in Cameroon. When ivory traders destroyed the elephants' habitats and used hand grenades to slaughter their herds, the animals began attacking villages in response." She paused and the audience's attention swelled. "Smaller animals can't do that. Plants can't do that." Her voice became a whisper in the microphone. "But we can do it for them."

Jeremy listened to every word, without crossing his legs or fidgeting on the thinly padded gray chair or glancing to see what Tim thought. No, listen wasn't the accurate word, not strong enough. Mary's words tunneled into his flesh, swam in his bloodstream, and sidled up to every circulating cell, already seeded with vigils of Latin deaths. Her sentences inserted into his DNA. He couldn't stop looking at her, at Mary the eco-terrorist. Why didn't she deny that awful title? How did she become so sure of herself?

"You may wonder," she said, clearly able to read his mind, "about the eco-terrorist label. That's how the folks in power attempt to demonize people who challenge their self-serving lies. They portray us as bogeymen." She grinned. "Bogeywomen."

He liked her smile, her ability to joke about such a desperate situation.

"The big fossil fuel companies run the show. They write the laws that make it legal to rape our planet and plunder its natural resources. Biodiversity is vanishing. Thousands of species are becoming extinct. The energy companies and their buddies in government are massively powerful. We must fight back with everything we have."

Mary crossed her hands over her heart and looked around the audience, her intense gaze stopping on individuals for brief moments. Look at me, Jeremy thought.

"Please join us. Join me. Dedicate yourselves to saving our planet," she said quietly. "For ourselves. For our children. For the whole earth of connected living organisms. Thank you."

Jeremy stood and clapped wildly with the audience. He swayed, light-headed and dizzy. He realized he'd been holding his breath.

Tim punched him in the shoulder. "Didn't I tell you? Right up your alley."

Jeremy nodded. He couldn't speak, even if he really needed to, even if he had to yell fire or something critical and life-saving. His brain was ablaze from her words, as if they held a match to the dry tinder of all those dead plants he held inside and ignited, exploding into flame. The oddest part was that what she said also expanded him, stretched his skin wide open to let these other people in, all these other people who also mourned the dying and wanted to help. His brother was looking at him oddly, expecting some sort of verbal response, but he couldn't make conversation out of a conflagration.

～～～

Standing on the sidewalk after the lecture, Tim suggested they head over to the burrito joint. "The people who organized the program will be there. Pink girl and Carl and Sari and others."

"I'd rather go home," Jeremy said. "Back to your place."

"I mentioned your radio show to some friends," Tim said. "They want to meet you."

Well, they weren't actually his friends; none of his buddies from the business school had shoulder-length hair or nose studs, but he knew Carl from freshman dorm. Tim wondered if introducing Jeremy to the eco-nuts was a smart idea, but he had to do something to shake his bro out of his solitary funk. He liked the idea of Jeremy as part of a group, any group, and this one seemed harmless, despite their rhetoric.

"Nah," Jeremy said. "I don't think so."

"Mary will be there." Tim grinned. He'd noticed how Jeremy stared at her.

"Just for a few minutes then."

Tim had to practically drag his brother into the line at the counter of the crowded restaurant and then push him into an empty chair with their food.

"This is Carl." Tim punched the shoulder of a guy with a ponytail who looked like he lifted weights, then pointed to the dark-haired woman next to Carl. "That's Sari."

"Tim told us about your radio show," Carl said, wiping salsa verde from his chin. "Sounds amazing. We don't have anything like that here."

Jeremy shrugged. "It's just about species that are threatened or going extinct."

"It *is* amazing," Tim said, crossing his fingers under the table. "Don't be so modest. Music and chanting all these Latin names."

"Maybe you could do a program like that here," Sari suggested. "We've got a college station."

"I'm not a student here," Jeremy said. "Besides, the UMass station master didn't like it. They shut me down."

"Exactly!" Carl banged the table. "That's what Mary was talking about, how they attack us when we organize around environmental issues."

"Nah," Jeremy said. "My show wasn't political."

Sari touched his arm. "It *so* was, Jeremy. Everything about the environment is political."

Someone brought two pitchers of beer and that changed the subject, so Jeremy was off the hook. Mary never showed up.

"Let's go," Jeremy said when he finished eating. As he and Tim left the restaurant, Sari touched Jeremy's arm again.

"We're meeting with Mary tomorrow at 4:00, to plan our next action. Why don't you join us?"

Carl glanced sharply at Sari, raising his eyebrows. "Too soon," he mouthed.

Sari shook her head slightly at him. "It's okay, Carl. He's okay, the radio show and everything." She turned back to Jeremy. "Please. Join us."

"Maybe," Jeremy said. "I'll think about it."

⁓⸲⸱

The brothers were quiet on the train, but later, climbing the stairs at Borough Hall, Tim interrupted Jeremy's thoughts. "That's cool, that they invited you to a meeting. I hear they're usually pretty paranoid. Secret handshakes and crap. You going to go?"

"I don't know." He slowed his steps and turned to Tim. "I'm not sure I'd be comfortable with your friends."

"Those guys? They're not my friends. Just some people I know a little." Tim paused. "My friends are like me, business majors."

"I've been thinking about that," Jeremy said.

"About what?"

"You being a business major. Isn't that strange, what with our family and everything? I mean, couldn't you at least study sustainable business or something? Green business?"

Tim laughed. "Don't you get it? That's the point. I don't want anything to do with what happened to us. I'm building a new life, one that's all mine."

"And all white?" Jeremy asked.

"What do you mean?"

"Your friends. Are they all white?"

"Yeah. Aren't yours?"

"I don't have that many friends," Jeremy admitted. "But they're like me, brown or mixed, mostly. Tomas is Puerto Rican. Danny is Korean-American."

Tim shrugged.

A few minutes later, Jeremy broke the silence. "Speaking of brothers, did you see the email from Gabe?"

"Half-brother. You mean about his birthday party?"

"Yeah. So are we going to help him? It's in two weeks."

"I'm not sure," Tim said.

"Why not?"

"Because it means getting in the middle of that mess again. Dad and Mom and Pippa and her new family."

"That's the point. They're family."

"I guess," Tim said.

They lapsed into silence. As they walked, Jeremy murmured under his breath, *Fitchia mangarevensis. Dryopteris ascensionis.* The sounds soothed him, slowed his breathing. The Latin names burrowed through his pores and into his cells like a sedative. They waited for the light at Atlantic.

"You ever think about them?" Jeremy asked.

"Them?"

"Abby and Terrence."

They almost never spoke about their siblings, half-siblings, whose deaths in Forest Park started the cascade that ended with Pippa leaving and their dad going to prison and the commune breaking up. He and Tim had been shielded from most of the ugliness and the trial, but he had some clear memories, like the night Abby was born.

The Pioneer Street greenhouse had shimmered with candlelight and the smell of damp earth. All night, while Murphy played music and Tian and Francie chanted and the midwife spoke softly to Pippa, Tim and he sat under the planting table building castles from wooden blocks and catnapping. He remembered putting his lips close to Pippa's stretched out belly button and telling Abby to hurry up, promising to teach her to draw. At eight, he had already filled notebooks with pictures of plants and flowers.

What bothered Jeremy most was that he couldn't remember the babies' faces. Sure, it happened years ago, but how could a person forget something like that?

"Won't you ever let it go? Tim said. "Aren't dying plants bad enough?"

Chapter Seven

That same early April evening, Flo pushed her bike into the wooden lean-to behind her apartment building, where the landlord grudgingly allowed her to park. Even if it weren't a clunky old-fashioned model—just like she was—there was no way she could carry a bike to the second floor. She wove the chain through the spokes and around the drainpipe and snapped the lock shut, spinning the numbers. She had a moment of panic that she would never remember the combination. Then she reminded herself that the numbers were written in indelible ink inside her left sneaker. What would happen, she worried, when she forgot the backup plan? Disaster, that's what.

Flo saw disasters everywhere. She always had. She collected them and deconstructed them into their worrisome component parts. Starting in eighth grade when her best friend's mom died of breast cancer, Flo made mental lists every night before falling asleep. Lists of potential catastrophes poised to derail her and her family. She planned her responses too: how she would cope if her father lost his job or her mother fell into an inexplicable coma or their house collapsed into one of those giant sinkholes they had down in Florida, possible even though they lived in Maryland. Over the years, Flo grew to firmly believe that this mental exercise would prevent ruin, but only if she imagined each one specifically.

It was an endless task and one she took seriously. But when it came, the calamity wasn't a sinkhole or a falling air conditioner. It was in her head and it stole her ability to inventory and list and plan and respond.

Trudging up the stairs, she acknowledged that her son probably considered her bike a disaster. At least once a week he begged her to donate the old contraption to Goodwill and stop risking life and limb. That was easy for him to say. Her two-speed bike, with its wicker basket and simple backpedal braking system, had carried her around town for over forty years, thanks to the elderly mechanic on Orange Street who kept it lubricated and working. Her evening ride around the central circuit in Forest Park was a better soporific than any of those stupid pills waiting to expire on the medicine cabinet shelf.

At her front door, she jiggled the doorknob and stared at the lock.

Locks required keys. Locks and keys and combinations and numbers meandered around her brain, circling and spiraling and refusing to line up right. The numbers stashed in her shoe weren't the right answer, but nothing else came to her. She could hear the phone ringing on the other side of the door. Probably Sam, checking up on her. Now he'd be bound to lecture her again about carrying a cell phone, just in case of emergencies, along with nagging about giving up the bike. She liked her landline. She loved her bike. Where was her bike anyway? It must be inside the apartment. She had to make sure and she had to pee.

She turned the doorknob again, hard, but it stubbornly refused to open. Charlie meowed on the other side of the door. Closing her eyes, she leaned her forehead against the door and gave in to the images swirling in her head: the heavy iron keys she found in her father's desk after he died. Leaning a different bike against the wire fence at Glen Echo to join Charlie—the human Charlie, not the cat—on the picket line. He wore a deep red dashiki. She carried a plastic-covered bike chain with the combination padlock and the string of numbers and voilá, she had it. She tugged on the leather cord around her neck and grasped the key. Yes!

Sometimes it took a while, but her brain didn't let her down.

Sam couldn't help himself. He left another phone message. "Ma, it's me. Could you please call me when you get home?"

Flo hated it if he hovered too much, but she infuriated him with her stubbornness. If only she'd give up that damn bike, at least stop riding at night. Flo made her thoughts on that subject abundantly clear: "Butt out, buddy," she'd said more than once. For the thousandth time, he wished that he had a sister to share his anxiety, or that his father were still alive. Not that Brad had been much good with emotions, and not that the man ever won an argument with Flo, but he might at least be an ally in the worry department.

It was bad enough having a teenager to fret over. Sometimes he thought that Anna got the easy part, living with Zoe for her first twelve years. He had been deliriously happy when Zoe moved upstairs into his half of the house, had eagerly built a ramp and wheelchair lift. But now he was the parent on the front lines of the potential major adolescent battles: cars and boys and drugs.

He shouldn't have to worry about his mother every night too, listening for the phone until their ritual evening call, picturing Flo wandering off somewhere on that clunker of a bike and forgetting how to get home or neglecting to look for cars. He'd been thinking recently of attaching a small GPS transmitter to her bike. He would do it too, if he could be certain that she wouldn't find it and get on her high horse about invasion of privacy or something. A tracker might be a drastic measure, but since the lunch with Zoe two weeks ago when he mentioned Assisted Living, Flo was barely speaking to him. She refused to talk about the place he found, refused to visit to check it out, wouldn't even discuss the subject in general terms.

The whir of the wheelchair lift announced Zoe's arrival home.

"How was study group?" he asked.

"Okay. Our project is cool."

"The immigration thing?"

"That's the one," Zoe said. "We mostly agree on national policy, including college admissions and steps to citizenship. We had a good time. Except for Xander. He's being a jerk."

"A jerk how?" Sam pictured the boy hitting on Zoe, even though they'd been friends since kindergarten days of painted macaroni necklaces and Cookie Monster lunchboxes.

"About immigration reform. He wants to send all the undocumented workers back to wherever. Like that's worked so far." Zoe swiveled away and headed down the hallway toward her bedroom.

"Goodnight," Sam called after her.

Zoe had her grandmother's liveliness. Maybe the girl also inherited Flo's attitude about changing the world. Sam wondered what a twenty-first century Stalinist would believe and shuddered at the possibilities.

He checked his watch. Only 9:30, not too awful. Flo would no doubt get home soon and call. In the meantime he couldn't stop thinking about her stubbornness, trying to come up with a strategy to change her set-in-concrete mind. Maybe Mimi could help. She and Flo had been friends forever. Last month when Flo tried to take a bus to the mall, she ended up in Agawam and called Mimi. Mimi was stuck in the dentist's waiting room and sent Sam to the rescue. Mimi must have noticed Flo's decline. He touched the phone screen and listened to the dialing beeps. Would Mimi feel disloyal talking to him? Probably, but it was worth a try.

Mimi did sound uncomfortable when he explained his purpose. "I don't know about this," she said. "Your mother is my best friend."

"I know," he said, "and I hate putting you in an awkward position, but I'm really worried about her. Have you noticed her, um, odd behavior recently?"

"She's more forgetful," Mimi said, "but so am I. It goes with the territory."

"Yeah." Flo would kill him for this. "I guess maybe she hasn't told you that she has been diagnosed with Alzheimer's?"

Mimi didn't say anything for a long time. Then she sighed, loud enough to create a breeze in Sam's ear. "She didn't mention it. But she wouldn't."

"I don't think she remembers the doctor telling her. When I reminded her, when I tried to talk to her about moving into Assisted Living, she looked at me like I was hallucinating."

Mimi sighed again. "The thing is, your mother has always been such an outrageous person that it's hard to know what's her normal quirkiness and what's something worse. Her mind works in odd ways. A few weeks ago she announced that she had given names to the three bridges in her mouth: the South End, Memorial, and the North End."

Sam laughed. Those were Springfield's bridges over the Connecticut River. That was just Flo's eccentric brain at work, not dementia. "Naming the dental work—that's Ma all right. But other things, like getting lost all the time and some belligerent behavior, that's what got her banned from Food Castle." He paused. "I'm afraid she's not safe living alone any more."

"I can't conspire against Flo. What are you asking me to do?"

"I'm not sure. Talk with her, maybe. Come with us to visit this place I found?"

"I can do that if Flo agrees," Mimi said. "And Sam? I'm so sorry."

⁓⊷

From her bedroom, Zoe eavesdropped on her dad's side of the conversation. He had been pretty distracted since the Food Castle debacle. Zoe couldn't imagine her grandmother in a nursing home, or whatever new kind of place Sam was talking about. Flo would rather ride her clumsy old bike down Sumner Avenue off into the sunset.

Zoe transferred onto her bed and dumped the contents of her chairpack. Fifteen minutes writing up the changes in their civics project and then she could put on her headphones and relax.

Her cell phone buzzed and Gabe's photo flashed on the screen. The kid lived downstairs; why was he calling her instead of talking in person?

"Hey, Gabe."

"Hey. Listen. I'm gonna have a birthday party here, Saturday after next. Dancing, you know, boy-girl and everything? My parents and your mom say they'll butt out if you and the twins are here to be, like, you know?"

"Chaperones?" How weird was that, being considered mature enough to be a chaperone. Except that some people didn't think a girl in a wheelchair could get into much trouble. She'd do anything for the opportunity to prove them wrong. Like tonight, working on their immigration project, she kept looking at Xander's scowling profile and wondering what it would be like to touch the fine brown hairs sprouting on his upper lip.

"Yeah, chaperones. Will you?"

"Boy-girl, huh? Is there a girl you like?" Zoe teased.

"Not really. Will you do it?"

"Did Tim and Jeremy agree?"

"I haven't heard back from them yet," he said.

"Well, if they say yes, I'm in too."

Chapter Eight

The next afternoon, Jeremy hesitated at the door of Sari's apartment. He considered turning back. He really wanted to see Mary again, but he had no connection with those other people. He could leave right now and nobody would know and no one would care. They only invited him because of Tim.

Footsteps in the hallway behind him scuttled that plan.

"Hey, Jerry," Carl said.

"It's Jeremy."

Carl's laugh was high-pitched, almost feral. "I think of you guys as Tom and Jerry. Like the cartoon."

"Well, I'm Jeremy. And my brother's name is Tim, not Tom."

"Whatever," Carl said. "You know, it's hard to figure you guys as twins. You look alike but otherwise you're like, opposites. Like cat and mouse." He laughed again and grabbed the doorknob.

Now Jeremy wanted to leave even more. There'd been a boy like Carl, all jokey and full of himself, on their block at home. A kid who read every newspaper article—about Abby and Terrance, about the trial and Tian going to prison—and made sure that everyone in school knew every detail. Tim ignored it all, just played sports until he fell exhausted into bed every night. Jeremy didn't much like sports. He drew pictures, of plants and flowers mostly, and look where that got him.

Instead of opening the door, Carl turned back to Jeremy with a sly expression.

"What?" Jeremy asked.

"I saw how you looked at Mary. You know, she's got a kid and that's all the family she wants. Just saying." Without bothering to knock, Carl pushed inside the apartment and let the door shut behind him.

Jeremy leaned against the corridor wall, feeling his cheeks flame. Had he been that obvious? Now was definitely the time to leave, before anyone else arrived for the meeting. Carl stuck his head back into the hallway. "You coming or what?"

Sari, Mary, and two other women sat in the living room and three guys walked in right after them. Jeremy added his jacket to the pile on the floor and took a seat slightly outside the circle, where he could watch Mary but as far away from Carl as possible. The pink-haired senior from the other night sat to his left. Pink wasn't a very sustainable color, was it? Maybe she regretted it, because she'd jammed an old brown felt hat low over her hair. She turned and introduced herself as Greenhope. Was that a name? What parents would call their baby something like that? She must have named herself.

"I'm Jeremy," he said.

"Are you a student?"

"Not here," he said. "At UMass. You?"

"My last semester."

Sari brought a teapot and cups to the table and general conversation morphed into a discussion about Earth Day and he realized the meeting had begun. Jeremy mostly watched Mary. Today she wore jeans and a sweater rather than her elementary ed outfit. She listened intently as people proposed teach-ins and sit-ins and take-overs. Greenhope suggested picketing the Park Slope home of an oil company CEO. Carl shook his head. "That won't do anything except make his neighbors feel sorry for the bastard." He started to talk about the evil of SUVs and how easy they were to target, but Sari touched his shoulder and he stopped.

Jeremy slouched in his seat. He didn't belong in this room. These people called themselves Green Warriors and believed in civil disobedience. He just cared about the plants. Still, when Mary passed around a dog-eared paperback book, he thumbed through it.

"If you haven't read it," Greenhope said to him, "you really should. The author explains it all. Everything fits together and make sense."

"We call it the Big Green Book." Carl laughed. His hyena snort was starting to really annoy Jeremy.

Mary must have noticed Jeremy's blank expression. "Like Mao's little red book," she said quietly. Jeremy nodded. Her glow was less intense than the night before, but he could only take his eyes away from her face for a few moments at a time, to look at other people or at the piles of books and magazines leaning against the apartment walls. When she spoke, he knew that her sentences were simply words lined up in order, but he savored every word. He wondered about her son, about her life. Then she announced to the group that she was returning to Oregon the next morning and after that it was hard to listen to anything else.

"Whatever actions you folks decide on for Earth Day," she said, "it's important to collaborate with environmental groups in the community, not only at the college. I think your actions should accomplish two goals: to make people feel deeply connected to the movement, and to move them forward in their commitment to stop the corporate rape of our planet."

"We need to recruit people, too," Greenhope added. "For the different levels of activism. Like they say in the Green Book."

Mary looked directly at Jeremy. "As someone who is new to this group, I hope you'll help plan the Earth Day programs. Sometimes we old-timers just talk to each other, forget to reach out to potential new allies."

Sari opened her arms to the group. "Let's not forget what Mary said last night. We are all family; we've *got* to work together. Climate change is killing our planet and our kinfolk."

An older guy spoke up then. "It's not that simple. Some of us from the community aren't satisfied with teach-ins and administration building take-overs. The problem is bigger than that and requires more aggressive tactics."

Carl nodded. "We want to save our planet, not take over the university."

On the train home, Jeremy tried to decide if he was disappointed or relieved that Mary was leaving. Relieved, mostly. And what was up with Greenhope? At the end of the meeting, she pulled him aside and said she was available if he wanted to talk about the Green Book. He promised to read it before the Earth Day committee meeting next week, so he stopped at the bookstore on the ground floor of Tim's apartment and bought a copy. "The bible of the deep green ecology resistance movement," claimed the blurb on the front cover. "A concrete blueprint to stop corporate destruction and save our planet."

Save the planet. Save the plants. Those words mattered. Jeremy took the stairs to Tim's apartment two at a time. Maybe this book was what he was looking for.

Upstairs he paced, too wired to sit down right away. He wandered down the hall and dumped his backpack on his bed, wondering for the umpteenth time why Tim assigned him the larger bedroom, the big room with two windows and a cross-breeze. Tim always kept his bedroom door closed and Jeremy had never been inside, not once in the weeks he'd been staying with Tim. He hesitated for a minute before turning the doorknob.

His brother's room was small and stuffy, with a single smudged window facing a trash-littered alley. An ordinary room with a twin bed covered with an Indian print bedspread, desk piled with laptop and textbooks, dust bunnies scooting across the floor. Ordinary except for the posters.

They were the same posters taped on the walls of their childhood room on Pioneer Street, then moved to the small Sumner Avenue apartment after Tian went to prison. They weren't the *exact* same ones—Jeremy could tell because there was no rip across Wolverine's left leg repaired with tape—but Tim must have bought new copies and replicated their bedroom gallery of X-Men characters and glory.

It was unsettling, seeing the posters here, and they transported Jeremy a decade back in time to the years he and Tim were nine and ten. Their dad was on trial and then sent away, leaving their mom to cope with the verdict and the move and their failing tea room business. Francie worked night shift on the hospital switchboard and Jeremy and Tim watched movies, preferably X-Men but anything with superheroes would do. Two or three times a week they stopped at the video store on the way home from school, their backpacks bulging with tapes, and spent their allowance on movie posters—when the owner of the store wouldn't give up the old or tattered ones—taping them to the wall of their shared bedroom.

They idolized Wolverine and his image ruled the gallery of posters on the walls. Jeremy's favorite, the one with the ripped leg, hung at the foot of his bed, placed so that he saw it first thing every morning. Bad things had happened to Wolverine too. He'd been hurt and abandoned and didn't know exactly what happened. Wolverine was a mutant, all alone in the world, but he didn't sit around feeling sorry for himself. At least Jeremy had a twin and he knew what hit him, though he never completely understood why. Tim and he collected every poster, every T-shirt, every magazine photo they could find. They bickered over who got to be Wolverine when they played X-Men, and who had to be Cyclops.

If Wolverine could survive the pain, then Jeremy figured he could push through too. If only the school for mutants were real. Of course, being a half-black commune brat with a dad in prison was nothing compared to having blades for hands or turning friends to ice with your touch or creating storms with your brain. Jeremy liked to imagine twin superpowers for Tim and him to balance the bad stuff. Tim said their situation didn't bother him; he didn't need any mutant assistance. Even so, their whispered super-power fantasies filled many hours when their mom was at work.

Looking at the posters on the bedroom wall, clearly Tim was affected more than he claimed. Tim had re-created their childhood refuge. Except that this room had a door, a privacy strictly forbidden in the commune. Jeremy closed the door behind him, stretched out on his bed and opened the Big Green Book.

~~~

"Reading in the dark?" Tim asked from the doorway. He switched on the overhead light and studied his brother, hunched over a thick tome. Jeremy had always been odd. Their childhood pledge was important, but having Jeremy stay with him wasn't helping; his brother was growing weirder instead of getting his act together. "What's the book?"

Marking his place with his finger, Jeremy held it up to display the cover. "It's like the bible of the deep green resistance movement," he said. "You know, the folks you introduced me to last night."

Uh-oh, Tim thought. That lecture really hadn't been a good idea at all. "Deep green resistance, huh. Is that what the eco-nuts call people who mourn dead plants?"

"Yeah, at first I thought it was just the plants too. That we could deal with it by freezing all the germplasm seeds like they're doing in that bunker in Norway or Iceland. But the problem is so much bigger than that. Our whole planet is at risk."

"If that's true, then it's too big. You can't stop it."

Jeremy shook his head slowly and pointed to his laptop. "I've been reading online. People *are* doing things. Things they won't talk about in a book or public lecture."

"Eco-terrorism, like that speaker said? Is that what you're getting into? Great. How about just sticking to dead plants? Maybe you could dress in all black and advertise to everyone that you're a really deep guy, mourning all these stupid dead species?"

"Go ahead. Make fun of me," Jeremy said. "Make fun of everything that matters. That'll make things better." His brother thought he had all the answers. Tim just stood there with his ridiculous dumbo ears sticking out from his business school haircut, not a self-doubt in the world. Well, Tim didn't have to know that Jeremy bought three six-packs of black T-shirts at Penney's and wore them every day against his skin. Out of respect. In mourning.

"Sorry, Bro," Tim muttered. He couldn't stand the wounded look on Jeremy's face. This situation wasn't working out well at all and he had no idea how to get out of it. Maybe when they got home for Gabe's birthday, Jeremy would stay in Massachusetts.

"You thought about going back to school?" Tim asked. Anything had to be better than Jeremy's Chicken Little gig.

"Listen. If you want me to leave, just tell me."

"That's not what I meant." Tim started backing out of the room. "Stay as long as you want."

"I'll stay here through Earth Day. We—they—the people in the Green Warriors group—are planning a bunch of actions."

"When's that?"

"April 22. The weekend after Gabe's party. You're going to help chaperone, right?"

"I guess," Tim said. "And April's cool. My roommate's not due back until June."

Maybe, when they were home for Gabe's birthday, he could talk to their parents about Jeremy. He could even call that nurse practitioner at the Health Service. She had sounded concerned about Jeremy.

～～

At dawn, Patty locked her office door and walked down the darkened corridor of Health Services. Even though she lived alone, sleeping during the day was tricky and she wasn't good at it. She wouldn't miss the night shift when she finally rotated back to days next week. Nights were quieter, so it was minimally easier to keep up with dictation and signing notes and scripts, all the tasks that computers were supposed to stream-line but didn't, not really. And the wee hours often brought in the urgent or unusual patient situations, the ones she had trouble forgetting.

Like that odd kid with the dead plants obsession. Turning into the urgent care hallway, she passed the exam room where Jeremy and she had talked. She'd tried to tune in to his program a few nights after his visit but it had been replaced with ten-minute radio plays produced by the theater department. When she called the registrar, they told her that Jeremy Beaujolais had dropped out for the semester.

This was a distressing part of the job. She would most likely never see Jeremy again, never know if he was okay, and that was tough. There was something peculiar about him besides his odd coloring, something she didn't quite understand. Some patients just got to her.

At the front desk, she waved to two day shift staffers and signed out, then hesitated. Maybe she could access his old radio program online.

"Oops. Forgot something," she murmured to the intake clerk and retraced her steps to her office. Jeremy's computerized medical record yielded the date February 25 for his Health Services visit and his broth-er's phone number. She scribbled it on a post-it note and stuck it in her pocket. On the website of the university radio station she quickly located the audio file for his program that night and opened it.

She recognized the Kyrie from Missa Luba in the background and heard the tremor in Jeremy's voice. "*Begonia eiromischa* was discovered in 1886 in Palau, but its forest habitat was cleared for agricultural cultiva-tion and no evidence of the herb has been reported in over a century." His voice sounded moist and porous, barely containing his sorrow. No wonder he ended up at Health Services. But he was no longer her patient, and psych wasn't her specialty, so why was she listening to this?

The Latin names contained more emotion than she would have guessed possible, and Jeremy's reading of them was elegiac. "*Orbexilum macrophyllum. Thismia americana,*" his voice especially trembled on that one. "*Camellia sinensis sinensis. Camellia sinensis assamica,* those were teas," he said. "And *Vanvoorstia bennettiana,* a victim of sewage contamination in Sydney Harbor," a place she had never been and where she would most likely never go. *"Nesiota elliptica."*

Listening to the kid's voice and the feelings trapped in the words and sentences, it was pretty amazing that he could function at all. How would someone help him, she wondered? Not her, of course. She specialized in adolescent sexuality and STDs. Psych was the last specialty she would pursue. She'd known that since nursing school, when a schizophrenic inpatient apparently didn't like her looks and smashed a fist into her head. Still, just out of curiosity, how would a counselor approach this kid's issues?

She'd probably never see him again, and would never know. Enough of this. She interrupted the program and shut down the computer. Ten weeks of night shift must be affecting her judgment more than she'd realized.

Chapter Nine

Before pulling into the traffic on Belmont, Sam double-checked Flo's seatbelt.

"You're going to love this place, Ma," he said. "It's homey."

Flo stared out the window. "So many wooden houses around here," she said. "I can't get used to them."

"What do you mean?" Sam frowned. "You've lived here for decades."

"In Maryland, the houses were brick."

"That's where you lived before I was born, right?"

She nodded. "Glen Echo. We made big history in 1960."

"Really?" Sam said. Flo rarely talked about her life before she moved to Springfield, before she married Sam's dad. "What happened in 1960?" he asked.

Flo turned and looked at him. "You know. The amusement park. The picketing and we won."

"How could I know? You never told me about this." He turned onto Mimi's street. "What pickets?"

"The students from Howard. Because the park was segregated."

"What happened?"

"I was arrested on the carousel," she said with a wide smile. "But we won. Me and Charlie."

"Who's Charlie?"

Flo turned back to the window. "So many wooden houses," she said again.

Sam braked in front of Mimi's house, making a mental note to Google Glen Echo.

∞≈∾

Mimi was sitting on the front stoop, waiting. Mimi was always early. That was the thing that bothered Flo about Mimi. Infuriated really. Like it mattered in the epic battle of good versus evil in the universe if Mimi got to a food coop meeting or a yoga class ten minutes early or ten minutes late. Flo never missed a chance to challenge her friend and ask, "Why are you so uptight?" "It's a matter of respect," Mimi would respond.

Mimi settled herself in the back seat and leaned forward to kiss Flo's cheek. Flo felt a surge of love and admiration. Mimi was brave. That time they were protesting in Washington—against the invasion of Iraq maybe, or was it Vietnam?—and the mounted police charged and Mimi grabbed her elbow and they stood their ground, even when the cops came at them with Billy clubs.

Looking back, Flo wished *she* had been braver when the clinic nurse gave her the news, so many years before. She could have called Charlie. It's even possible that things could have been different. Months of embarrassment and years of evasions—okay, of lying—could have been different. Her actions—her feelings—*should* have been different. She considered herself liberated. Her life's work was to fight—to flaunt—the stupidities of patriarchy, of class and racial privilege. So why was she ashamed about this? It made no sense, and yet it was and had been so. Regret ballooned in her chest and she had to concentrate on breathing while Mimi talked and Flo tried to put words that made sense into the empty bits of quiet.

∞≈∾

Merging onto 91, Sam tried to follow Flo and Mimi's discussion. Mimi seemed to elicit more coherence from his mother than he did. Maybe because they'd been friends for decades and were equals, instead of the shifting power differential between mother and boy, elderly mother and adult son. Still, the women's conversation followed Flo's current brand of nonlinear discourse, zigzagging wildly and bouncing off names he didn't recognize. Charlie never came up. Sam wondered if Mimi knew about him.

"Would you look at that?" Flo pointed at the car ahead. "What kind of person pays for a vanity plate reading Ya Hoo?"

"You're a snob, Ma," Sam said.

She'd always been a snob. He had often benefitted from her strong opinions and rules, reading *To Kill a Mockingbird* instead of *The Hardy Boys*, not allowed to exceed his one hour of television and even that was carefully monitored. One evening when Flo was out at a meeting, Sam found his dad watching an old science fiction film and asked, "Does Ma know you're watching that?" His father had laughed. "Your mother keeps us on a tight leash, doesn't she?"

He took the first Holyoke exit and turned onto Hillside Village Lane, rubbing his upper lip. He'd shaved off his distinctive handlebar mustache at Zoe's request two years earlier. Sometimes he missed it. He'd always figured it was his mustache that made people want to tell him their life stories. But even with a naked upper lip, people still spilled their guts, and his own finger still migrated there when he was worried. Today he was definitely worried; there was no way Flo was going to agree to Assisted Living, even with Mimi along as cheerleader.

Halfway up the hill, they turned into the parking lot. The pseudo-do-chalet architecture was annoying but the building overlooked the Connecticut River with a view of the western hills and the city to the south. Sam didn't see why they reserved the most spectacular setting on the mountaintop for the affiliated nursing home, when those patients couldn't fully appreciate it. Of course, he might feel differently if his mother were living there. Would she need a nursing home? How soon?

He turned off those questions and tried to remember the details of Hillside Village. When he'd called to make the appointment, the Assisted Living director explained that any potential new resident would have to be evaluated by their physician.

"She has her own doctor," Sam said.

"Of course," the director had said, "but we have different care options, ranging from Independent Living to the nursing home. For example, Assisted Living is for those residents needing extra care with ADL, activities of daily living. We're very proud of our new Memory Unit. It's designed to reflect the latest thinking in dementia care. Our physician will determine which is the best fit for your mother. He'll also review her current medications. Some individuals with early dementia can benefit from medications that primary care providers may be reluctant to prescribe."

Reluctant to prescribe? That sounded ominous, but Sam had agreed. It was hard to believe that his mother would be a good fit for the restrained grace of Hillside Village, with or without medications. In his experience, she took pride in not fitting in, from disrupting PTA meetings to picketing the high school performance of West Side Story for its cultural stereotypes. Picketing. That made him remember her comment about Glen Echo and Charlie, whoever he was.

The director met them at the door. "I'm Trixie. Welcome. You have an appointment with Dr. Robertson, and I hope you'll join us for lunch, but first I'd like to show you our home." She took both of Flo's hands in her own and smiled. "We have wonderful activities. I think you'll like it here."

Trixie led them to a sunny room with couches and easy chairs arranged in small conversation groupings. Flo played her hands along the bank of multi-paned windows, but the place reminded Sam of Colonel Mustard in the conservatory with the candlestick. He trailed behind the three women as they toured an empty apartment with freshly painted white walls and new gray carpet, the elegant dining room and informal snack bar, the gym and heated pool and puzzle room. It reminded him of visiting preschools with Zoe. He wondered where the block-building area was, and the dress-up corner.

Flo was underwhelmed too, until they walked into the art studio.

"Oh!" She hurried to the potter's wheel and scraped a fingernail across the dried clay on the metal wheel head. She settled her tush on the molded plastic seat and straddled the wheel. She belonged here.

"Clay?" she asked.

Trixie dug a damp brown clump from a plastic barrel and handed it to Flo. She held the fragrant earth close to her face and inhaled deeply, then placed it in the center of the wheel. She dipped both hands in the water pail and tenderly covered the clay. She pressed softly on the pedal and the wheel began to turn.

Her hands cupped the spinning mound, smoothing the bumps and holes. She eased the clay up into a tall cylinder and pressed it back, lifted it once more and pushed it down again. The clump was now symmetric. Centered. Pressing harder on the pedal, she dug both thumbs into the center of the mound and pulled them slightly apart to form the bottom of the bowl. Her fingers urged the sides up toward her face. She leaned closer, opening herself to the earthy smell, the feel of clay molecules sliding elegantly against each other and through her fingers. Her swiss-cheese brain didn't matter here.

"Wow," Sam said when the wheel stopped spinning and the bowl glistened. "Where did you learn to do that?"

"Charlie," she said. So many years since her fingers danced with clay. So many lost years. So many losses.

"Charlie?" Sam asked.

Flo remembered how clay caked on Charlie's overalls and how it flaked off on her when they kissed in the bisque drying room at the Corcoran. She let Trixie lead her to a sink to wash her hands and guide her down another identical hallway to the medical office. She sat alone in the exam room with arms crossed. She scraped a bit of dried clay from her shirt and put it in her mouth, savoring the taste. She didn't need a damn doctor, unless this one could fix her brain or give her a transplant but she was pretty sure they hadn't invented those yet. Her brain lost things, lost words and memories and ideas and names and even essential things like this morning, when she stood in the kitchen holding a piece of metal with two parts and a tiny wheel in the middle—with sharp edges—and unable to remember what it did or why she needed it.

How odd that some things were lost and some memories lived razor-sharp in her head, in her body. Her skin remembered the scrape of Charlie's beard when he skipped shaving and the webbing between his first and second toes, while so many other things wobbled in her brain, important things she was supposed to know like the route home from the park and how to scramble an egg. When that happened, and it happened more and more, she tried to hold fast to whatever the vanishing thing was in her brain but her heart raced and she breathed faster and faster until she thought she'd die of breathlessness and dizziness and sometimes the thought swelled and burst, leaking bits of ruined images from her useless head.

After the exam, the nurse escorted Flo back to Mimi in the waiting room, and gestured Sam to follow her.

"Dr. Robertson will speak with you now," she said.

The doctor sat behind his desk making notes on a yellow pad. Sam took one of the matching plaid chairs. Was plaid supposed to make him feel comfy?

"Your mother's dementia is moderately advanced." The doctor spoke without looking up. "Early Stage Five. It's too late for Assisted Living, but I think she'll do well in our Memory Unit."

Sam tried to hide his reaction. Why not call it an Alzheimer's Unit, or Dementia. It seemed cruel to call it a Memory Unit when the residents were losing theirs.

"What's the difference?" he asked.

"More staff for one thing, to monitor pharmacotherapy."

"Why drugs, if there's no cure?" Sam asked, aware of the argument in his voice, the annoyance threading between the words of his question.

"We can sometimes slow the progression." The doctor finally looked up and made eye contact with Sam. "Help people feel less agitated."

You mean easier to handle, Sam thought.

"Also the physical layout of the Memory Unit addresses the behaviors common to these conditions. For example, the hallway is circular, so our residents can walk and walk and never get lost."

"Don't they notice they're going in circles?"

"No, Mr. Tobin. They do not. In any case, with your mother our goal would be to get her settled with the appropriate services now, before the disease progresses."

"Progresses how?" Sam asked, even though he'd read the entire Alzheimer's Disease website carefully and had memorized the seven stages. He knew the symptoms to come: the wandering, the suspiciousness and delusions, the incontinence, the belligerence.

Except, of course, Flo had a long history of belligerence.

"We'll address new problems as they come up," the doctor said. "I think your mother will do well here, as long as we address her anger issues. I'd like to start her on a medication for that."

"What medication?" Sam asked.

"It's an off-label use." The doctor handed him a folded brochure. "Ignore the black box warning about side effects in elderly patients with dementia. They have to say that, for liability."

"What kind of side effects?"

"Everything from dry mouth and drowsiness to cardiac arrhythmias and sudden death. This drug is routinely prescribed for patients like your mother and it's pretty effective."

"If we don't agree to the medication?"

Dr. Robertson stood up. "Then perhaps you should look for another placement. I don't think your mother will do well here without appropriate pharmacologic modification."

"Isn't it reasonable for people like my mother to be angry, given how much they're losing?" Sam remained sitting. He wasn't finished. "She's always been healthy. A little arthritis, but that's all. And now *this*. Aren't there kinder ways to treat the symptoms? Like pet therapy? Ma loves her cat. Can she bring him here?"

"We have a couple of resident cats in the Memory Unit and on the nursing unit," he said. "But residents may not bring their own pets from home. Liability issues."

That won't go over well, Sam thought. Still, he and Zoe could adopt Charlie and sneak him in to visit.

"What about, you know, encouraging them to talk about it, in a group or something, instead of just sedating them? Alternatives like using art or poetry or humor?"

Not that humor was all that effective with Flo. He stifled a smile, thinking of the time two, three years earlier, when he wrapped a bag of marbles for his mother for their Chanukah gift exchange. Flo's memory loss was evident but not yet frightening. It had seemed like a good gift. Funny even. Sam and Zoe had picked out a rainbow of purples and deep reds, Flo's favorite colors, and put them in a thin muslin pouch. *To replace the ones you've lost*, he wrote on the card.

Flo had not been amused.

The doctor didn't respond right away, but the tight lines around his mouth and the flare of his nostrils conveyed his reaction. "I suppose that theoretically that might be an interesting approach if we had unlimited resources," he admitted. "But we don't; no facility does. It's imperative that we provide a safe environment for all our residents and for our staff."

Sam stood up; he got it. Drugs were easier. Not to mention paid for by Medicare. He didn't much like it, but what choice did he have? These people knew what they were doing; they had the highest rating in the area. The doc seemed arrogant but maybe he could be flexible. Sam offered his hand and his most conciliatory tone.

"I think I understand. Would you be willing to wait a while and see how she adapts to this place before starting any medicine?"

The doctor shook Sam's hand. "Sure, we can wait a few weeks, monitor her behavior, and see how it goes."

Even if he succeeded in convincing his mother to move to Hillside Village, she would be under surveillance. Great. Flo's behavior was iffy at the best of times.

Chapter Ten

The F train was just pulling into the station when Jeremy reached the platform on Saturday, so he was fifteen minutes early for the Earth Day meeting. When he picked up a spicy bean chimichanga and walked into the back room of the burrito bar, Carl and Sari were already at the table, talking with their heads close together. They looked up and their conversation stopped short, leaving two words hanging frozen in the air: Molotov. Cocktail.

Sari and Carl looked at each other, then spoke at the same time.

"Hey, Jerry," Carl said.

"You're early." Sari pointed to her watch.

Molotov cocktail. Jeremy's face must have reflected the two words because Carl fumbled. "We were, you know, just shooting the bull."

"Shooting the bull," Sari repeated. "Nothing important."

The first time Jeremy heard the words Molotov cocktail was in the visiting room at the prison. It must've been very early in their father's sentence because he and Tim were still terrified by the place—the beefy guards, the ugly smells, the other prisoners with their shuttered faces. Their dad had already put on that waxy face too—Francie explained that it was a mask to protect him in the rough prison—but the day he mentioned Molotov cocktails his mask slipped for a moment.

That day it took Francie and the twins longer than usual to get through the multiple checkpoints, the bag inspection, waiting for the slow computer processing and finally, the approval. Then they were at a round table. The red line painted on the floor bisected the visiting room and the prisoners weren't allowed to step over. The vending machines lined up along the wall, forbidden territory to prisoners, but Francie wouldn't let them buy any cheese doodles or soda anyway. They ate hummus and veggie sandwiches from the old white Styrofoam cooler that shrieked when Francie pulled off the lid.

That is, the twins ate. Her face flushed and shiny, Francie tried to interest Tian in morsels of neighborhood gossip. It drove her nuts that she couldn't touch him. Hugs were allowed only at the beginning and end of a visit; Francie called them bookend hugs and claimed it was cruel and unusual punishment and that was against the law. In between hugs, Francie talked nonstop and Tian rarely responded, his face hard and fragile at the same time. Jeremy imagined his dad's skin was eggshell thin, and a little crack would let his thick feelings ooze out. They didn't though, not all the years in prison, except that one day.

"What can I do to cheer you up?" Francie asked Tian that day. "Bring you something special next week? A cake or something?" She rested her forearms on the table and leaned forward toward Tian, smiling broadly. Jeremy flushed at the way her breasts pushed up when she leaned like that. He looked down at his Batman sticker book.

"How about a Molotov cocktail?" Tian said, his whisper fierce enough to make Jeremy and Tim stop playing and stare at him.

"Quiet!" Francie gestured at the guard with her chin. "They hear you talking like that, they'll stick you in solitary and never let us back to visit." Tian looked away and Francie hid her face in her arms. Jeremy crumpled the Batmobile sticker in his hand and stared at the guard on his stool, willing him not to hear his father's words.

On the long ride home, Jeremy asked his mom what a Molotov cocktail was, the bad thing his dad wanted.

"An explosive device," she had said. "Nothing you need to know about."

People crowded around the big table strewn with bean-stained napkins and splotched with salsa verde. Jeremy nibbled at his food while loud conversation spiraled and the room grew warm and the meeting went on and on. He kept losing track of the argument. Teach-in versus sit-in. The discussion spun in circles, with tactics and goals and strategies and objectives twirling wildly in the air like smoke. At the center of the murky language tornado, two words stood motionless. Molotov cocktail. Unspoken but loud.

"We should focus on getting the university to divest in fossil fuel," Sari said. "Economic pressure will force the industry to pay for their carbon emissions and that'll level the playing field for renewable energy sources."

"Divestiture is fine," said a man Jeremy recognized from the meeting after Mary's lecture. "But it's not enough. It ignores global overpopulation and resource depletion. We've got to create a new structure for society, like massive permaculture projects. We've started a small farm on campus, but it could be so much more. Maybe we could take over the botanical gardens or Prospect Park and grow food to serve the people. Occupy the land!"

A woman Jeremy hadn't seen before shook her head. "Come down to earth, Tommy. We need stronger local regs about recycling and emissions. People need to take individual responsibility for their carbon footprint, you know?"

Greenhope looked around the room and spoke slowly. "Turning this monster around is going to take more than outlawing plastic bottles or driving a hybrid car. The big carbon polluters are criminals. If we don't stop them, our children will inherit a dead planet."

Jeremy couldn't imagine having children. He tried to picture Mary as a mother.

"This is not only about students," Carl said. "A teach-in could offer avenues for activism both on campus and in the community. Education is critical."

"Maybe a radio program, like the one you did at UMass, Jeremy," Sari said. "I listened to a few of the podcasts and they're amazing."

Jeremy leaned back and closed his eyes. Sari listened, so why wasn't she—or anyone—talking about the dying plants? Why wasn't *he* saying something?

As the meeting broke up, the guy called Tommy came over. "Hey," he said. "Did Sari say you were from UMass? I hear they've got this awesome permaculture project going. Have you been involved with that?"

Jeremy shook his head. He'd seen a course listed in the bio department.

"Forget gardens." Sari touched his arm. "Did you read the Green Book?"

"Most of it."

"What'd you think?"

"I'm not sure. They seem to believe the only way to save the planet is to bring down civilization. Sacrificing 90 percent of the earth's population." He shrugged. "That's a little hard to stomach."

Sari nodded. "Still, they make a pretty compelling argument, don't they?"

Greenhope interrupted her. "Compelling but totally unacceptable." She turned to Jeremy. "Will you be at Saturday's planning meeting?"

Jeremy shook his head. "I have to go home this weekend for my brother's birthday, but I'll be back for Earth Day."

"Good," Sari said. "Because I want to talk with you about the Green Book. And about some other actions we've been thinking about."

Like Molotov cocktails? No thanks. He turned to leave. "I haven't finished the book yet," he said over his shoulder.

~≈∼

Jeremy walked toward the subway. Images of the Green Book and Molotov cocktails ricocheted inside his brain. Did any of these people even care about plant genocide? His feet played a dirge beat on the sidewalk.

His lips found the syllables of species lost from the planet and chanted their names in mourning. *Pluchea glutinosa*. In the air around him, deep musical notes grew from the mantra of Latin nomenclature, the melody faint and familiar but not quite recognizable. *Shorea cuspidata*.

Odd that he never before noticed the gated park on his right, so luxuriant and lush for mid-April that the tall metal fencing couldn't contain the exuberant growth. Leafy branches heavy with buds twined around the metal balusters and climbed to the ornate spindles sharp against the afternoon sky. Broad leaves escaped between the fencing and reached for him as the music swelled and then he knew it. Of course he did—it was the Kyrie from Missa Luba. He hadn't played that CD since the awful night of his interrupted radio program and visit to the Health Service. None of that mattered now. The music expanded to fill the air and he added the harmony of his offerings: *Radula visiniaca. Psiadia schweinfurthii.*

The music grew louder, more orchestral, more salutation than requiem now. Thick branches squeezed through the fence stakes and pushed at him. The metal itself began growing and changing, morphing into organic shapes, shiny metal limbs and delicately veined leaves, and they reached for him too. A long twig—was it vegetable or mineral? How bizarre that he couldn't distinguish between them—wrapped itself around his right arm and squeezed, sending minuscule green shoots pricking through his skin into his flesh, into his cells, into his circulating blood. The branch tugged at him and the fencing spread itself open. As the forged steel railings curved apart to welcome him, Jeremy stepped off the sidewalk and into the garden.

Chapter Eleven

Even though Flo's ancient bike zigzagged across the bike lane, threatening to spill Flo into the gravel ditch, Zoe still had to push hard to stay close. Two wheels were faster than four, Zoe reminded herself, but she was about a fifth her grandmother's age so she should be able to keep up, right?

"Wait," Zoe called. "Let's watch the ball game for a few minutes."

Flo dragged her foot on the pavement to slow down, ignoring the brake. She leaned her bike against a bench with flaking green paint facing the ball field and looked back at Zoe. "Can't keep up with an old lady, huh?"

"Busted." Zoe swiveled her wheelchair alongside the bench. Her grandmother might be losing her marbles, but she still had moments of awesome smarts. And she had never been easy to fool. Her dad had asked Zoe to try to find out what Flo thought about the Assisted Living center they visited, since Flo refused to discuss it with him. But if Zoe brought it up, her grandmother would see right through her.

Zoe watched the skinny kid at the plate, spitting in the dirt and knocking his bat against the ground in a parody of professional players. He wiped his hands on his green shirt, positioned the bat, and waited. Why did baseball involve so much standing around? Life was too short to waste time. Flo sat on the bench with her hands on her knees, fingers positioned in that yoga secret hand signal. Did that mean she was meditating or something, and didn't want to be disturbed? Zoe studied Flo's face wondering what it felt like to have your brain disintegrating, swirling right down the toilet and sucking your life along with it. No wonder she didn't want to talk about Assisted Living.

The skinny kid hit the ball hard. It arced over the infield and bounced twice before a red-shirt player caught it. The batter made it to third base and his grin made Zoe smile too. He looked about Gabe's age, eleven or twelve. He was probably a Forest Park kid; maybe he'd be at Gabe's party next Saturday.

That was going to be so weird, chaperoning a dance party. Gabe wanted retro decorations—crepe paper streamers and a rented strobe light. Her friends never had parties with themes and dancing and decorations. Or maybe they just didn't invite her.

"Zoe?" Flo said.

Zoe looked at her grandmother. "Yeah?"

"What's on your mind?"

"Can't a girl take a ride around the park on a beautiful day with her grandma without having an ulterior motive?"

"Sure. But I know you, and you're preoccupied with something."

"A couple of things," Zoe admitted. "Like, I'm worried about you living alone and everything. Have you thought about that place on the hill?"

"Don't be a stool pigeon for your dad. What's the other thing?"

Zoe blushed. She *told* her father it wouldn't work.

"The other thing is that Gabe is having a birthday party next weekend, and I'm supposed to help chaperone. I'm nervous about that."

"Gabe?"

"You know. He and his mom—that's Pippa—live downstairs with my mother and Emily?"

Flo still looked puzzled. Like a cloud covered her face, all shadows and gray air.

"Remember? Gabe's dad was in prison because of those two little kids dying a few years ago in the park? They all lived in that commune. His parents weren't married or anything."

"Charlie and I weren't married," Flo said slowly.

"Who's Charlie?"

Flo stood up. "You can tell your dad that I'm not going to that place. He can live there if he likes it so much." She grabbed the handlebars of her bike and awkwardly settled herself on the seat. "I'm perfectly fine and I'm going home. Alone."

Zoe watched Flo peddle back along the bike path. What just happened? What did she say wrong? Should she follow her? Better not—Flo would be majorly pissed off.

And who was Charlie?

∽ɘɔ

Flo had to get away. She didn't want Zoe seeing her blubber like a baby. Not that she didn't have plenty of reasons to cry and more reasons cropping up every day. Just that morning she found herself sitting fully clothed in the bathtub with no water and she couldn't remember getting in, or why. She had sniffed her armpit and figured out she needed a bath, but by the time she climbed out of the tub to take off her clothes, she decided to brush her teeth instead.

Maybe she'd better add that to her list: take off clothes and put water in bathtub before getting in.

And that wasn't the only item to add. There was Charlie. Decades ago she promised herself never to mention him, and she just did it again, to Zoe. If she were a superstitious person instead of a communist she might think that Charlie was trying to contact her, hurling surprisingly potent ghost memories of their time together across lost decades. But that was the substance of paperback romance novels, not real life.

She wobbled under the arch at the park entrance and pressed the crosswalk button at Sumner Avenue. When the signal changed, she pushed her bike across the street and then stopped. Which way was home? The buildings all looked the same, even though she could see they were different colors, shapes. Unfamiliar houses, wooden houses in yards rich with trees and shrubs, some squat brick apartment buildings. She had a feeling she belonged here somewhere, but she recognized nothing. She had no idea which way to turn.

How could her brain betray her like this?

If only Mimi were here with her, to say, "Earth to Flo" and remind her where she was going. If only she were back home in Maryland; she would remember how to get to the apartment on River Road. If only that arch across the street could be the entrance to Glen Echo Amusement Park. If only Charlie were here with her. If only.

She leaned her bike against a wrought iron fence and sat down on the curb. She let her head settle into the cradle of her arms. Just for a minute, to rest. Then she'd get up and figure out how to go home.

∿♪

Sam put the finishing touches on a new website for the Hampden County Home Care agency. The irony of the situation wasn't lost on him. His ex-wife's cousin Emily used to work for the place and her job got them all into trouble. His part of the trouble was rescuing Jeremy and Timothy from the forest, when their parents broke the law. He was fond of the twins, although he hadn't seen them in ages. Zoe said they'd be in town for Gabe's birthday party and that she was chaperoning the party. Of course, he wasn't invited, but Zoe said it was happening downstairs so he might manage to bump into them. He was thinking about ways to make this happen when the doorbell rang. He rolled his desk chair to the front window and looked down.

A police cruiser? Uh-oh. Did something happen to Zoe? He flew down the outside staircase.

Next to the mailbox at the foot of the stairs, an officer stood with his mother, holding her arm. Flo looked down at her feet but he could see tears staining her cheeks.

"Do you know this woman?" The officer asked.

"She's my mother. What's wrong?"

The officer's voice was kind. "She was wandering around the farmers market at the X, looking confused. She, uh, doesn't seem to know where she lives, but we found this in her pocket."

Sam took the folded flyer from the officer, one of dozens Flo had helped him distribute promoting his website design business, offering a discount to neighborhood residents. It had his photo—not your best side, Flo had criticized—and his address.

Sam took Flo's hand in both of his.

"My bike," she said, finally looking up at him. "I've lost my bike."

He guided her to the stairs. "We'll find it, Ma. Later. Come inside. I'll make tea." He turned back to the officer. "Thank you."

Halfway up the steps, Flo stopped.

"Do you need to rest?" Sam asked.

"I'm fine," she said. "But don't even ask. Because I'm *not* going to that place."

Chapter Twelve

The strobe light snapped into the ceiling bracket with a sharp click, pinching the tender web of skin between his thumb and index finger. Jeremy yelped and yanked his hand back.

"What's wrong?" Zoe asked. She wheeled to the center of the living room, trailing black crepe paper and looked up at him.

What was wrong with him? Jeremy had been asking himself that question for the past week, ever since a metal fence twisted open and green fingers pulled him into that impossible garden, lush with plants that no longer existed on earth. Afterwards, he dug through his wallet for the card that the nurse practitioner gave him, because maybe he should talk to someone. But he didn't call, because whatever it was that happened there, whatever hallucination or crossed cerebral synapses, he'd felt happier in that place, more peaceful, than he could ever remember. It felt like a family reunion with all the dead kin come back to say hello, patting his shoulder with their leafy hands and murmuring, "Haven't you grown into a fine young man?" Sure the kin were dead plant species but still, who knows, he might still be there, growing roots into magical soil, if it hadn't been for the screaming fire engines and ambulances blasting down the street, breaking the spell, and then he was back on the sidewalk, stunned and shaken and clueless.

But that probably wasn't what Zoe meant.

Jeremy put his injured hand in his mouth and sucked, then climbed off the stepladder. "I'm clumsy, that's all." He showed her his hand and they both watched the blood puddle in the hollow web.

"Purlicue," Zoe said.

"Huh?"

"That's what that space is called, between your thumb and pointer finger. You should clean that," Zoe said. "Bandage it."

"When I get home. To my parents'."

"No. Come on." Zoe turned away. "We'll do it now."

Jeremy followed her chair down the hall to the bathroom. Purlicue. He'd never heard the word, but it sounded like her hair looked, curly. Curlier than he remembered. Bouncier. He tried to recall the last time he'd seen Zoe and couldn't. A couple years at least. Probably at one of Gabe's soccer games, before he started at UMass and moved into the dorm. However long it had been, she had certainly changed.

"How old are you?" he asked when they squeezed into the bathroom.

"Sixteen." Zoe turned on the faucet and pushed back, out of his way. "Wash it," she told him. She pulled sterile gauze, tape, and a small tube of ointment from a drawer. "You don't want an infection."

Bossy, he thought, letting her dry his hand and wind it in gauze. He liked her attention. He liked the way her hair smelled, a combination of almonds and fruit, when she leaned over to tape the bandage. Like the marzipan Pippa once helped him and Tim make for a cooking project, back when their commune was good.

"There," she said. "Don't get it wet when you shower."

"You want to be a nurse or something?" he asked, then added, "A doctor?"

"Nah. My Aunt Emily's a nurse, so I grew up with blood and guts. I want to be a medical researcher, find a cure for birth defects."

"Like what's wrong with you?" he asked.

"Nothing's *wrong* with me," she said. "I was born with a spine problem." She swiveled her wheelchair and pushed out of the bathroom.

He watched her leave, then checked his watch. Three hours until Gabe's party. He'd better get back to his parents' place to clean up so he could be back in time to chaperone, whatever that meant. Keep the kids from sneaking off into the bedrooms, he figured, or getting into the liquor cabinet. His assigned job was manning the music system but Gabe had already made a mix of his favorite bands and told Jeremy no substitutions. So he might have a chance to hang out with Zoe.

How do you dance with a girl in a wheelchair? he wondered.

$\sim$

After Jeremy left, Zoe went back to twisting crepe paper. Pippa cut eight-foot-long strands from the roll, tied one end from the living room chandelier, and handed the other end to Zoe. Her job was to twist the crinkly paper and attach the long loops to lamps and plant hooks and curtain rods around the room. Black and blue wasn't the most cheerful decorating scheme, but that's what Gabe wanted and it was his birthday.

Gabe had always been kind of strange, which wasn't all that surprising when you took his family into consideration, his dad in prison and Tian's other kids, Gabe's half-siblings, dying like that. Plus Gabe grew up in her house, which wasn't the most normal situation either. It used to be great, when it was just Zoe and Anna and cousin Emily. When Gabe and Pippa moved in, it grew too crowded, too noisy and cluttered with little boy energy.

Zoe remembered the day she decided to live with her father. She was twelve and came home from school to find Gabe and his friends lying across her bed reading her diary aloud and laughing.

"I've had it," she screamed at her mother. "I'm moving upstairs."

Gabe apologized and he looked like he really meant it, but the diary was just an excuse. She was almost a teenager and needed privacy. Sam looked shocked when she told him. Stunned and then delighted. His joy bothered her a little. "I'm not so great to live with," she warned him. The day she moved upstairs she gave up playing spoonerisms and retired her baby-name for her father. No more Papa; now she called him Dad.

Mostly, it had worked out well. Sam was easy to live with even though he worried too much. Sometimes she worried that her presence might scare off his potential girlfriends, but her dad never brought anyone home. He was pretty cute, for a father, with curly brown hair and tanned even in winter. Mom always joked that he tanned from the inside, didn't even need to be in the sun. Sam looked a lot like Jeremy, actually, although she didn't think they were related. Hard to tell with their complicated and interwoven families. They had the same coloring, same mop of curls. Maybe that's why she liked Jeremy's looks so much. She blushed.

"Hey. You're falling down on the job," Pippa said. "Should I hang these?"

Zoe nodded. She'd been daydreaming and twirling, curling and daydreaming, and a mountain of twisted strands lay heaped in her lap.

"Sure," she said. "I'm going to go upstairs and get dressed."

～❧～

"But today's Saturday, isn't it?" Flo said into the phone. "The Club meets on Thursdays."

"Emergency meeting," Mimi said. "I'll pick you up in half an hour."

"What's the emergency?"

"You," Mimi said. "You're the emergency."

Flo was quiet for a moment before responding. "I'll be ready."

Marlene, Fanny and Claire had already claimed one blue sofa at the Coffee Hut. While Mimi stood in line for their Mocha Delights, Flo settled on the matching couch and watched her friends. As long as she could remember everyone's name, former career, and hot drink of choice, how bad could her brain be, right? Fanny: divorce attorney, skinny decaf latté. Marlene: Women's Shelter, skinny decaf latté but she sometimes forgot the skinny part. Claire: still worked part time as a nursing supervisor, green tea, couldn't speak a declarative sentence.

And Mimi, who handed her the steaming drink. Mimi: used to run the Food Pantry, mocha delight, best friend for more decades than Flo could count.

"Can we talk about our name?" Fanny asked. "I've been thinking, how about the Sisterhood?"

"More like the geezerhood," Mimi muttered.

Claire shook her head. "Sisterhood reminds me of the Hadassah, from when I was a kid?"

"We can appropriate their name," Fanny argued. "Make it ours."

"I like the girls' club," Marlene says. "Or maybe the babayagas, like those old women in Paris who decided to make a commune."

Flo didn't care about the name, but wasn't it upside down that when they were in their twenties and thirties they weren't allowed to call themselves girls and now in their seventies and eighties it's okay?

Mimi held up her hand. "We're here to talk about Flo's . . . problem."

Flo looked at her lap and tried to name the conflicting feelings clogging her throat: Annoyance that Fanny won't shut up about names. Frustration that Claire thinks that everyone's health is her concern. Irritation at how bossy Mimi can be, sticking her nose in other people's business.

Gratitude that her friends came on a Saturday because she has a problem.

What was her problem? Something was wrong but she couldn't quite remember what. Words had always been her friends but now they deserted her. Without her words, who was she?

Claire reached across the table and patted Flo's knee. "What's going on?" she asked.

Marlene nodded. "And how can we help?"

Next to her on the sofa, Mimi leaned close and took Flo's hand. "Do you want to tell them, or should I?"

Flo felt the heat of their stares on her face. "You."

Mimi looked from one woman to the next, around the circle. "Flo has been having some problems with her memory."

Fanny jumped right in. "Of course she has. At our age we all have lapses."

Claire shut her up with a glance. Claire took her role as the group's health professional seriously. She was solicitous and generous with advice and offers of help, even when no one wanted it. Flo hid a smile behind her other hand, the one Mimi wasn't holding, remembering the time she had cataract surgery and Claire came over every morning to read to her. The books she chose were so boring that Flo kept falling asleep, blaming her non-existent pain meds.

"These memory lapses are more serious," Mimi said. "One day last week she forgot where she lived, couldn't get home. A policeman rescued her and brought her to Sam's apartment."

Flo closed her eyes, remembering the rough curb where she sat for what felt like hours, waiting for a clue about which direction was home, then walking aimlessly until the cop found her wandering through stalls at the farmers market. How shamed she felt when the he talked to her like a little lost girl.

"The thing is," Mimi continued, "Flo has been diagnosed with Alzheimer's."

No one spoke for a long moment. "The dreaded A," Marlene said softly. "The scarlet letter of our generation."

Flo knew that word. Alzheimer's. When Mimi paused and took a sip of her mocha, Flo saw that her own mug was full. She put it down. She wasn't thirsty.

"Sam has decided that Flo can't live alone any longer." Mimi took a sip of her mocha. "He's looking at Assisted Living facilities. The place he's chosen is pretty nice, actually, but Flo doesn't want to go."

Her voice trailed off into more silence. Flo couldn't think of a time they had been quiet for this long, not since Mimi's beloved Joanna died without warning and they were stunned with her into the silent vacuum of profound grieving. This was like a death too, Flo thought, and it was the demise of her brain they were mourning.

Claire reached across again and took Flo's other hand. "How do you feel about the diagnosis, Flo?"

"How do you think she feels?" Marlene interrupted. "Maybe now really is the time to make our own babayaga commune. My house is big. You could all move in and..." Her sentence disappeared into the sad black hole in the center of the group.

A distant section of her brain flared slightly. Flo pictured a thought being born and pulsing into life. Clumsily, like when Sam was an infant and first discovered that his fingers could move to his mouth and he could suck them and it felt good. Her thought felt good too, if she could just hold onto it long enough to form it into words and push them through her mouth.

"Does it ever happen to you?" she began, the words raw and stubborn and slow. "You are someplace and all of a sudden you don't know where you are and all the landmarks disappear and you're lost?"

She faltered and stopped talking. How impossibly hard this was, to try to grab onto something so alarming, so intrinsically wordless, and translate it into sentences. But if she couldn't tell these women, her closest friends in the world since Charlie, she was lost for certain, so she had to try. "Do you know what it's like, to try to grab onto a familiar thing—a house or a corner store or a park bench—but things and places turn slippery and they slide away before you can get a good grip?"

She could tell by their faces that they didn't know. And they pitied her.

"We'll come to you," Marlene said. "Have our weekly meetings in the place, you know, where you'll be living. And we'll visit, lots."

"I'll make a schedule," Claire added.

"Nothing is settled yet," Mimi said. "But I thought you would all want to know what's happening. And it didn't seem right to talk about Flo without her here."

Flo pulled her hands away from Mimi, from Claire. That was the problem, wasn't it? Even when she was right there, sitting with her best friends, it happened. The words she needed slid out of their sentences and tumbled from their paragraphs. At some point, soon, all her words would be gone and she would disappear.

Chapter Thirteen

No one answered Sam's knock. That wasn't surprising because the volume of music blaring from Anna's half of the house was impressive. Staggering, even. He always had a moment of disbelief knocking on Anna's door anyway, after living behind it for years. But that was before Zoe's diagnosis and birth and all the troubles with Anna culminated in his move to the upstairs apartment on Zoe's first birthday. Things changed again when Pippa moved in with baby Gabe, and he was even more isolated. So he got it that he hadn't been invited to Gabe's birthday party, even though he helped Zoe pick up the strobe light and lugged bags of crepe paper rolls from the party store. He knocked again, then let himself in.

The music blasted from the living room, the pulses of bass melody somehow coordinated with colored flashes from a strobe light and waves of laughter. The red-faced birthday boy was flanked by two girls who were demonstrating a stomping dance step that rattled the walls of the old house. Sam turned left, away from the party, and pushed through the kitchen door.

Four adults sat around the table. Pizza crusts littered their plates. Four faces turned to him, neither surprised nor welcoming. His ex-wife Anna and her cousin Emily sat on one side of the table, long necks held in identical position. When Emily moved to Springfield and needed a place to live until she found a job and apartment, he joked about the long-necked Maine island cousins, but neither found it humorous. Sam didn't expect much welcome from Tian or Francie either. The first time he met them they were on the receiving end of a police raid in Forest Park and he had—at some risk to himself—taken charge of their twins and brought the boys to safety. Tian had never really thanked him for that, but the guy had bigger problems back then. From the way he was fiddling with a jumble of rubber bands around his wrist maybe he wasn't out of the woods yet.

Anna didn't look so welcoming either, with that deep, vertical worry crease between her eyebrows. But then, their relationship was so complicated that he never knew what kind of response to expect. The last couple of years though, once she got used to Zoe living upstairs with him, they'd been doing pretty well.

Pippa was the really thorny one, with her spiked yellow hair and old-fashioned glasses. She didn't look a day older than the afternoon she showed up at the children's hospital during Zoe's emergency shunt surgery when she was five. He hadn't exactly been the knight in shining armor when Pippa was under house arrest, but he *did* rescue the twins, and they *were* part of her family, or whatever the commune members called themselves. He had thought, back then, that there might have been something special between them, even though she was still involved with Tian and pregnant with his kid. Then Tian went to prison and Gabe was born and Pippa moved them into this apartment with Anna and Emily and Zoe, and nothing happened with Pippa. The story of his life.

"How's it going?" Sam asked. "I couldn't work upstairs with all the noise, so thought I'd come down and see if you need any help." He looked around the table. "Guess not, huh?"

Anna patted the empty chair to her right. "Help yourself to pizza, Sam. The kids don't seem to need any of us in there."

"You got any beer?" Francie asked.

Anna shook her head. "I thought we'd better not have alcohol around, with the party and all."

"We should still check on them every once in a while," Pippa said. "Gabe is only eleven, and this is his first, you know, teenager party."

"He's too young for this," Tian said. "If you ask me. Which you didn't."

Pippa frowned. "Gabe asked and you agreed. It's what all his friends are doing."

"Which is a really terrific reason he should do it too." Francie took Tian's hand and brought it to her lips. She muttered something that sounded like "lemmings."

"Gabe's a good kid," Pippa said. "And there's nothing wrong with a party like this. Besides, Zoe and the twins are in there with them, and they'll make sure nothing bad happens."

"I don't know about Zoe," Francie said, "but Tim isn't exactly responsible where girls are involved and Jeremy isn't the most mentally stable guy in the world."

"The twins are solid," Tian said, snapping a rubber band. "They'll keep Gabe's friends in line."

Sam felt the heat of Anna's stare and turned to her. He knew that look. "Why don't I just go check it out?" He stood up. "I haven't wished Gabe a happy birthday yet." When no one objected, he flashed Anna a you-owe-me glance and walked toward the living room.

It was hard to believe these kids were, what, eleven and twelve? They looked like small high school kids, with make-up and weird hairstyles and acting both knowing and infantile. He supposed parents always looked down on the youth culture of the next generation. His dad always seemed disappointed in him, telling him to "be a man"—whatever that was supposed to mean. Brad gave him the third degree every evening and clearly suspected the answers were lies. Flo was different. She never forbade him anything. When he was a teenager, she reminded him about the potential consequences of smoking weed in the alley near the movie theater, or getting caught with a fake ID, or not wearing a condom—which made him blush furiously but didn't seem to faze her—but rarely questioned him about his activities. Sam had evolved his own parenting style, such as it was, in direct opposition to his memory of how his father handled things, with a small dose of Flo's unconditional trust thrown in for good measure.

Trying to locate his daughter in the dark living room pulsating with drum beat and intermittently illuminated by action-stopping flashes of strobe lights, Sam wondered how effective his parenting amalgam would turn out to be. He didn't see Zoe, but there was one of the twins over by the refreshment table surrounded by sixth grade girls. From Francie's comment in the kitchen, that was probably Tim. Sam looked away, telling himself that he'd check again after he found Zoe.

There she was, pivoting her wheelchair to the heavy bass rhythm. She twisted her head too—side to side and up and down so that her hair flashed and twirled around her face like a fierce and rowdy halo. He couldn't tell if she was dancing alone or with someone, but it didn't seem to matter because Zoe looked like she was having great fun. Sam leaned against the wall and his gaze swept around the room.

He wasn't the only one whose attention was riveted on Zoe. The other twin, Jeremy, was staring at her too. He was the quiet one, a little pathetic, always had his nose in a sketchpad drawing plants when he was younger. Sam wondered how he fared when the family broke up and had to leave their greenhouse. Anna had mentioned he was studying botany at the university. Good for him, but why was he staring at his energetic and outgoing daughter?

⁓⊸⊷

Jeremy watched Zoe dance. Elbows jerking akimbo, she swiveled her chair sideways to the music, whipping her head back and forth so that her hair bounced, the long sandy-brown curls alive and electric. You'd think a wheelchair would make a person earthbound, but not Zoe. He wished he could dance like that, uninhibited and totally into the rhythm, not caring how awkward he looked, how uncoordinated.

How do you dance with a girl in a wheelchair, he wondered for the umpteenth time.

It shouldn't be a problem for fast dancing, if she didn't mind being partnered with a klutz, that is. He had never been all that social, didn't like parties or school dances, but he'd watched enough other people enjoying themselves to fake it. He on his feet and Zoe in her chair could wildly gyrate around each other just like able-bodied couples do. Was that term, "able-bodied," politically correct or offensive? He didn't know and at that moment being PC wasn't the most critical question. No, the most important thing in the universe was wanting to dance with Zoe, slow and close, their arms entwined tightly around each other. That yearning pushed doubts about terminology out of his brain, replacing it with the one really important issue: how could they slow dance if Zoe couldn't stand up? He pictured himself leaning over her chair, his butt sticking out, and that couldn't be right.

The song ended and Jeremy glanced at the music system, his assignment for the party, as the next song started without any help from him. Gabe's iPod was loaded with the music Gabe and his two best buddies selected, groups like One Direction that he never heard of but Gabe said the girls loved. It left him nothing to do except watch Zoe and daydream. Across the room his brother clearly had no compunctions about leaving his assignment at the refreshments table, hanging around instead with a group of Gabe's female classmates.

Always looking out for his twin, Jeremy scanned the room for possible adult interference, but no grown-ups were in view. He didn't expect his parents to actively chaperone. It just wasn't their style. Tian and Francie were probably chugging beers in the kitchen, wishing they were back home in their dark apartment six blocks away. But he expected Gabe's mother to be keeping tabs on the group. Pippa seemed like a hovering kind of parent, always worrying that Gabe would hurt himself playing soccer. And Zoe's mom, Anna, seemed even more overprotective.

Wait, there was Zoe's father, Sam, scanning the room. Maybe he would say something to Tim, stop him from hanging around those girls.

Tim didn't mean anything, but still. And at least Zoe was sixteen, only four years younger than him.

And here she came, wheeling in his direction.

∽ഛഛ

Zoe wiped her sweaty palms on her thighs. One silver lining of paralysis was that skinny jeans fit really tight, much better than her friends who were always lamenting their chunky legs. She pushed her chair toward the far corner, where Jeremy stood leaning on the wall next to the iPod system trying to look nonchalant and pretty much failing.

She liked him, even if he wasn't outwardly hot like his brother. They both had curly light hair that contrasted with darker skin, kind of like her father's coloring. Was that Oedipal or something? Jeremy wasn't all buffed and polished like Tim, but he was cute and had been so easy to talk with that afternoon when he cut his hand on the strobe light.

Now in the yellow and pink flashes of the spinning ball, Jeremy looked even more like a scared rabbit, but she wasn't going to wimp out now. She pushed right up next to him and held out her hand, really glad she had just wiped it dry.

"Dance with me?" she asked.

She'd chosen a really fast number and the dance floor—well, the living room—was crowded. It wasn't easy to dance close together without rolling over his feet or someone else's. She kept losing herself in the music and the movement and the drumbeat, but she always knew where he was. Whenever she caught his eye, she couldn't help smiling. When the song ended and a slow number began, neither one of them made any move to leave the dance floor.

He raised his eyebrows. She nodded. Yes.

Honestly, she had no idea how to do this. She had googled "dancing in a wheelchair" every way she could think of. Some of the results made her laugh—scantily clad women in Quickie chairs shaking their boobs on a stage and troops of disabled dancers doing synchronized motions to Aretha Franklin and men in chairs with regular girls draped on their laps. Nothing that helped her at all.

But she had thought about this a lot over the past few hours and she remembered how she used to dance with her papa when she was little. So, pushing her chair back toward the wall, she locked the wheels and leaned down to swivel the footplates out of the way. She put her feet on the floor and motioned Jeremy closer. Extending her hands, she gripped both of his and pulled herself up.

"Mind if I stand on your feet?" she asked.

He looked dazed but shook his head. No.

She placed one ballet slipper on each of his black high tops, angled outwards for a stronger base of support. Then she positioned her arms loosely around his neck and grinned.

"So what are you waiting for?" she asked. "Dance."

~~∽⌒∼~~

Relax, Jeremy told himself with every exhaled breath. But it was hard when every inspired breath carried the aroma of Zoe's marzipan shampoo. Silly idea, marzipan shampoo. He smiled into her hair, couldn't help it; it was right there, tickling his nose. How could he help being so aware of her hair? It did smell like ground almonds and fresh squeezed oranges. He liked it. And he liked her feet in those soft little shoes standing on his sneakers so that every step he took, every sway back and forth to the music, she was right there moving with him. His hands were planted on the small of her back, which was warm under the satiny fabric of her shirt, just above the waistband of her jeans. He liked how her arms rested on his shoulders and her hands circled his neck.

But he didn't like how his body sprang to attention. He knew her legs were paralyzed, or partly so, but what about the rest of her? Maybe she couldn't feel a boner. Still, he leaned back and looked at her. He had to say something, but couldn't think of a thing to say.

Zoe smiled at him. "So, I've been wondering. Are we related or something? Like, cousins?"

"I don't think so." Not by blood or marriage anyway, but she felt so familiar even though he hadn't seen her in years. Maybe people could become related by circumstance, by geography or history or the strange things their families got involved with.

She nodded, as if she could read his mind and agreed with him. "My mom said you dropped out of college. How come?"

"I'm just taking a leave of absence, while I figure stuff out."

"What kind of stuff?" She tilted her head just a little and the gesture was delicate and expectant, as if she really wanted to know the answer. It made him want to tell her everything but how could he explain it right? It was so important that she understand how significant the extinctions were, how tragic. He took a deep breath of marzipan.

"It's the plants," he said. "They're dying, hundreds of species every day."

"I didn't know that. Why?"

"Global warming and pollution and poisons in the air and water. It's our fault."

"What can we do about it?"

He loved that she said we. "That's the problem. I don't know how to stop it. I'm not sure it's possible."

She closed her eyes then and rested her head on his shoulder. He felt her touch the curls at the nape of his neck, twisting them around her fingers. He emptied his mind of vegetable disaster and focused on the music. And her fingers. He was so glad he hadn't gotten around to a haircut. If only he were brave enough to touch *her* hair but no, his arm couldn't do that. The thought raced through his mind that Tim would go for it, but he pushed the knowledge away because this wasn't about Tim.

This was about him. Jeremy. About how every inch of his body felt new. How each place where they touched contributed a singular and astonishing note to his orchestra of longing. How the inch of space between their bodies was electric, with hormone-charged molecules spinning wildly.

He wished the song would last forever.

A wisp of her hair danced into the air and landed on his cheek. He closed his eyes and felt the strands curl around his ear. Strange how hair could feel so alive, so green and growing, even though he knew that growth was from the follicle and the hair itself was a matrix of protein, filaments of keratin and melanin, husks of dead cells. Her hair was totally animate—the strand on his face was a vine, twining around his ear. Another curl spiraled around his shirt collar, tendrils grabbing the cotton fabric, tiny suction disks attaching to his neck. A third thicket of hair reached across to his arm, sending adventitious runners grasping his skin and burrowing into his flesh.

"Jeremy?"

He opened his eyes to a quiet room, buzzing with between-song conversation. Zoe regarded him half smiling, half concerned. "You okay?"

"Yeah," he said. "I'm great."

∽∾∾

The moment he saw Sam coming toward him, his expression grim and disapproving, Tim winked at the gaggle of girls and started back to the refreshment table. He hadn't seen Sam in years, but even without his crazy mustache the dude was totally recognizable, and so was his attitude. Not that he had any authority over Tim, no way, but Tim didn't need anyone ratting him out to Tian. His father had always tended to overreact to ordinary stuff and Tim planned to avoid being on the receiving end. He grabbed fresh ice from the cooler under the table and packed it around the cans of soft drinks in the metal tub. That's when he noticed Jeremy.

Whoa. His brother was dancing with the crippled girl. His goofy face was all dazzled and befuddled and he looked down at her like she was some hot actress and she was looking at him with the same silly grin. The funny part was that his brother was probably still a virgin and didn't have a clue about moving this along. She was just a kid, but not too young for those sparks sizzling around the two of them.

Watching his brother twist a long strand of the girl's hair and weave it in and out around his fingers, Tim couldn't help feeling both smug and envious. So this was how a botanist gets it on.

Chapter Fourteen

Luckily, Flo's telephone had speed dial and Mimi's number was near the top of the list. Number three, right after Sam and Zoe. Flo counted the ring tones as they echoed in her ear—five, six, seven—and a picture formed in her mind: her best friend Mimi spending Saturday evening with Marlene, sharing a bottle of cabernet, and gossiping about her. Over decades, Flo had tried to squash her jealous feelings. It was childish for grown women to worry about best friends and who liked whom more. She knew that, but that didn't mean she could stop herself, any more than she could stop worrying about potential disasters. Besides, at this point in her life she needed Mimi more than ever. Needed her loyalty and her full attention, undivided and undiluted.

The recording clicked on and Mimi's voice commanded her to leave a message. Flo froze and couldn't think what to say.

"It's me," she stumbled over her words. "Please call." She shook her head. How dim-witted she was becoming. Some days, she barely recognized herself.

Maybe music would help. She turned on the thingy that Sam gave her for Chanukah and stood staring at it. Amazing how that small machine could contain all her music. Sam had transferred CDs and audio tapes, even her old vinyl records into that tiny rectangle. She always left it on scramble, partly because she forgot how to use the menu, but mostly because she loved being surprised at what came next. How would Aretha Franklin feel about following Blondie? What fun to hear the final notes of Smokey Robinson fade into Donovan or Sweet Honey and the Rock.

It took a few seconds to identify the song that came on, but then she did and it was a revelation. "I always cook with honey," Judy Collins sang. "To sweeten up the night." She wanted to sob, thinking how nights used to be sweet. And—that was it—she wanted to cook, to bake, to make something sugary and satisfying, something that would fill her up and make her happy. She danced a little, a grapevine step and a twirl, imagining that Charlie was dancing with her in the small apartment he had never seen, in the city he had never visited.

She two-stepped into the kitchen and looked at the shelf of cookbooks. She rarely cooked any more, other than making a salad with some tuna fish, or nuking a frozen organic burrito. The kitchen table was half-covered with junk, items that belonged someplace else but she didn't care where. Charlie-cat was curled up and sleeping, his gray fur a shadow in the wooden salad bowl. A slatted box that once held clementines was cluttered with bills waiting for Sam's attention and grocery store flyers, a bottle of her favorite coriander-scented body lotion, worth every overpriced penny. She picked up an ancient photo of Sam wearing Zoe in a baby carrier. Poose, he used to call her, short for Papoose.

Flo shook her head. How wrong she had been about Zoe. After the ultrasound, she had advised Sam and Anna to have an abortion. There were very few things in her life she regretted, and that one topped the list. She didn't regret Charlie, though maybe she shouldn't have married Brad, but she regretted being so wrong about Zoe. She kissed the photo and returned it to the salad bowl, under the little bag of marbles Sam gave her as a gift. Mildly amusing, really, if it hadn't been so insulting.

But tonight she didn't care about insults. Tonight she wanted to cook, to make something special, from scratch. She ran her finger across the dusty spines of the cookbooks, stopping at *Diet for a Small Planet*. She pushed the box of junk away and sat at the table, thumbing through the recipes and listening to Charlie's uneven purr. Years ago she would've tossed him off the table, but now it didn't matter. Let him sit wherever he wanted to. She smiled at the lentil recipes, remembering how Sam loved the soup but wouldn't touch the loaf, no matter how many times she told him they were both made from the same ingredients—lentils and brown rice and carrots.

She found the recipe for honey and nut granola, but who was she fooling? She didn't have any of these ingredients in the house—steel cut oats and walnuts and organic orange blossom honey. She had nothing in this house. She threw the book on the floor, kicked it into the corner on her way to the refrigerator. Well, she didn't need a cookbook. She'd make something up, using what she *did* have.

Precious little, it turned out. But there were eggs—eggs didn't go bad, did they?—and an omelet would be great. Savory was even better than sweet, and healthier. She could cut those mold spots off the cheddar and chop those slightly wilted scallions and somewhere in the cupboard there was a can of artichoke hearts. Yes, cooking was just the thing to feel better.

She scrambled the eggs in a bowl and chopped the scallions, the wrinkled green pepper and limp celery, swaying as Janice Joplin belted out a little piece of her heart. Sad she had died so early. So many of Flo's heroes died young: Malcolm X and Judi Bari and Che Guevara and Rachel Corrie. And some heroes dropped out of sight, and you never heard from them again. She wondered what happened to that IRA woman, Bernadette somebody? Was she still standing strong or long gone?

The butter sizzled in the pan—it smelled so good—and Flo dumped the veggies in to sauté. Charlie lifted his head, sniffed the cooking aroma, then went back to sleep. Maybe it was better to go out in a blaze of youthful energy instead of this incremental wilting of nerve cells, crumbling of synapses, spots of mold eating up her memories. She caught her reflection in the kitchen window, framed by the curtains she hung when Sam was a little boy and worried about people looking in at them. The curtains were more gray than yellow and the hemming was coming undone. She'd take care of that tomorrow, wash them and mend them and they'd be good as new.

The phone rang and Flo hurried into the living room to answer it. Sam nagged her about trading in the landline for one of those smart phones, but at least with this one she always knew where it was and couldn't lose it. Besides, she didn't feel very smart, not any more.

"Hello?"

"It's Mimi. Are you okay?"

Flo smiled. "Sure. Why wouldn't I be?"

"Your message sounded—I don't know—frantic maybe? Desperate."

"Message?"

Mimi didn't answer for a few seconds. "Didn't you just leave me a message, to call you?"

Flo tried to think, but all that came were images of cooking with honey and Mimi sharing a bottle of red wine with Marlene. "Hmmm," she said. "What are you up to tonight?"

"Watching an old movie on TV. What about you?"

She and Charlie used to love the movies. Their first date was a Godard film, *Breathless*, in a small cinema near Dupont Circle. July of 1960, a few weeks after they met on the picket line at Glen Echo, two young people fired up and determined to integrate the amusement park. Charlie and his friends from Howard University sat in on the carousel and were arrested. Flo had just graduated high school and lived in the neighborhood. That park had defined her childhood summers—riding the ostrich on the carousel and swimming in the magical Crystal Pool—so of course she had to be part of the protests. Her parents forbade her to go, but she went anyway, carrying a hand-lettered picket sign. Bumper cars for all, or something silly like that. "I like your sign," Charlie had said, falling into line next to her.

"Flo?" Mimi's voice replaced the image of Charlie's face, shiny in the summer heat. "You there?"

"Where else would I be?" Flo said.

"I don't know," Mimi said. "But sometimes these days you're . . . missing."

Mimi had always been direct. It was one of the things Flo loved about her friend, except when the directness veered across the line into bossiness. Mimi liked to make pronouncements about things, and once pronounced, she rarely changed her mind. Not too good with the gray areas. That was probably why Flo had never told her about Charlie.

Charlie was all hers, her secret. It might be the most important part of her, what defined her, along with Sam and her women friends. When she met Charlie, she was already involved in civil rights with a city-wide group of high school students. They called themselves SAD, Students Against Discrimination. An unfortunate name, she later realized, but SAD and the Glen Echo movement and Charlie introduced her to the grown-up politics that changed her forever. That connected her, intensely and viscerally, to something big and world-changing. She studied Marx and his framework, his sharp focus, helped her make sense of it all. Sure, the Party made mistakes, but no one else had come up with a better way to understand and try to change the world.

It wasn't just the politics. Charlie opened her ears to new music too. That summer, while her neighborhood friends were swooning to Cathy's Clown and Teen Angel, Charlie introduced her to the exciting sound coming out of Detroit. Motown, he called it, with groups like The Miracles and the Marvelettes. They danced to "Shop Around" and "Please Mr. Postman" in the living room of his apartment near the university when his roommates were out.

"Like now." Mimi's voice was insistent. "Are you still with me, Flo?"

Maybe it was selfish, but she never told Mimi about any of it. Not about that first summer, and how she didn't want to go to college in September, but Charlie wouldn't let her stay. Not about trying to find him when she came home for winter break and he had moved. Not about going to Glen Echo every Saturday when she was home the next summer, when the park was finally integrated, and riding the carousel and the bumper cars but Charlie never showed up. And certainly not about what came later.

"I'm really worried about you," Mimi said. "How your attention wanders. Your memory loss is getting worse, isn't it?"

Her memory wasn't disappearing, just recalibrating. She might not remember calling Mimi but she remembered the swirly pattern of the gilded spirals painted on the winged horse Charlie rode on the carousel the day he was arrested. She remembered the old things, the most important things, the people she had loved. The struggles she cared about.

"I remember a lot," Flo said.

"You are my best friend in the world and I love you." Mimi's voice trembled. "And this is very hard for me to say. But I think Sam is right. I think Assisted Living would be a safer place for you to live."

So there it was, bossy Mimi in full display. Flo placed the receiver carefully in the phone cradle. Maybe bossy Mimi wouldn't even notice and would keep talking to an empty phone line. Flo didn't want to hear about Assisted Living. She wanted to remember.

Charlie broke her heart when he disappeared like that, leaving no way to contact him. She called the registrar at his university several times, but they didn't believe she was his sister and refused to give out any information. She haunted his old neighborhood, sat on the steps of the house he no longer rented, harassed the one friend of his she had met. Eventually, she stopped looking. She told herself it was humiliating and she tried to care about her dignity. She went back to college and her life there was full enough and she spent summers doing political work. A few years later when she volunteered for Freedom Summer, she thought maybe she'd run into him in Mississippi, but no such luck. No Charlie.

The phone rang again, but Flo ignored it. She didn't need Mimi lecturing her. And she didn't want to interrupt these memories, even if she couldn't quite remember when they happened. 1969 or '70, she thought. She coughed. If only she had a lozenge handy for this scratchy throat.

Of all the places she'd dreamed of finding Charlie, she never expected it to be at work. It was a sunny May afternoon and she was considering leaving early. He walked into the community radio station and right up to her desk.

"Are you the person to talk to about getting coverage of an event?" he asked.

She had stared at his face. The face that required two shaves a day or it was sandpaper on her skin and she never cared except that it made her mother suspicious that maybe she wasn't actually staying over at Susan's house so often.

"Charlie?" she whispered. "Is that really you?"

He didn't answer, but his eyes glistened. That evening, over dinner and drinks at her apartment and talk that lasted on and off until morning, they caught up with each other's lives. Her college and journalism school and work for public radio until they fired her for being argumentative and having a political agenda, how she loved working for a community media cooperative. His return home to Detroit to organize autoworkers, his marriage and two young sons.

"Why did you disappear like that?" she finally asked him.

He answered into the thicket of her hair. "Because Jim Crow was alive and well in D.C. in 1960. You would've gotten us both killed."

Ten years had thickened her waistline a little but also taught her a lot about what her body needed and this time she wasn't afraid to let him know. She remembered every detail about that night: the sparking of skin cells ordinarily tasked with simple barrier duties, holding insides in, keeping microbes out, separating her from other organisms. That night her skin committed dereliction of duty. It opened up and welcomed foreign proteins. Her bones melted and dissolved. Her muscles relaxed and sang.

Flo wrapped both arms around her chest and swayed back and forth to the lament of Smokey Robinson seconding that emotion. She remembered how the scratchiness of his beard left red marks that lasted for days. When he slipped away from her apartment just before dawn, she knew he wouldn't be back.

She didn't cry until five weeks later when the clinic nurse called with the results. And then she couldn't stop. Between bone-shaking bouts of weeping, she argued with herself for three days. Then she called Brad, her on-again, off-again boyfriend, who had just accepted a job in Massachusetts. She let him think the baby was his, without actually saying so. He was delighted at the pregnancy. She gave notice at the radio station and they moved to Springfield. She started freelancing to work from home, met Mimi and they started a women's group. Brad was a solid man, a good socialist and a good father. Not his fault he wasn't Charlie.

She coughed and blinked away the tears. Took a tissue from the box next to the phone and blew her nose. Soppy old woman.

Okay, so maybe she should have shared the story with Brad, with Mimi. Or even with Sam. Maybe it was cowardly. But she couldn't share Charlie.

She coughed again and blinked her eyes several times to try to clear her hazy vision. Was she getting a cold? And why were clouds filling up her living room? No, not clouds.

Smoke.

There was knocking. Hammering. On the apartment door? Was someone out there? Who would be visiting? She stood up to answer but the smoke made her cough so hard she had to sit down again. More knocking.

And a screaming sound. Was that her? Why was she screaming?

~╯╯⌇

A few blocks away, Sam couldn't take his eyes off Zoe and Jeremy dancing. He told himself he should return to the adults in the kitchen. He could report that Tim was manning the refreshment table, that Gabe was slow-dancing with two girls at once, and all was well. Instead he meandered over to Zoe's wheelchair, abandoned and pushed back against the wall. He rested his hand on the crinkly vinyl seat back and watched Zoe swaying on Jeremy's feet, the way she used to dance with *him*, her papa, when she was a little girl.

Sam closed his eyes. The music was slow and dreamy and the melody was familiar, a remake of a song he and Anna once danced to, in the same sweet musical embrace, in the early days before Zoe. For a moment, he was back in college with Anna, at a party in someone's living room. The furniture was pushed to the walls and they moved through the fog of smoke, fragrant weed and cigarettes mixing in lazy, hazy clouds. Anna's hair was long then and the furrow between her eyes hadn't yet formed and they danced closer than skin. He knew within weeks that she was the forever one, and for once his mother didn't offer an argument.

Sam and his mother were both wrong about Anna and forever, but after an admittedly unimpressive beginning, Sam became a pretty good dad. His half of the two-family house was always open to his girl. He never cancelled their weekends together, was always available last minute when Anna had to work late or attend weekend meetings. He shared the hospital vigil when Zoe had shunt surgery and he learned to do Zoe's stretching exercises and her caths, until she became independent with both. At ten years old, when she decided to give up her crutches in favor of the wheelchair, he didn't argue because she was right, she *could* move faster and expend less energy in a chair. At twelve, he welcomed her decision to share the upstairs apartment—an ironic echo of his move eleven years earlier—and adapted good-naturedly to the takeover by her clothes and books and music.

But this guy and his hormones all moony and horny over his girl? Sam wasn't ready for this and neither was Zoe. She was too young, too vulnerable. He recognized the way Jeremy's body was bent over, to maximize his contact with Zoe's chest and arms and conceal his erection. He knew that move. He remembered high school dances, yearning for the slow numbers and dreading them. But that was different; Zoe was his little girl.

In his wistful state, he confused the first vibration in the front pocket of his jeans with his worry about Zoe and a young man's hormones. The second time he realized it was his phone, but he didn't recognize the number on the screen.

He stepped into the hallway. "Hello?"

"Sam Tobin?"

"Speaking. Who're you?"

"Springfield Fire Department."

~~~

Arms in a green jacket enveloped her on the narrow ambulance stretcher.

"You could have been killed," the man in green said. "Burned to a crisp."

Flo couldn't respond. Couldn't answer him because the cloud of smoke was all around her, in her eyes and mouth and nose and clogging the plastic thing over her face and all over her clothes and in her hair and inside her thinking. She must have been sobbing because the man was patting her shoulder and saying, "It's okay, Ma. Don't cry." It was hard to see with the smoky fog and flashing lights, red ones and yellow, fire trucks and ambulances and cop cars and for a moment she thought the man might be Charlie. But no, the man's face was close to hers and it was closer in hue to hers than Charlie's and the voice was Sam's, saying Ma, and they were his arms, his green jacket. When Sam was a baby, the white privilege of her skin bothered her, to have her color weigh more than his father's. Later, she was grateful, because Sam could pass as an easy-tanning boy, or a throwback to her eastern European relatives. Then the man said something about tea and offered a cup and she knew for sure it was Sam because Charlie hated tea, said it tasted like fishy dishwater. She inhaled the aroma of it, a deep breath, and that made her cough and cough but then she was glad because it pushed some of the smoke away. Sam held the tea close to her face and the steam was cleaner than smoke and what a good boy he was.

"We'll get you home, Ma. Home to my place, and out of those smoky clothes, okay?"

She pushed the mask off her face and pulled a plastic clamp from her finger but Sam put them back.

"The EMT said you can go home soon. Apparently if your eyelashes and nose hairs aren't singed, your airway is most likely fine too. But until she returns you need the oxygen, and that thing on your finger. Okay?" His voice broke. "You were very lucky."

She wanted to comfort him but her arms were too heavy and the world was still too smoky smudged.

"If your neighbor hadn't smelled the smoke and called 911 and kicked in your door, well, I don't want to think about it." He paused. "The EMT said I've got to keep an eye on your breathing tonight. I'll make up the sofa bed in my office."

But what about her apartment? What about her cat? She looked down at her clothes, rumpled and sooty and where was her pocketbook and her pills and what about all her books and her photo albums and her favorite jacket Anna made from pieces of Sam's outgrown blue jeans that Flo had saved for years and lined with red satin, and how badly was her apartment burned anyway? Sam wiped her face with something soft, a tissue, and left his hand there. She was too tired to drink the tea even though it smelled so good. She rubbed her cheek against Sam's hand and closed her eyes. But then the smoke was thicker and she couldn't breathe for coughing and then she was sobbing hard and grabbing at Sam's face.

"What is it, Ma?"

She couldn't remember, but there was something important to ask him. About the smoke and the fire and her things. She didn't have much but they were hers. Her photographs and scrapbooks, even though the corners were chewed up by sharp cat teeth. That was it and she cried harder.

"Does something hurt? Should I get the EMT?"

"Charlie? Is he okay?"

"Your cat?"

The cat Charlie? The man? She wasn't sure. Yes, the cat. She grabbed his hand and nodded.

Sam shook his head. "I don't know."

Chapter Fifteen

The music in Zoe's brain was exuberant and insistent and way louder than the crank and racket of the wheelchair lift. Jeremy had promised to come upstairs after he helped clean up from the party. "Half an hour tops," he said. Holding tight to the image of their dancing, she wondered if they had any good snacks she could put out and maybe some soda—and wondered what they would talk about. She wheeled into the living room to find her dad dozing in the recliner and her grandmother asleep on the sofa.

No! That would ruin everything and the living room smelled bad—murky and nasty and thick.

Sam's eyes opened at the sound of her wheels on the wood floor. "Shhhh," he said. "She needs to sleep."

"What happened? What's that smell?"

"A fire in her apartment," Sam whispered.

Zoe's eyes filled. "How bad?"

"Bad. Luckily a neighbor heard her smoke alarm and called the fire department. He said Flo was just sitting in the living room surrounded by smoke. She could have died." Sam stood up and motioned for Zoe to follow him to the kitchen. "She can't go back there, can't live alone any more." He sat at the table and slumped over into his hands.

"She could stay here with us," Zoe said, and then she thought about her two afternoons a week helping Flo. She pictured mornings, when she and her dad by mutual agreement didn't speak during breakfast, their matching noses buried in books at the kitchen table. She pictured every day after school and every evening. Every single dinnertime, watching her grandmother eat bloody hamburger while claiming she was a vegetarian and drawing with ketchup on the table. It wouldn't be easy, but when she had to, she could escape to her bedroom to do homework. What a selfish person she was for even thinking like that. She looked up at her dad. "Couldn't she?"

"That's sweet of you," he said. "But she could start a fire here too. She needs supervision."

"You want to put her away in that nursing home, don't you?"

Memory unit, Sam thought, remembering the doctor and his circular hallways. "The thing is, her condition will get worse."

"But she'll hate that. She won't go. You can't make her, can you?"

Sam's face and arms sank onto the table. His hands covered his head so his words were muffled. "I don't know."

Zoe wanted to comfort her dad and she felt terrible about her grandmother. She hated asking for this, but she deserved a life too, didn't she?

"Could we talk about this tomorrow? I invited Jeremy up, just for a little while. He has to go back to Brooklyn tomorrow. He'll be here soon."

"So you want me to get your grandmother out of the living room."

She nodded.

He hesitated and for a moment she thought he would say no. "I guess. I made up the bed in my office for her." Zoe felt his glance, sharp and worried, as if he was looking at someone he didn't know.

While Sam picked up his sleeping mother wrapped in her smoke and her blankets and carried her to the futon in the small back bedroom he used as his office, Zoe opened the windows and waved her arms to disperse the burned smell. She folded the quilt over the back of the recliner, plumped up the throw pillows on the sofa, ran a damp paper towel over the coffee table. It wasn't like she invited guys over every weekend so it was odd that her dad didn't ask about Jeremy. Especially about Jeremy, a guy from the *other* family and someone she had never mentioned. The blush burned her neck and covered her cheeks. Sam must have been downstairs. Might have seen them dancing.

She heard the soft click of the study door closing, then footsteps in the hall and water running in the bathroom. She found a basket for the chips and emptied a jar of salsa into a bowl with a vine of flowers around the rim. She arranged them on the coffee table and rearranged them until the placement of basket and bowl and napkins and orange soda and cups looked perfectly casual. She bit her lips to make them puffy and red, leaned forward in her chair and ruffled her hair to make the curls bigger and more bountiful. Then she waited for Jeremy's knock on the door.

∽≫

Jeremy hesitated at the door, looking at the wheelchair lift. He could tiptoe back down the staircase, return to Brooklyn tomorrow, and pretend tonight never happened. He wasn't sure what scared him most—Zoe's disability, or simply the fact that she was a girl who seemed to like him and invited him over after a party, or the way her marzipan hair grew around his fingers and sent runners up his arm that burrowed into his skin.

The door opened. Zoe looked flushed and expectant. Pretty.

"I heard you on the stairs," she said, wheeling back to let him enter.

The room smelled funny. Burnt. "You been cooking?" he asked, before thinking. Great. Now she'd think he was dissing her domestic skills or something. He was so not good at this.

Zoe laughed. "I'm a decent cook. My dad made all these changes to the kitchen so I'd have full access and everything. I had to learn so his money wasn't wasted." Her smile dissolved. "That smell is from my grandmother, her clothes and hair. There was a fire in her apartment tonight, while we were at the party."

He followed Zoe into the living room and sat on the sofa. "That's awful. What happened?"

"We don't know yet." She parked her chair and engaged the brakes. With a smooth motion, she vaulted onto the sofa. "Soda?"

He nodded, accepted the glass. How could he get her to move closer, to play with the hair on his neck again? What could they talk about?

"Tell me more about the plants," she said. "About endangered species?"

He leaned back. This he could talk about. "I've always been interested in plants. When I was a kid," he started and then stopped. She probably knew about his crazy family because of her Aunt Emily. Amazing that she wasn't totally scared off by his father and prison. "We had this greenhouse. I used to sit in there and draw the plants because they were so intricate, so perfectly imagined, all those spirals and coils and whorls."

The greenhouse was where it happened the first time, the plants coming to him, during the end-of-life ceremony for Bast. Jeremy remembered leaning against the hard leg of the potting table and then the candles flickered and the green started moving and the branches and leaves and vines reached out to him, their sucker fingers circling his arms and moving over his back and his neck. How they became part of him and he knew they were family, just like the people around the funeral circle.

Zoe touched his arm. "You were telling me about the spirals and coils and whorls?"

"Yeah, I got totally caught up in how mathematically perfect plants are, how people have even written formulas that describe them." He hesitated, remembering trying to explain it to the nurse practitioner and her blank look.

"I know what you mean," Zoe said. "In math class we studied Fibonacci numbers, the patterns of the seeds on flower heads and the spirals on pine cones. So totally cool. But if it's the drawing part you like so much, why didn't you become an artist?"

"My dad—Tian—insisted that Tim and I choose practical majors, so we can support ourselves when we graduate. He said botany was better than art and I could still draw plants for a hobby."

"What about the endangered part?" She offered him the basket of chips.

He looked at her face, familiar but still unknown. Could he talk to her about this? He never discussed his family, not even with Tim. But Zoe was different. She must know what happened, even if she was young at the time. He took a big breath. Yes.

"After my brother and sister—my half-siblings actually—died, and then our cat was killed, his head cut off, and then the trial and after that our commune fell apart too. You know about this all, right?"

Zoe nodded. "It so totally sucks."

"We had to move out of the house and it was just Mom and Tim and me in this apartment and I just, I don't know, couldn't stop thinking about how fragile it all is."

She took his hand. "What do you mean?"

No, he thought, can't go there.

He switched gears. "With the commune gone there was no more homeschooling so I started school. I was excited to be in a regular classroom, with lots of kids. Problem was, most of them called me cult-boy or taunted me about my dad being in prison. I made a couple of friends, but their parents said no way, like my family's trouble was contagious."

"Did you blame your parents, for all that?"

What an odd question. He thought about it. "No, don't think so. I mean, do you blame yours, for being born different?"

"Sure. Sometimes." She laughed a little. "So how'd you deal with school?"

"A teacher saved me, when she offered extra credit to pick an endangered species and write a biology report on it."

"What did you choose?"

His finger traced the leafy vine on the salsa bowl. "*Thismia americana*, a shy little plant from the Lake Michigan wetlands. It had a tiny white flower like a pearl. I chose it because it lacked chlorophyll and our teacher said plants all had chlorophyll and I liked that she was wrong. And because it was declared extinct the year I was born."

"So did you think the pearl flower was reincarnated into you?" she teased, letting go of his hand.

What could he say to get her hand back?

He dipped a tortilla chip into the salsa. He didn't actually think that, didn't believe in reincarnation, but sometimes he did suspect that his DNA was missing something essential. Like chlorophyll if he'd been a plant, which might be preferable. Carrying the chip to his mouth, he splotched salsa onto his pants and they both laughed. This wasn't hard. Zoe was so easy to talk to.

"Is she going to be okay?" he asked. "Your grandmother?"

"She's okay from the fire. But she has Alzheimer's. My dad wants her to move into a place for people with dementia. So she'll get supervision and everything."

"Over my dead body." Flo said from the hallway.

~~~

Flo had woken up in a strange room. Well, not totally strange because she recognized Sam's office, where he ran his website design business. More like out of the ordinary because she didn't usually sleep there and she smelled like a campfire. The other bizarre thing was her brain, which should have been groggy with smoke and trauma and her increasingly warped and twisted neurons, but instead it felt sharp, jazzed even. This disease didn't play fair. Or maybe that oxygen in the ambulance juiced her brain cells.

Whatever the reason, she wasn't going to let this lucid moment, this opportunity for clarity, however fleeting, pass her by. She should probably shower and get dressed, but she could do that when her hazy lazy brain returned. She stood up, wrapped a blanket around herself, and walked into the hallway. The most important thing to do now was talk to Sam and change his mind about Assisted Living. Oh, she knew she couldn't avoid that genteel incarceration forever, but not today. Not yet.

And find out what happened to her sweet kitty.

Sam was asleep on top of his covers, his laptop open, but she heard voices in the living room. Zoe and someone she didn't recognize, but maybe the smoke had affected her ears, pickled them or something. She peeked around the corner and saw Zoe on the sofa with an unfamiliar young man.

". . . Alzheimer's," Zoe was saying. "My dad wants her to move into a place for people with dementia. So she'll get supervision and everything."

Flo stepped into the doorway. "Over my dead body," she announced.

Well, that certainly startled Zoe and her young man. He stood up, in a gesture of respect, and Flo narrowed her eyes at him. Who did *that* any more? Was he a human anachronism, a figment of smoke inhalation?

"This is my friend Jeremy." Zoe rested her hand on Jeremy's arm, a gesture that made Flo think, Hmmmm. "He's Gabe's brother. Remember I told you about Gabe's birthday party tonight? Jeremy, this is Flo, my grandmother."

Flo did recall something about a party. It was somehow connected to Forest Park and those dead babies but she wasn't about to admit the holes in her memory to a stranger—to anyone, if she could help it—so she just nodded.

"Do you want some soda?" Zoe asked. "Or tea?"

"Tea, please." The caffeine would help keep her brain in gear until she had a chance to talk with Sam. When Zoe transferred into her wheelchair and pushed into the kitchen, Flo took her end of the sofa.

"Now, tell me who you are again," she said to Jeremy.

"He's an artist and a botanist and wants to save all the plants from becoming extinct," Zoe called from the kitchen.

"Can't the man talk for himself, you bossy child?" Flo yelled back, then started coughing.

"It's okay," Jeremy said. "I don't mind."

"Nonsense. What's your shtick with the plants?"

He leaned forward. "Two hundred species go extinct every day."

"More nonsense," Flo said. "Where'd you get your numbers?"

"The United Nations, I think. I'm not sure. But I know it's not a natural process. People are causing it. Industry and pollution."

Balancing the brewing tea on a lap tray, Zoe pushed back into the living room. Flo could smell the cinnamon through the veil of smoke and smiled, because it was her favorite hard-to-find blend that Sam kept around for her visits. Such a good boy.

"So what are you doing about it?" Flo asked, putting the steaming mug on the coffee table. What an interesting young man Zoe chose—maybe the gene for political activism skipped a generation, like diabetes and retinitis pigmentosa. Sam had never seemed interested in politics, but maybe Zoe would carry on her struggles.

"Come on, Grandma. Don't give him the third degree."

"No, that's okay," Jeremy said. "I like talking about it. It helps me figure things out. I went to some meetings in Brooklyn with these environmental activists. They're doing teach-ins and Earth Day programs and trying to educate people about global warming. But the plants in their apartments are dead from neglect."

"Global warming, huh? How does that fit into class struggle?" Flo asked.

He looked confused. "I'm not sure. And I'm not sure about some of the people in the group. I'm worried they might be doing other stuff too." His voice grew brittle. "I heard them talking about Molotov cocktails."

"Then why are you going back?" Zoe asked.

He shrugged. "Next Saturday is Earth Day. I promised I'd be there."

"With Molotov cocktails?" Zoe asked.

"Not me," he said. "I'll be careful."

"Sometimes you have to fight dirty," Flo said. What was wrong with these kids? Didn't they understand how important the struggle was? "You think those oil companies play nice?"

"I know," Jeremy said. "But if you do ugly things, even to make the world better, doesn't that make you as bad as *them*?"

"You do what needs to be done." Flo crossed her arms. "Sometimes you have to fight dirty."

Zoe put her hand on Flo's arm. "You already said that, Grandma."

"I don't know if I can do it, can break the law. Look what happened to my family." He glanced at Zoe. "And yours."

"Some laws are wrong," Flo said.

"So change the bad laws," Zoe added.

Flo smiled. "It's not that easy, sweetheart. Some things are urgent."

"Yeah, like dying plants," Jeremy said. "But some of the things the Brooklyn activists talk about are pretty intense. I mean, if you do stuff like that, how can you live with yourself?"

"You mean like blowing things up?" Zoe asked.

He nodded.

"You'd be surprised what you can live with," Flo said.

She felt tired, so tired. Young people didn't have the fire, the passion, of her generation. How would they ever make the sacrifices needed to change the world? You couldn't get away from the dirty underside of political work. The tactical arguments that turned personal, the nights spent in filthy jails, betrayals by people who turned out to not be on your side after all. But she wouldn't trade it for anything. Even after the Washington chapter kicked her out before Sam was born, she still considered herself a communist and spent interminable evenings in troublesome gatherings of like-minded people. "You can put up with a lot if you're doing the right thing."

"But I'm not sure what *is* the right thing," Jeremy said.

Back then, she'd been pretty sure about that: organizing people against racism, against bosses and their wars.

"Some people in the Brooklyn group think the basic problem is how society is organized," Jeremy continued. "But when I consider it from the point of view of the plants and the planet, human civilization itself is the problem."

Flo frowned. From the point of view of the plants? Maybe this guy was off his rocker. Or maybe not. When was the last time she asked a plant what it thought? She knew what she *should* say; that whatever his question, the right answer was with the working class. But the tea wasn't helping and she felt her mental sharpness fading away into fog.

Jeremy leaned closer. "And another thing. How do you stay true to the people you care about?" he asked in a small voice. "While you're trying to change the world?"

Flo closed her eyes. She had asked Charlie that same question once, a lifetime ago, when he told her to go to college and get the skills to organize the workers. "But what about us?" she asked him and he answered something very smart—he always had the right response ready—but she couldn't remember what it was.

Her thoughts and her sentences were starting to slip-slide away. So much for the effect of oxygen on brain cells. She felt herself tumbling down a steep hill of defeat, losing words as she fell. Using the arm of the sofa and the coffee table, she hoisted herself up.

"So tired," she said. "Got to sleep."

~∞~

Sam woke to a burst of laughter from the living room. He stretched his neck in a circle roll and closed his laptop. He hadn't meant to fall asleep, not with Ma's breathing not so good and Zoe alone in the living room with that boy. He'd better check on them all, but first he should call the fire station again, see if they'd learned anything. He both wanted to know the results of their investigation and was afraid to find out. Maybe it would be just the ammunition he needed, to convince his mother she couldn't live alone.

Hanging up ten minutes later, he felt much worse. The firefighter's report was preliminary, but it didn't feel like ammunition. It felt inevitable and inescapable. The fire had started in the kitchen, probably on the stove and then the curtains. The apartment was uninhabitable, would need to be completely gutted. And the cat, Ma's beloved Charlie-cat, was dead. Flo would be devastated, but maybe it would convince her of the seriousness of the situation.

Later, he would have a solemn talk with Flo. About Hillside Village.

The clock said 1:15 but there was no way he could sleep. Besides, maybe it wasn't such a great idea to leave Zoe alone with Jeremy, not after the way they danced, the way the kid looked at his daughter. He had always trusted Zoe, had often gone to sleep when Xander and other friends were visiting, listening to music in the living room or working on school projects. Sam wasn't proud of it, but he had felt protected by her medical condition. Sure, he hoped Zoe would find love and romance and everything, but her mother and all the books said it was likely to be later in life than regular people. Trust Zoe to ignore the experts and forge ahead.

The door to his office was slightly open and he could hear Flo's raspy breathing. He tied his bathrobe belt and peered around the corner into the living room. Zoe sat on the sofa, facing Jeremy, her skinny legs crossed in the position her orthopedist recommended for good hip development. Was she wearing lipstick? And when did she start wearing tight sweaters?

Sam leaned against the wall and listened.

"Did you like the Oz books?" Zoe was asking. "Not just the Wizard, but the ones about Winkie Country and Glinda. And Ozma—she's my favorite."

"I don't know," Jeremy said. "I only read the main one, and saw the movie."

"I've got all the books. You could borrow a couple. They're downstairs, in my mom's apartment. I always have Sunday breakfast with my mom. Maybe you could come tomorrow, if you have time before your bus. You know, so you can take a look at the books."

Sam couldn't help smiling. Where did Zoe learn these moves?

"Sure, but I don't know if I'll like the Oz stories. I was more into the X-Men. Tim and I must've read every comic book and seen every movie a dozen times. Our bedroom wall was covered with their posters."

"Really? Those mutant characters—that one-eyed man and the girl who makes storms, right? Oh, and the guy with the knife hands?"

"That's Wolverine. You should give them a chance. The stories are all about good and evil, about prejudice and racism."

There was a silence, then Jeremy spoke again. "You know, I'm kind of like a mutant myself. My dad's an ex-con, a felon. My mom worships an ancient Egyptian goddess. Five years ago, I would have given anything to attend Professor Xavier's School for Gifted Youngsters, except that I had no superpower."

"You don't seem like a mutant to me," Zoe said, her voice both soft and teasing.

Sam couldn't quite take it in. His little girl sounded so adult, flirting with Jeremy, drawing him out. A surge of memories pushed Sam deeper into the hallway. Breathtaking memories. Little girl memories of spoonerisms and stretching exercises and purple headbands and finger puppets and that silly stuffed rhino she couldn't sleep without—what was his name? Rufus, that was it. Where was Rufus now?

There was another silence and this one went on and on until Sam couldn't stand it. He peeked quickly around the corner into the living room.

Zoe sat close to the boy. Their arms were entwined and their faces close. Kissing.

Sam closed his eyes and listened hard. Okay, eavesdropped. A father's right and his responsibility.

Chapter Sixteen

Walking to Zoe's mother's house the next morning, Jeremy realized he was whistling. Whistling meant happy. Weekend visits home weren't usually happy; normally he couldn't stand more than an hour at a time of his father's inarticulate grimness or his mother's palpable anxiety. Like when he got home from Zoe's the night before and Francie was waiting up for him with a barrage of questions.

"When are you moving back home? You're not dropping out of school, are you? Why didn't you call us when you freaked out and were sent to Health Services? Why'd you go to Brooklyn?"

Luckily his dad was already asleep. Francie was much easier to placate than Tian would have been, Tian with his sad eyes and snapping rubber bands. Jeremy explained that he had to be in Brooklyn for Earth Day but planned to return to UMass in a couple of weeks. He might have to take an incomplete or two, but he could make up the work over the summer. He didn't actually know he'd made the decision to leave Brooklyn, but when he spoke the words, Francie let up with the third degree and he felt his chest relax and soften. Tim would be so relieved.

But none of that would make him whistle. So it had to be Zoe.

Did that make him a major loser? Falling for a sixteen-year-old girl stuck in a wheelchair. If anyone had told him a year ago that he'd feel this way about a girl who had to pee through a catheter, he would have laughed. Not that Zoe had told him about that, but he had read all about spina bifida on the Internet. No way, he would have said. But a year ago he didn't know Zoe.

He stood facing Zoe's house, with the stairs and wheelchair lift to her dad's second floor apartment on the left. He shifted his weight from one foot to the other, his thoughts bouncing back and forth between wanting to stay in Massachusetts with his plants and Zoe, and the pull of Earth Day at the Brooklyn courthouse. Either way, he wouldn't let the plants down.

But first, there was breakfast with Zoe and her mom. He'd ring the doorbell in just a minute.

～●～

Zoe glanced at the kitchen clock. She hoped Jeremy wasn't one of those chronically late people. Sometimes her friend Xander did it on purpose, because he knew it pissed her off. But Jeremy wasn't like that, was he? Didn't he understand how stressful it was for her to introduce him to her mom? Anna had always been the hard-nose parent, tough and demanding, and Sam the softy. How could Jeremy keep her waiting like this?

"Relax," Anna said. "He's probably standing on the sidewalk out front, not wanting to appear too eager."

"Come on, Mom. He's not that insecure." Or was he? How much did she really know about the guy, other than he liked those mutant characters and how easy he was to talk with? And the taste of his tongue. She blushed and turned away, taking an extra mug from the cupboard. "I wonder if he likes coffee."

"Maybe make a pot of tea too?" Anna said.

Zoe put the teapot on the table, then looked at her mother. "Hey, where are Pippa and Gabe?"

"They wanted breakfast at the diner."

"Really? Not so that you can interrogate Jeremy without interference?"

Anna smiled. "You invited him, Sweetie. I just want to get to know him a little. Your first real boyfriend."

"Come on, Mom. I'm sixteen."

"Only a couple of years younger than I was when I met Sam."

"And look how well that worked out."

"Don't worry," Anna said. "I promise not to embarrass you. By the way, I heard your Jeremy is planning to return to UMass in a couple of weeks."

Zoe spun her wheelchair around to face her mom. "How did you hear that? He didn't tell *me*. And he's not *my* Jeremy."

"Relax," Anna said. "His mom mentioned it when she called this morning to thank me for hosting Gabe's birthday party."

"Then why didn't he tell me?"

Anna took Zoe's hand and squeezed. "Don't expect too much of boys in the communication department."

"Dad's pretty good at talking."

"They get better with age, if you can hang in there."

Zoe pulled her hand back. She hated it when her mom talked that way, woman to woman, as if they shared a way of looking at the world because of their gender. Just because her parents failed at marriage didn't mean all relationships were doomed. Jeremy had been so easy to talk with the night before. So why would he keep something important from her, like moving back?

～∽～

Jeremy followed Zoe into the kitchen. The air felt charged and not in a good way.

"You didn't tell me you were moving back," Zoe blurted.

He looked at her in surprise. She sounded irked, like he should have already told her. But he didn't decide until after he left the night before, so how could he?

"I didn't actually make the decision until late last night," he said, then added, "after you and I talked about it. My mom ambushed me when I got home. But I'm still going back to Brooklyn with Tim this afternoon, so I can be part of Earth Day next weekend."

"Coffee?" Anna held the carafe over his cup. He nodded. "What's the purpose of the Earth Day event?"

Jeremy grinned. "Depends on who you ask. Some people want their colleges to divest from oil and gas companies, others want the borough to beef up recycling and emissions regs, and still others think that organizing around global warming is the way to move the US toward socialism. Take your pick."

"What about you?" Anna tilted her head slightly to the side with the question.

Anna's gesture zoomed him right back to the evening before, when Zoe cocked her head that way while they danced. He felt his face flush and took a sip of coffee even though it was too hot and he hated it without milk and sugar. Zoe had done that thing with her head right before she touched the curls on his neck and then he touched her hair and it came alive, all green and growing like vines down his arms and into his skin. Amazing that Zoe and her mom had the same gesture. Or maybe it wasn't so amazing because of genetics, but he couldn't think of anything he did that mirrored his folks. Or he didn't want to.

"Jeremy?" Zoe asked.

His face flushed again. Blazed, it felt like. "Sorry, I was thinking about something," he mumbled, then turned to Anna. "What did you ask me?"

"About Earth Day?"

"Yeah. To be honest, I'm not exactly sure what I think. I'm still trying to figure it out. I can see all the perspectives, but I care about vanishing plant species." He shrugged. "Not as interesting as divestiture or revolution, I guess."

"You're a biology major, right?" Anna asked. "What will you do when you get back to school?"

"Take botany courses. Drawing classes when I can fit it in. I've got to catch up on the work I missed, but I'd really like to learn about permaculture and sustainability studies."

"I bet there's a global warming action group on campus," Zoe said. "We've got one at my high school."

He smiled at Zoe. "Yeah. I'll look into that." Jeremy reached for the sugar bowl. "But first there's Earth Day."

The next Saturday, the demonstration turned off Atlantic and stretched down Court Street as far as Jeremy could see. He teetered on the curb, searching, but saw no sign of Carl or Sari or Greenhope or the five-foot-long climate change banner he'd helped paint the night before. The banner was striking—floods and blizzards and tornados whipped across the canvas of water-starved fields and crumbling city blocks. His major contribution was a border of leaves of dead species resurrected to frame the devastation, to illustrate the coming catastrophe. Stem-like green letters formed the words "Biodiversity is shrinking," woven among the broken branches. He was proud of his work, even though he expected no one would appreciate the attention to detail or recognize the accuracy of the drawing.

He stood on tiptoe and looked north toward Borough Hall—maybe he missed them. Maybe he should go home. Well, to Tim's. Or he could try to catch up with them for the sit-in. Except that he couldn't make up his mind whether or not to be arrested.

It was too warm for April and the air shimmered. His mouth was dry and he was thirsty. Maybe he could grab a bottle of water from one of these stores before joining the march.

A troop of drummers marched by, their explosive syncopated thumps so insistent that they hijacked his heartbeat. Too loud. Too intense. He turned away and elbowed through the crowd of gawkers, trying to imagine how Zoe would maneuver her wheelchair in the crush of people.

"Hey, Jerry. Over here."

"Jerk," he muttered. Carl thought calling him Jerry was funny. Carl was an ass.

Carl and Sari leaned against a brick wall near the corner of Court and Livingston, a large backpack between them on the sidewalk.

"Where's the banner?" Jeremy asked. "And the rest of the committee?"

"Borough Hall lobby," Sari said. "Waiting for the marchers to arrive for the rally and civil disobedience."

"Are you marching?"

"Soon," Carl said. "We'll meet you there."

"You got any water?" Jeremy asked.

"In the pocket." Sari pointed to the backpack and Jeremy reached for the zipper.

"Not inside!" Sari's whisper was fierce. She grabbed his hand and pulled a water bottle from the side pocket. "Here."

Jeremy stared at her, frozen by her fury. What could she have in the pack that was so secret? Her words from the burrito bar exploded in his head, flung him back into his boy's body to that prison visiting room, to the look on his father's face, half despair and half ferocity and totally scary.

"No, thanks," he said to the air as he hurried up the hill to Court Street, away from Carl and Sari and his father and the guard and the prison visiting room.

～∘⌐

His heart was still racing fifteen minutes later as he rearranged his butt on the linoleum floor of the courthouse lobby and wished for more natural padding. Nothing much was happening at the moment and he was grateful for that. He had found Greenhope and Tommy and they'd draped the banner around their bodies so the message and the border of painted leaves were visible. The uniformed cops stood in straight lines against the lobby walls, helmets and shields ready. They stared at the protestors while the suits with ear buds conferred. Jeremy wondered what they were thinking. Greenhope ignored them and watched streaming news coverage of Earth Day events around the country on her tablet, complaining that each of them looked bigger and more exciting than their puny college sit-in.

A cop wearing a black NYPD-stenciled vest stepped out of the huddle of suits and raised an electronic bullhorn to his lips. A thin squeal became static and then words. "You are trespassing. This is your last opportunity to leave the building. In five minutes, we will begin arresting those individuals who persist in breaking the law."

Tommy got up to leave. "My wife will kill me if I get busted again," he said.

Jeremy still hadn't decided. Stay or go? Even if they won their demands and the university agreed to divest their fossil fuel holdings, thousands more species would become extinct in the meantime.

Greenhope pulled her hat lower over her face and elbowed him. "You staying?"

He shrugged. It didn't matter, not really, but he had to decide. "What's with the hat?" he asked, more to buy time than because he wanted to know.

"It's a cloche. It was my mom's," Greenhope said. "I always wear it to demonstrations. But don't change the subject. What are you going to do?"

Jeremy had no idea. What good would it do to get arrested? Tian said that civil disobedience delivered people right into the clutches of the system. But it was also a badge of honor to the students crowded into the courthouse. Flo would be proud of him. Maybe Zoe too. The thought made him smile.

"Getting busted is not for everyone," Greenhope said, leaning close. "I mean, maybe you've got a good reason to leave. Like you're wanted for arms smuggling in Omaha or you're the single parent of infant twins and the babysitter has to leave at five sharp."

"Nope," Jeremy said. "Neither of those." Did having a sort-of girlfriend back in Springfield count?

"This isn't a game, you know. This is life and death and you've got to choose. Are you with us, or not? I mean, if it's just that you're scared, welcome to the club. Everyone in this room is scared and every one of us is worried that we'll lose our scholarship or daddy won't keep paying tuition or a police record will follow us all the days of our lives and we'll never get a good job and be able to retire in Florida."

She paused for breath, but continued before Jeremy could respond. "You know, Brooklyn will be as warm as Florida in a few years anyway. Beachfront, even. So I'm staying right here." She patted the floor. "You?"

He shrugged. He couldn't decide.

"You've probably heard horror stories about what can happen in jail, especially if they think you're a troublemaker. But it's not that bad and we've got to take a stand. What's more important than this, than our Earth?"

Jeremy pictured his father's empty eyes in the visiting room and the incessant snapping of rubber bands. Greenhope didn't know the half of it.

"Holy shit." Greenhope pointed to her tablet.

A large photograph of Mary filled the screen, her round-collared blouse incongruous with the handcuffs and SWAT cops flanking her. DOMESTIC TERRORIST ARRESTED IN BOMBING screamed the headline.

Bombing? Mary? He tried to read the story but his eyes blurred. He pictured Mary and her elementary education clothes and her story about the elephants in Cameroon getting revenge. "An eco-terrorist," she had said. But she had a little boy—didn't Carl say she had a son—and what would happen to the kid? Did he have a dad?

"You okay?" Greenhope asked. "Your face is white."

This time, it was different. He recognized the foreshadowing of the green tingle, like the migraine aura his mom described. Different in another way too, because the plants were growing inside his body this time. They germinated in the muscle fibers of his forearms and grew their way through the mesh of tendons in his wrists, their insistent sprouts stiffening in his fingers, joint by joint. Stems pieced the skin at the end of each tender fingertip and pushed through. Leaves unfurled in quick-time, urgent with the need to find sunlight and grow.

He recognized a few of the leaf patterns, like *Sterculia khasiana* and *Wikstroemia villosa*, but most of them were strangers, unknown and exotic species.

"Welcome," he whispered to the newcomers.

"Time's up," the officer with the bullhorn said. The lines of uniformed cops stepped forward, toward the seated protesters.

"Jeremy?" Greenhope shook his shoulder, her voice worried. "You could probably still get out, if you want to leave. Are you sure?"

He wasn't frightened. This felt so right. He belonged here, in this forest of green crusaders woven together with the branches growing from his hands, the green vines twisting around the protestors' arms and legs, sprouting deep green leaves perfect against their backpacks and hooded sweatshirts.

"Save the earth," people around him chanted. "We have no Plan B."

"*Melicope paniculata*," he sang with them. "*Ochrosia nukuhivensis.*" He waved his arms high above his head, helping the resurrected plants reach for the sky. In the distance there was a loud answering boom, and he heard it as the voice of the universe joining in. "*Centaurea pseudoleucolepis*," he responded.

The cops began grabbing arms, dragging the protestors up from the floor, fastening plastic cuffs around their hands. He and Greenhope were tied together, by yellow plastic and the glorious tangles of vines, because the plants were everywhere by then.

Greenhope whispered in his ear. "Did you hear that explosion?"

He didn't answer. The magnificent and heartbreaking architecture of extinct leaf patterns filled his ears and his head and the building and the world.

"You need a shower," Tim said Sunday morning. "I can't believe you just spent a night in jail."

Jeremy blinked at the bright sunlight. "Thanks for posting my bail."

"It's just a loan," Tim said, guiding Jeremy down the stairs and toward the subway. "You've got to pay me back, and soon."

"Jeremy—wait!" A woman's voice called from the top of the stairs. Both men turned around.

"That's Greenhope," Jeremy said. "We were arrested together."

Tim tried not to smirk at the woo-woo name and pink hair. Didn't he know her from someplace?

"Are you okay?" The way she touched his brother's arm made Tim wonder if there were other things Jeremy hadn't told him. Probably not. Girls had always liked his bro but Jeremy was clueless.

Jeremy nodded and withdrew his arm. Maybe not. "Just tired. I think I'm glad I stayed, although I have no clue if we accomplished anything."

"You were pretty strange there, you know, before they busted us. Muttering Latin names and waving your arms around." She paused. "I was worried about you."

Terrific, Tim thought. Was Jeremy going to freak out again?

"He's fine." Tim turned to leave. "We've got to get home. I've got an econ exam tomorrow."

"Wait," Jeremy said. "Have you heard from the others? Carl or Sari?"

"Nothing. I don't think anyone else from our group was arrested." Greenhope hesitated. "Did you hear the explosion, right before they dragged us out?"

"Explosion?" Tim asked. This gets better and better.

"I'm not sure," Jeremy said. "Maybe. And what about Mary? I'm so bummed about her."

"There was an email from her collective saying that the terrorism charges were totally bogus. A frame-up. Look." Greenhope touched her tablet screen and brought up the message and photo.

"Hey," Tim said, looking over Jeremy's shoulder. "Haven't I seen her before?"

"It's Mary," Jeremy said. "Remember her lecture?" He turned to Greenhope. "How old is her kid?"

"I don't know. Eight or nine, maybe?"

A hard age to lose a parent to prison, Tim thought. He looked at Greenhope. "What did she do?"

"Maybe nothing. I'll call you when I hear details." She touched Jeremy's shoulder and turned away.

"Terrorism and explosions? What the fuck have you gotten me into now?" Tim asked.

"Hey. You're the one who dragged me to that lecture, bro."

"Just to try to shock you out of your dead plant funk," Tim said. "I totally regret it now, introducing you to those people. You're pathetic, but they're nuts, off their rockers."

"So what are you supposed to do," Jeremy asked, "when you care so much about something and no one in power will listen?"

Tim shrugged. "No idea. But what exactly did this accomplish today, besides throwing away four hundred bucks?"

Not that he expected Jeremy to have a good answer. Damn, one of these days his bro had better get his head straight and fly right. First he wastes his time studying dead plants and now he's turning into some kind of Greenpeace terrorist. Jeremy had always been odd, even in high school. Sketching flowers instead of playing soccer, staying in their room with Wolverine instead of hanging out with girls who liked beer and messing around. But this was truly weird.

"Mom and Dad are going to be majorly pissed off about this," Tim said.

"So don't tell them," Jeremy said. "You'll get the money back."

"It's not just that," Tim said. "What was going on with you, with the Latin chanting and all? Sounds like you even weirded out your pink punk friend. You're here to get over that craziness, remember?"

Jeremy stopped in the middle of the sidewalk, forcing people to walk around them. "You know, Tim. You can't spend your whole life running away from things, from what happened to us. From Abby and Terrance."

Wouldn't Jeremy ever let up about the past?

"Don't you think about them at all?" Jeremy asked. "I wonder about Abby and Terrance all the time, like if they're buried with Bast—you remember how much they loved that cat? Don't you ever speculate about what they'd be like now, like teenagers? About where their graves are, what plants grow in the earth above them?"

It seemed like he was going to say something more, and Tim waited. But Jeremy shook his head and turned toward the subway entrance. "You wouldn't understand," he muttered.

Probably not, Tim thought, and he didn't think he wanted to. Truth was, Jeremy frightened him.

"Listen, bro," he said. "I think it's time for you to go home. Today."

Chapter Seventeen

"It's a beautiful morning," Flo said. "Don't you ever go out? Ride a bike or take a hike? Go on, you can leave me alone. I'm fine."

Sam sat next to her on the sofa. "We have to talk."

I'm fine, Flo repeated to herself. She closed her eyes but that made the smoke smell stronger so she opened them. How long would her skin secrete this smoky scent? Anyway, she knew this conversation was coming. In the week since the fire, Sam had been unnaturally kind—cooking the comfort foods she once made him as a boy and bringing mystery novels home from the library, even though she couldn't seem to follow the plots. Several times he brought up the topic of Assisted Living. So far she had been able to postpone the discussion, but she knew it was coming and she didn't want it. She shook her head side to side, willing him to go away. I'm fine.

Sam took her hand. Another bad sign; he wasn't going away. "Ma, it's time. Your apartment is ruined and it's not safe for you to live alone."

She pulled her hand back and squeezed her eyes tighter.

"I've signed the papers for Hillside Village. A special Memory Unit there. It's a nice place. You move today. Zoe will help us."

She shook her head. "No."

He persisted. "You have Alzheimer's, Ma, and it isn't going away. You've got to be someplace where you can get the help you need."

I'm fine, she thought or did she speak the words out loud? She knew they weren't exactly true, but words contain power. "I'm fine. I'm fine. I'm fine."

"You're not fine, Ma. You lost track of time and caused a fire and your cat died. Next time it could be you. We have no choice."

Sometimes when she tried to concentrate on something, like proving to Sam that he was wrong, the words slid away and were replaced by a buzzing. It started in her ears like a thousand bees and it moved into her brain and it got so loud she couldn't think. The sound grew enormous, vibrant and electric and insistent and it pushed everything else out of her head. First it banished the words and sentences, then moved on to feelings. Right now, the bees were demolishing her sorrow about her poor Charlie-cat who didn't deserve to die of breathing smoke. It was her fault, but the brain-buzzing meant she didn't have to feel so bad about him any more. Maybe the bees would sting her skin a thousand times and she could just die and not hear them buzzing any more, not feel so lost and scared. She leaned forward until her head fell onto her lap and hugged her knees and gave in to the terrible and welcome noise.

"I'm so sorry." Sam put his arms around her.

⁓⌇⌇

Sunday mornings were made for sleeping until afternoon, but Zoe hadn't argued the night before when Sam asked her to set her alarm for 9:30. Not when he told her where they were going.

"Flo wants you to come with us," he said. "To the place."

"You mean *you* want me to come."

"That too."

In the morning, Zoe was groggy as she stood behind her grandmother. Leaning her belly against the chair back for support, she helped Flo towel off her wet hair. She had never before noticed the spiral cowlick on the crown of her grandmother's head, like a tornado had touched down there and flattened the sparse gray fields. People in wheelchairs rarely had the opportunity to look down at anyone's head.

She brushed Flo's slate gray hair, trying not to tug the tangles too hard. When she was finished, she pulled a few thin strands from the new hairbrush and tucked it into the small duffle bag with the other necessities Sam had bought, the pajamas and underwear, sweatpants and flannel shirts. The duffle was covered with daisies but it still wasn't cheerful and neither was Flo. Zoe would be devastated if she lost her things. Zoe couldn't begin to imagine how it would feel to lose all her clothes and books, all the silly things saved because they meant something, even when nobody else got why. Like those olden albums of Sam as a baby that Flo loved. Steadying herself with one hand, Zoe leaned forward and kissed the tornado place on her grandmother's head.

"You okay?"

"I'm fine," Flo said.

"It won't be so bad. You know? I'll visit lots, and my dad too."

"I know. I'm fine. Now scram. I can dress myself."

"Yeah," Zoe said, settling back into her chair.

She pulled the office door behind her with a soft click. She *would* visit, she promised herself. Every week, twice even.

Sam sat on the sofa, head in his hands. Zoe rolled up close to him, as knee-to-knee as the footplates would allow. She let her head fall forward to rest against his.

"Sad, huh?"

"Just thinking," he said.

"Hey," she said. "Can we go through the apartment and see if anything survived the fire. I bet she'd love some of her things."

"Tomorrow," Sam said. "Her landlord said I could go in before the clean-up crew starts. He warned that there isn't much to salvage. The fire burned really hot."

"I want to go with you. I know the things she treasures."

Sam nodded. "But first we have to survive today."

Sam drove slowly. He didn't want this short trip to end and he couldn't wait for it to be over. Next to him, Flo stared out the window. She had refused his offer to put her new duffle bag in the trunk, cradled it instead in her lap. In the back seat, Zoe was plugged in to her music. Sam wished he could zone out too.

Flo's voice broke into his worries. "I miss my car."

"I know," he said.

"Where is it?"

"You sold it two years ago, remember? After the accident."

Her car had been part of the negotiations. She agreed to sell the Dart, and he promised no Assisted Living. He bit his lip. That was then and this is now, he told himself. Circumstances change.

"Whenever you need a ride," he said. "Just call. I'll drive you wherever you want to go."

She looked at him like he was the demented one.

"I'm sure Mimi will too," he added.

"Where is Mimi?"

"Home, I guess," Sam said. "She'll come visit soon."

"Visit me in prison?" She paused. "How long until spring?"

"It *is* spring," he said. "Late April."

"Oh." She was quiet for a moment before continuing. "You know, the trees are beautiful. They have dignity."

He gripped the steering wheel harder, to resist crumbling at the image of dignified maples and elms.

She shrugged. "It bugs me that the houses here are made of wood, that's all. They're brick, where I live."

It wasn't worth reminding her that she'd lived in Springfield for forty-five years, since before he was born.

"How long until spring?" she asked again.

Sam sighed. "Sometimes you ask a question when you already know the answer, don't you, Ma?"

"I'm getting used to the wooden houses," she said. "It takes a long time."

"Yes," he agreed.

"You know what I love?" she asked.

"What?"

"The trees. Do you think they'll cut them down and build houses here someday?"

"I don't know."

"They do that. Cut them down. I miss my car. I miss driving. If I had my car, I could escape from this prison place you're taking me to."

"I know, Ma."

"I don't know what I'd do with a car any more." She closed her eyes. When he turned off the engine at Hillside Village, she opened them. "I like the trees. We don't have them, where I live."

~~~

Zoe hated medical facilities of all kinds. At least this place was totally accessible, which made getting around and helping Flo easier. But easier movement meant more energy and more room for memories. Whenever she rolled into a medical facility, ghosts of disease and difference appeared—the sicky-sweet smell of the brown soap and the scratchy elastic of the hat she wore to the operating room, and the prick of the needle stuck in her arm.

She'd been lucky, she knew that. Her last surgery was over a decade ago, and it was hard to remember much about it because she'd been so young. Other kids with spina bifida had it much worse—bladder surgeries and spinal fusion and wounds that wouldn't heal. She knew because she lurked on the SB websites. She never posted. She'd spent her whole life being as normal as possible.

This place wasn't so bad, Zoe thought, if you ignored the piano. After his first visit to Hillside Village, Sam told her about the two old women who'd had strokes and played two-handed, together. Sure, that was very cool. But he didn't mention that the grand piano, sitting right in the middle of the lobby, was where they put the announcement when people died. With framed photos taken decades earlier and a few pathetic paragraphs about long-ago jobs and awards and when they moved to Hillside and a little guestbook for people to record their memories in shaky handwriting.

The administrator, Trixie, met them at the piano of death and showed them to the Memory Unit, punching in a code on the keypad to unlock the door. Prison, just like Flo said. Trixie introduced Sam to the social worker to sign papers, and walked Zoe and Flo around a peculiar circular hallway to Flo's new home. The room wasn't too awful and at least there was no roommate. A little generic, but no hospital bed or rails or bars or anything. Flo glowered at Trixie so Zoe thanked her, and followed her grandmother into the light blue room.

"Hey, that's nice." Zoe pointed to the recliner in front of the window, with table and lamp next to it. "Perfect for reading."

"It's stupid." Flo kicked the bedside table, although Zoe couldn't see anything wrong with it. "Stupid," Flo muttered again, then slumped onto the bed, curled up on the blue and green paisley comforter, and closed her eyes.

Before the fire, it would have been impossible to fit all her grandmother's belongings into the room. That morning it only took a few minutes to unpack the clothes they'd bought her, and arrange the framed photographs Sam had selected from their fireplace mantel along the top of Flo's new dresser.

With a permanent marker Zoe printed "Flo Tobin" on the white label inside each nightgown, each stiff new flannel shirt and elastic-waist denim pants, before stacking them in the drawers. This was *so* not how Flo dressed. Maybe they could plan a trip, in a day or so, to the mall to get the right clothes—real jeans and bright T-shirts with outdated political slogans about boycotting grapes and sisterhood is powerful—so Flo would feel like herself again instead of some generic some old lady.

That thought made Zoe stop writing, because you probably couldn't buy those political T-shirts at the mall and maybe Flo would never find herself again. Flo Tobin, she printed on the last pair of sweat pants. She hoped Sam would return from doing paperwork at the nurses' station soon, before she got to the underwear.

When Sam got back, he sat on the bed next to Flo.

"You awake?" he asked.

"Go away."

"I signed the papers," he said. "The social worker will be in soon to talk with you." He hesitated. "They suggest that Zoe and I leave, so you can start getting accustomed to the place." He touched her cheek. "Why are you crying?"

"Duh," Zoe whispered but Sam ignored her.

"Tell me, Ma."

"I miss Charlie."

"I know," Sam said. "He was a good cat."

"Not the cat. The man Charlie."

"What man?" Sam raised his hands, palms up, in a questioning gesture.

"I loved your father," Flo told him.

"I know. He was a good man."

That is so lame, Zoe thought. She never knew her grandfather, but couldn't his son think of any adjective other than *good?*

"Not Brad," Flo said, opening her eyes and looking into Sam's. "Your real father's name was Charlie."

Charlie? Sam heard his mother's words but they didn't make any sense. More and more often her words came zooming in from some other planet, like her comment about dignified trees on the drive. The Alzheimer's website recommended not arguing with the imagined memories, the untrue statements, because you couldn't use logic or evidence against the disease. He knew all this, but his mother was one of the smartest people he knew. When she talked nonsense, well, he couldn't stand it. He leaned down and kissed Flo's cheek and tried to keep his voice from breaking.

"Rest, Ma. I'll sit here with you."

Flo pulled the pillow over her head. She didn't have the strength to hear Sam's response. Why did she say that, just now, about Charlie? She hadn't planned to, at least not right now, not today, but the words just came pouring out of her mouth. She'd been thinking about Charlie more and more recently, as the barricade she had constructed to not-think about him disintegrated and tumbled away. Her memory, her apartment, her clothes and her photos and her sweet cat—how much loss could one woman take? Still, she had not planned to blurt it out like that to Sam. He deserved better.

Or maybe not. Maybe he deserved being clobbered over the head with his paternity, and she hadn't even mentioned the zinger. Maybe that was exactly what he deserved for locking her up in this place just because she had a little accident with a stove and some kitchen curtains.

Okay, a big accident—a fatal one to the feline Charlie. But still, this place was a prison and she wasn't going to accept it, not without a fight. Because she was a fighter, always had been, and a survivor too. And no matter what this disease thought it could do to her brain cells, she would win.

I'm fine. I'm fine. I'm fine, she told herself. But like many of her favorite words, her recent sentences, that one was made of glass. Not ice, as she first thought, but glass, thin and smooth and fragile as an infant's skull bones. And slick, so that words that one moment were poised elegantly on the glossy surface of a paragraph would the next moment slide off into some nether void and disappear. And there was always the possibility of breakage. That thin glass plate on which her sentences, her brain, her life, balanced could crash and shatter into shards. Sharp and glistening and deadly.

Chapter Eighteen

Stretched out on his bed, Tim listened to a screaming siren race closer and then fade toward downtown Brooklyn. He was massively relieved that Jeremy was on the train home, but he still didn't sleep much the night before, so he might have dozed off. Three sharp knocks on the apartment door startled him.

"Police." More knocking.

Tim opened the door to two uniformed officers.

"Are you Jeremy Beaujolais?" the tall one asked.

"No. He's my brother."

"Is he here?"

Tim shook his head. "He took the train home to Massachusetts this morning. What's this about?"

"We're investigating a firebombing yesterday afternoon, during the demonstration. We'd like to talk to Jeremy about it."

"What was bombed?"

"The offices of a fuel company, along the Gowanus."

That sounded like something Jeremy would be against, but Tim couldn't imagine his nerdy brother firebombing anything at all. "By now he's back at college. At UMass."

"Is he studying Molotov cocktail assembly up there?"

Tim studied the cop's face. Was he making a joke? "Botany. Plants. Dead ones, mostly."

"Was your brother involved in the demonstration on Saturday?"

Tim swallowed hard. "He sat in and was arrested. So he couldn't have been involved with any bombing."

The two cops exchanged looks.

"You'll have records of that, right?" Tim said. "The arrest and timing and everything?"

"We'll check it out. You involved with that global warming too?"

"Not me," Tim said. "I'm a business major. Supply chain management." He was babbling. Stop talking too much, he told himself.

"You know any of his friends? From the group?"

Tim shook his head. "No, but I met the punk girl he was arrested with. Pink hair and a bizarre name. Green something."

The cop looked at his notebook. "Greenhope Murphy. I need your brother's address and phone numbers. School and home."

Tim gave him the information, trying not to imagine how Tian might respond to cops at his apartment door asking for Jeremy. Trying not to picture Tian in Forest Park, the night he escaped from jail. The snowy night he charged the cops with a fury that still invaded Tim's sleep.

On the way out, the other cop handed Tim a business card. "Call me if you remember anything else."

Tim stood at the closed door for a few moments, resting his forehead on the painted surface and letting his heart rate slow to normal. Why was he so scared, when the cops were just doing their job? His brother might be a nut case but he wasn't a fire-bomber. Jeremy would never touch a Molotov cocktail, not after that day in the prison visiting room. At least, Tim didn't think so.

But how well did he *really* know his brother? Tim wandered down the hallway to his room. He stared at the posters covering on the wall. Wolverine stared back. Did Tim imagine his disapproval?

Tim didn't feel good ratting out his brother, disrespecting their pledge. It had been him and Jeremy against the world for so long. Against the people who broke up their Pioneer Street house, the ones who sent their dad to prison. The people who made their mom cry every night when she thought the boys were asleep. Sure, he got it—those people believed his dad was responsible for Abby and Terrence's deaths and maybe they were right.

But damn it—was it right to punish the whole family? He felt himself getting angry. He stood up. Three steps to the wall and he faced Wolverine, man to man.

Why did Jeremy have to dwell on the past so much? Be so damn sensitive? Sure, Tim thought about the babies sometimes. That's how he thought of them, generically, the babies. If he allowed himself to remember how fourteen-month-old Abby climbed into his lap with her princess book, or how Terrence at two-and-a-half tugged on his shirt and whined to play catch in the back yard, well, that hurt and Tim didn't like to hurt. He wanted to put all that weird history—the commune and his dad's prison and Jeremy's extinct plants, all of it—behind him. He wanted a normal life. That's why he left Springfield. That's why he was studying business.

That's why he hardly ever went back to Springfield. Just for a quick visit when his dad was released and again for Gabe's party. But he wasn't going back again, not for a long time.

And that's why he told Jeremy to go back to UMass. Because it wasn't right for Jeremy to get all nutso on him. He took a step closer to Wolverine and poked a finger in his chest. Not right and not fair.

He and Jeremy both liked Wolverine best, but Tim could see the strength of the others too, even that stiff Cyclops. Sometimes Tim fantasized that his parents had died in that plane crash like Cyclops' folks did, sending him and Jeremy to earth in parachutes. He knew that was wrong, but he dreamt about it anyway. He imagined having a wicked optic blast and hot women and everything. Being a stiff was better than prison and shame.

It wasn't right for Jeremy to make him think about the old days. Tim grabbed the top of their favorite Wolverine poster. He only hesitated for a moment, then started ripping. It felt good to tear the paper. He was so pissed off. He pulled harder and the paper tore jaggedly though Hugh Jackman's thick hair shaped like weasel ears and his never-smile face, bisecting the white muscle shirt.

Okay. So maybe Jeremy wasn't the only twin haunted by their past. But at least Tim fought it. He tore the poster again, in the other direction, ripping through the steel blades that crossed his angry face like prison bars.

Take that, Wolverine. Take that, greenhouses and tea and communes and everything else his crazy family stood for.

He tore again across the steel blades/prison bars and that made him stop for a moment. Was *that* why they both loved that particular poster best? The bars? Never mind. It felt good to tear the paper. Powerful even, and he moved to Cyclops next. Then on to the other Wolverine posters and Storm and the group shots with Xavier, ripping and tearing them into shreds. He got a trash bag from the kitchen, stuffed the tatters inside, then tied the top. Tomorrow he'd buy new posters, cool up-to-date ones that had nothing to do with the past. He was moving on.

But first he had to call their mom and warn her that Jeremy was losing it.

~·~

The city bus let Jeremy off four blocks from his parents' apartment. Tramping up Forest Park Avenue with his duffle bag, he thought he probably should be majorly pissed off. At Tim for kicking him out, at his parents for telling him to catch the city bus instead of picking him up downtown at the Greyhound station. Most of all he should be angry with Mary for doing whatever she did to get herself in big trouble. But he was so tired, and surprisingly glad to be home.

The glad feelings lessened as he climbed the stairs to his parents' second-floor apartment. By the time he unlocked the door they were mostly gone.

"I'm home," he called. He walked through the living room and dining room of the railroad flat, then detoured to the bedroom he once shared with Tim. He dropped his jacket and duffle on the bed and kicked off his sneakers. He spent a moment looking at the posters on the wall and wondered what it meant that his practical business-major brother, who said he'd left behind their oddball childhood, had replicated the décor of this room in his Brooklyn apartment. He touched the taped place on Wolverine's left leg, then rubbed his finger along the soft black leather covering his shoulder.

Secretly Jeremy had always liked Storm best. If he could be any X-Man, he would be her. She was closest to nature, to the world of earth and its plants; she *lived* inside the weather. Every molecule of her body was connected to the natural world and he was envious of that bond. Maybe Storm's powers could even reverse global warming. But of course he could never admit any of this to Tim, even now that they were grown up, because Storm was a *girl*.

The kitchen was empty. It was almost 6:00. You could never predict about Tian, but Francie was usually awake and cooking dinner by now, gearing up for her night shift on the hospital switchboard. When the hospital telephone systems went digital, Francie had worried her job would disappear too, along with her imprisoned husband and their commune, but the hospital still needed real voices to respond to anxious relatives and transfer not-quite-emergency calls to the right department.

He lifted the cover of a pot bubbling on the stovetop. Lentils. He smiled. Of course.

"Out here," his mother called.

If you ignored the slanting floor and mosquito-sized rips in the screens, the small back porch was the nicest part of the apartment. His parents sat at the round wicker table, Tian balancing on the back legs of his chair with his bare feet on the table and a book in his hands, and Francie hunched over the checkbook and a stack of bills.

"Hello, Son," Tian said without looking up from his book.

Jeremy hated being called "Son." It was generic, as if his father couldn't remember his name. Had he always done that, before prison? Jeremy couldn't remember.

"You still boycotting online banking?" Jeremy asked as he kissed Francie's cheek.

Tian looked up from his book then. "You still refusing to accept the fragility of the Internet?" he asked. "One brilliant hacker and the entire global financial structure will crash and burn, taking along civilization as we know it. Might not be a bad thing, either."

"Nice to see you, too, Dad."

Tian wasn't that old, forty-five or six last November, but during his last year in prison he stopped shaving his head and his hair grew in gray. Steel wool, Francie called it when she tried to tease him into shaving again. "I'm not that man any more," Tian reminded them. It wasn't clear what kind of man his father was, other than one who read a dozen history books from the public library every week and wore a mess of rubber bands on his wrist. The gray hair didn't bother Jeremy; it was his father's facial expression that haunted him, like he'd deserted his own life. That look and the rubber band bracelets drove Jeremy nuts.

"What's with the rubber bands?" Jeremy had asked.

"Cut him some slack," Francie said, but Jeremy couldn't stand the sharp crack of the rubber, over and over and over. "It's like a stress reliever. He's doing his best."

Francie closed the checkbook and put it on top of the pile of envelopes. "I'm glad you're home, Jeremy. We've been so worried about you. About what you're doing with your life."

"I'm fine," Jeremy said. "Spending a few weeks in Brooklyn was cool, even though now I'm going to have to hustle to make up the work."

"Tim called," Francie said.

Great. His brother probably didn't even wait until Jeremy was out the front door to tattle. "What did he say?"

"That the cops were at his apartment this morning, looking for you. Something about a firebombing."

It took a few seconds to catch his breath. "That has nothing to do with me." That must have been the explosion when he was in the courthouse. Sari's backpack flashed across his mind, but it didn't make sense. His friends wouldn't be involved in something like that.

Francie looked at her lap. "He also said you're having spells or something, chanting in Latin and acting really strange. He's worried about you and so am I. I want you to see someone, a counselor."

"I don't get it," Tian said. "What's your problem? Why can't you move beyond the dead plants?"

Okay, Jeremy thought. Here goes nothing. "Plant extinction is not my *problem*. It's my *work* and it's just as important as your history books. I can't stand by and let things fall apart. I want to make a difference." He hesitated, then decided to keep going. "Also, I can't stop thinking about what happened to our family and the commune. How everything fell apart for us."

Tian started fiddling with the rubber bands, pulling them and twisting them and finally letting them snap hard, one by one, against his skin. Jeremy rubbed his own wrist.

"What do you mean?" Tian asked, finally looking up. "*You* weren't arrested. *You* didn't spend all those years in prison."

Francie reached over and covered Tian's wrist with her hand, cutting off the sharp sounds. "That doesn't mean we didn't suffer too, Tian. You know that."

Jeremy stood up. "I lost a brother and a sister. I lost you. And ever since, I've felt like our family is on the wrong side of things."

Tian tapped his finger against his book and then pointed it at Jeremy. "If you studied history, you'd understand. That's what they do. They target us and lock us up. Then they blame the victim."

"I don't want to be a victim. I want to change things."

Tian's expression, part grimace and part frown, contained eons of sorrow and regret. It was the saddest expression Jeremy had ever seen on a human face.

"That's a young man's dream," Tian said. "It was mine too." He didn't add, *Look what happened to me.* He didn't have to.

Jeremy shook his head. He couldn't do this. They would never be able to talk to each other about this. He turned away and walked into the kitchen.

Francie followed him. "Don't give up on your dad," she whispered. "He's a good man. He's started attending a group for men just out of prison. He just needs some time." She took a deep breath. "And I think I get it, about the plants, about how important it is. But I'm worried about you. Will you see someone?"

"I'm heading up to school this evening," he said. "I have a lot of work to do if I want to finish the semester. But if it'll make you happy, I'll make an appointment at Health Services."

⁓≗⸽

Four hours later, Jeremy cracked open the window and curled up on his dorm bed, grateful for the gazillionth time that he had a single. It was chilly for late April, surprising after such an early spring, and the air in the room smelled stale. He wrapped his quilt around his shoulders and that reminded him of the banner he and Greenhope wore during their arrest. What happened to the banner? The cops probably saw no value in it and his careful work ended up in a landfill in New Jersey or on a trash barge, waiting to be dumped into the ocean, to poison small fish with specks of acrylic paint.

He reached into his backpack and took out his sketchpad, promising himself that tomorrow he would begin putting his life back together. He'd talk to his advisor and contact all his professors about missed work. If he groveled, his supervisor at the dining hall would assign him three or four shifts a week. He'd find Patty's card and call for an appointment. He'd find a climate activist group on campus and get involved.

But tonight he'd take a few hours to commemorate the plants that lived only on paper, and in his memory. It might calm him down. It might banish the competing thoughts and images and feelings ping-ponging around his brain.

Sari grabbing her backpack.

Mary's photograph with its impossible headline.

His father's nappy gray head and his disdain.

His own lack of clarity about how to live the kind of life he wanted.

The feel of Zoe's soft ballet slippers on his feet as they swayed back and forth to the music of their breathing.

His nine-year-old self, hiding huddled with Tim in a snowy clearing, smoke from a sodden bonfire hanging around them, watching the cops take his family away.

"*Pluchea glutinosa*," he murmured. "*Oldenlandia adscensionis. Myrcia skeldingii. Neomacounia nitida.*"

Chapter Nineteen

Nine days after the fire, Sam fumbled for the key at the door to Flo's apartment. The dead-campfire smell of smoke hung thick in the hallway. Inside, the damage from both fire and water was far greater than he'd expected. His shoes squished and sunk into the carpet. Good thing he'd persuaded Zoe not to miss school for this trip. He couldn't imagine how her wheelchair tires could roll across this soggy mess or how she would handle seeing the scorched ruins of Flo's home.

His throat ached at the blistered finish of the old upright piano that no one ever played. He traced the deeply charred wood of the admittedly rickety coffee table he made for Flo's birthday one year, the overlapping circular marks from her tea cups now almost obliterated by flames. Must've been ninth grade, the year he took wood shop. He felt particularly close to his mother that year, after his father's heart attack. Brad's heart attack.

Brad, who for some incomprehensible reason in his mother's jumbled and seared brain, was no longer his father. Not that he believed Flo for a split second, not about Brad.

His head spun—must be the smoke or toxic fumes—and he grabbed the arm of the blackened sofa for support. The fabric was soaked and he jerked his hand away. This room was a mess, and he didn't want to see the kitchen, where the blaze started, where the cat died. Maybe Flo's bedroom, down the hall and farthest from the fire, was less damaged. Maybe some of her special things could be retrieved.

He hesitated in the doorway. He grew up in this apartment but rarely entered his mother's bedroom. When he woke up with a nightmare, Flo came to him, and snuggled in his bed until he fell asleep. Sam's bedroom was now her office, stripped of his things two decades ago. Flo's room had always been hers alone, mysterious and private, even when she shared it with Brad.

The damage was minimally less in the bedroom, and draped across the bed was Flo's favorite jacket, a patchwork of Sam's outgrown blue jeans from toddlerhood through high school. Anna sewed it for Flo's birthday the first year Sam and Anna lived together and Flo loved it. Sam reached for it, then realized that it had become a mosaic of soot and scorch, a fabric corpse flame-fused to the comforter.

He backed out of Flo's room. He couldn't do this. He'd take a quick look at the rest of the apartment, just so he could tell his mom he checked, but there was nothing here to save. Nothing to bring comfort. In the kitchen, his foot kicked something hard and sent it skittering across the burnt and curled linoleum floor. Probably one of poor Charlie's toys, he thought, bending over to pick it up.

Not a cat toy; nothing recognizable. A bumpy blob of melted something, maybe a paperweight? Had the cat been playing with it? Sam spit on the blob and rubbed it against his T-shirt. Under the thick soot coating, emerald green appeared, and purple. They were marbles, fused together by the fire into a lump of glass.

There was a soft knock on the apartment door. Sam put the destroyed marbles into his pocket and squished across the rug to answer it.

～✑✑

Mimi wasn't sure *why* she needed to see Flo's apartment, except for her profound regret that she didn't come over that Saturday evening when

Flo had sounded so out of it and hung up on her and then wouldn't answer the phone. Of course Mimi should have gone over, should have checked on her best friend, should have at least called Sam. Flo could have died in that fire. Mimi would never forgive herself for doing nothing.

Now, she looked at Sam. Tears had washed lines through his soot-smeared cheeks. She opened her arms.

"I'm so sorry," she said. "I should have come that night. I could have prevented this. This is all my fault."

Sam stepped back, out of Mimi's arms. "Of course not. Something like this was inevitable. You know that."

Mimi walked to the middle of the living room and looked around. "I had no idea it was this bad." She opened the coffee table drawer and took out a framed photo, blackened and charred. The soot smudged when she tried to wipe it off with her hand. "That's Flo and me, the year we met," she said. "Can I keep this?"

"Sure," Sam said. "Take anything you can salvage." He hesitated. "Listen, I have a question. Did you know anything about Charlie?"

"The cat?"

"No. The man. Ma's lover." His voice broke. "She says he's my father."

Mimi shook her head. A lover? How could Flo have kept a secret like that, all these years? If that were true, she'd be furious at Flo. If she weren't already overwhelmed with guilt and sorrow.

"I never knew about any guy named Charlie."

"Me neither," Sam said. "It's probably just the dementia speaking."

❧

When he got home, Sam scrubbed the marble blob with dish soap and water, dried it carefully, and put it on his desk, next to his computer. It was grotesque, how the different colored marbles kept their basic spherical shape but their edges melted into each other. Beautiful too, in a way, and the only salvageable thing from her apartment.

He was procrastinating. He had promised to visit Flo this morning. But first, what about Charlie? The guy was probably just a fantasy or a phantom, but Sam couldn't stop thinking about him. He wanted to Google him, but couldn't quite bring himself to do it. For one thing, what was he going to do with the information? Confront his mother? She'd been through enough recently, hadn't she? On the other hand, if not now, when? She wasn't getting any better. Every week she lost a little more of herself.

Besides, he didn't know where to start. Well, that wasn't true. He had a few clues, facts that Flo had mentioned weeks ago in connection with Charlie: Glen Echo. 1960. Picketing. Of course, that was before she said who Charlie really was, and 1960 seemed so long ago. Irrelevant. At least, that's what he'd thought.

Now, he put those keywords into the search field, hesitated for a moment, and pressed Enter. Easy as pie.

He read old newspaper articles about Glen Echo, the segregated amusement park near Flo's childhood home in Maryland. Howard University students picketed, whites from the local neighborhood joined them, and counter-demonstrators came from the American Nazi Party. He searched files of black and white photos, reading each picket sign and every caption. He never found his mother's picture, not for sure, but there was one small, unidentified white face in a crowd shot that *could* have been a young Flo.

There was only one Charles, a tall guy who showed up in almost every photo. The caption identified him as Charles Elwood Anderson, a student at Howard and one of the picket organizers.

Charles was black.

Sam looked at down his hands, his skin dark against the white keyboard. Then he typed Charles Elwood Anderson into the search engine.

Flo closed her eyes to concentrate better on the radio program. She had heard about this research a few years ago and she understood it perfectly then, but either the science was getting murkier or her brain was. The reporter was saying that fetal cells circulate in a mother's bloodstream for decades after a pregnancy. It wasn't clear if these cells helped the mother, or hurt her, but they stuck around, even after the children grew up and moved away or even died. In one case, hundreds of fetal cells in a woman's liver cured her hepatitis or maybe it was pancreatitis, at least Flo thought that's what he said. Even if she got it wrong, it didn't matter. What mattered was she wasn't alone. Even when she could no longer talk with him, when she stopped recognizing his dear face—it was impossible to believe that could ever happen—Sam's cells would roam her veins, keeping her company. She wouldn't be alone.

"Knock knock." Sam's voice filled the doorway.

She didn't answer. Walking into her room, Sam couldn't tell if Flo was awake or asleep. She was curled up in bed and the radio volume turned up loud. She looked a decade older than before the fire, just two weeks ago. She was aging fast. Not so much in body but in her brain certainly, and maybe in her soul, if such a thing existed. Suddenly he wished that Zoe had come or that Anna were next to him, holding his hand.

He turned down the volume on the radio and Flo opened her eyes.

"Got two things for you, Ma." He leaned down to kiss her cheek. "A present and a question."

Flo smiled. "I like presents."

He sat on the edge of her bed and reconsidered. Should he give her the marble blob? Would it please her or upset her, making concrete the damage from the fire? Why would she want it now, when the marbles and what they represented offended her before?

"I went to your apartment, to try to save some of your things." He touched her hand. "But the fire destroyed pretty much everything."

"Everything," she echoed.

He nodded, then handed her the blob of multicolored glass. "It burned so hot. Look what it did to the bag of marbles I gave you."

She held it on the palm of her hand and stared, turning her hand this way and that. The morning light from the window flashed a prism of jewel colors onto the wall. Flo moved the glass so that the colors danced.

"So pretty," she said.

Sam closed his eyes. She didn't know what it was, didn't remember. No way would she be able to talk coherently about Charlie. Still, he had to try.

"Now the question." He moved to the bedside chair. Giving her space would be good, right? "Tell me about my father."

She rubbed her thumb across the marble glass, polishing the surface. "Brad died. Don't you remember?"

"Not Brad. Tell me about Charlie."

Flo smiled. "I loved him very much."

I loved Charlie and I was a coward, Flo thought. She didn't realize she spoke the words aloud until Sam answered.

"Coward? You're the bravest person I know."

That was not true. A brave person would have told Charlie about the pregnancy. A brave person would not crawl back to her old boyfriend and move north with him. A brave person would not lie to Sam about his father or keep the whole awful, wonderful thing from her best friend. Those were the acts of a coward.

Some things, some people, you know all your life, Flo thought, and they were true and solid and you trusted they would never change. Like Sam. Like Zoe. Like the memory of Charlie. So real, so sweet, so necessary.

But then they *do* change. People and places begin to unravel a bit at the edges, to fray like linen napkins washed too many times. The people were still there but not in sharp focus. The memories soften and begin to dissolve. Flo had always known that life could implode in an instant, in a moment of inattention, a routine lab test. But she had believed that if she worried enough, if she imagined each catastrophe, it would be a talisman against it happening.

She was wrong about that. Even with all her worrying, disaster arrived and she was unprepared. She could do nothing to stop it.

Chapter Twenty

Rolling her wheelchair past the piano of death, Zoe looked away from the framed photograph of a white-haired man with an oval mole on his cheek and a long list of accomplishments and community memberships. She felt sad for the man's grandchildren and didn't want to think about the day Flo's existence would be reduced to an 8 x 11 frame on that shiny wood surface. She'd read about Alzheimer's on the Internet and knew Flo could live for years. Her body could, at least.

She took Jeremy's hand. It was sweet of him to spend part of his Saturday visiting her grandmother. He said it was cool, that he really liked talking to Flo.

Next to the elevator, the activity room was being set up with booths and tables, for some sort of festival or fair. Hillside Helps, announced the banner over the double doors.

"Helps what?" Zoe asked.

Jeremy read from a poster on the wall. "Get involved with the organizations that work to improve our community."

"Cool," Zoe said. "Let's bring Flo down. She'll enjoy it."

Flo was sitting by the window in her room with a book closed in her lap. Her face lit up when Zoe and Jeremy entered. "Finally, some fun," she said. "I've been here a month and this place bores me to tears."

"You've been here a week, Ma," Sam said from his perch on the bed, computer on his lap.

Flo waved his comment away. "Feels like a month. I've been here long enough to hate it. The people here smell bad."

Zoe rolled her eyes and wheeled close to hug her grandmother. "In any case, today will be fun. There's a community fair downstairs."

Flo made a face. "Bunch of silly do-gooders."

Jeremy sat in the guest chair. "What's wrong with doing good?"

"Do you know the difference between liberal and radical, young man?"

"Don't get started, Ma," Sam said.

"The fellow asked me a question," Flo said. "He deserves an answer."

Sam shrugged and turned back to his computer.

"I'm not sure I know the difference you mean," Jeremy said.

Or that you really want to, Zoe thought.

"It's the difference between putting a band-aid on a gaping wound," Flo said. "A wound like poverty or racism, versus trying to correct what *caused* the injury in the first place. Making that commitment and following through, no matter what the consequences."

Jeremy had spent a lot of time considering consequences. How children are often the collateral damage of their parents' choices. Even if the parents mean well, even if the effects are hidden or subtle or dormant for decades. Not only the families of spies or serial murderers or drug dealers are at risk; the white picket fence can hide unforgivable error or neglect, pious fanaticism or cavernous sorrow. Kids are simultaneously fragile and resilient; who knows why one blooms in the dark and another withers in bright sunshine.

Why was Tim so untouched by their shared past, why was *he* the one with obsessions about fragility, about extinction, the one with hallucinations—or whatever they were—of plants growing out of his fingertips? Not that he would give it up, not entirely, not all of it. Looking at Zoe, so comfortable with herself despite how she was born, he wondered if he'd ever feel normal.

"Do you really mean that?" Jeremy asked Flo. "Because the consequences can be huge."

Flo's face had slackened and she didn't answer. Zoe told him on the phone that Flo was in and out of lucidity, sometimes floating off in the middle of a sentence. Too bad, because Jeremy really wanted to know the answer to his question and he didn't know that many people to ask besides Flo. Mary maybe. If he ever had the chance to talk to her again.

"What happened to you?" Flo asked without opening her eyes. "To make you ask about consequences?"

What could he tell this old woman? That Tian and Francie had lived their utopian dream, trying to repair the social damage they observed around them. Was it their fault that their dream became his nightmare?

"Bad things happened to my family when I was nine," Jeremy said. He was nine and hiding in the snowy woods with Tim, watching the cops kick and beat his dad, drown the bonfire, cuff and take away all the members of his family. "When you're a kid and bad happens, it sticks to you like superglue. Forever."

"But Jeremy . . ." Sam started.

"I know, Sam," Jeremy said. "You were there, with your crazy mustache, and you saved us and I'm really grateful. But nothing can erase what happened. It was like growing up in a war zone."

Zoe reached for Jeremy's hand. "Or like being a mutant."

Jeremy nodded. "That's right. Mutants are people who feel different and discarded. They've been pushed away and live on the edge of things."

Flo's eyes snapped open. "That's the lumpenproletariat," she said. "The only way to get power is to fight back, organize yourselves."

"I don't know about the lumpen-people," Jeremy said, "but Zoe and I are inheriting a world that is self-destructing. Even if I want to do the expected thing—get a good job, have a family—what's the use? Our kids will grow up to environmental catastrophe." Jeremy blushed furiously on the word kids, avoiding Zoe's gaze. "How fair is that?" he said, looking at the floor.

"Who ever told you life was fair?" Flo asked.

Sam stood up. "This is fascinating, Ma. But let's all go downstairs and check out the fair before lunch."

~~∞~~

Sam had to sign his mother out of the Memory Unit before punching in the four-digit elevator code. He knew the reason for the precautions, but when Flo muttered, "prison," he couldn't disagree. Still, she was safe here. No more wandering off and forgetting where she lived. No more fires.

Downstairs, the activity room was crowded. Every non-profit in town had a table, from homeless vets to domestic abuse, from global warming to civil liberties. Zoe and Flo wandered together from display to display and Sam followed, trying not to lose sight of them. He didn't know whether to hope his mother got involved with something or worry that she would join a group and let loose her particular brand of bossy passion on the unsuspecting members.

While his mother and daughter chatted with a ponytailed man about the battered women's shelter, Sam joined Jeremy at the climate change booth.

"There's great stuff here," Jeremy said, holding a flyer from 350.org. "These guys have a chapter at UMass and I went to my first meeting on Tuesday."

Zoe wheeled up to them, Flo leaning heavily on the wheelchair. "Grandma's tired of walking. Time for lunch."

Two young women holding clipboards flanked the exit. One stepped forward and asked, "Can you spare a moment for reproductive rights?"

Sam glanced at his mother, whose face was turning a deep red. Uh-oh. He had a bad feeling about this.

"How dare you?" Flo voice cascaded to a scream. "Look at you, you babies, asking *me* if I can spare a moment for reproductive rights? Do you have any fucking clue what we faced, how hard we fought to gain those rights you're talking about?"

Flo snatched the woman's clipboard and raised it like a club, then threw it at the two women, who cowered while the clipboard clattered across the tile floor.

"It's okay, Ma." Sam put his arm around Flo and tried to swivel her away from the women. Jeremy picked up the clipboard and handed it to its owner.

"It's not okay. It's insulting." Flo slapped at Sam's hands.

"Sorry," murmured the young woman clutching the clipboard to her chest. The other canvasser looked stunned.

Zoe grabbed her grandmother's hand and tugged. "Let's get lunch. I'm famished."

Flo turned back to the two young women. "Feh. You know nothing." Spittle sprayed with the force of her words. "Nothing."

Trixie appeared at Flo's side. "Is there a problem, dear?"

"I'm not your dear and yes, there's a problem. These insulting, stupid girls know *nothing*." Flo started walking toward the elevator, Zoe and Jeremy hurrying after her.

"I'm so sorry," Sam said to Trixie and the young women.

Trixie patted his arm. "You don't have to apologize, Mr. Tobin. It's the disease."

Sam wanted to be alone, to weep, but he had to pay attention. The director was still talking.

"This kind of aggressive symptomatology is not uncommon," Trixie said. "Unfortunately this is not the first incident with your mother. We have to consider the safety and tranquility of our community. I suspect that when Dr. Robertson hears about this, he'll decide it's time to begin the psychotropic medication he mentioned to you."

~≈≈~

After the incident with Flo and the canvassers, lunch was anything but cheerful. Sam dropped Zoe and Jeremy off at the library and went home. Instead of going upstairs and finishing building a website for the new

Asian fusion restaurant at the X, he rang the downstairs doorbell. Sam hated to ask Emily for medical advice but he didn't know where else to turn. She was a nurse, even if she refused to administer to family.

Anna answered the door. "Hey," she said. "How's your mom?"

"Not great," Sam said. "That's why I'm here. I'm worried. Is Emily home?"

"In the kitchen, kneading bread." Anna stepped back to let Sam enter and followed him down the hall.

"Hey, Sam. Talk to me while I take out my frustrations on seven grains who can't fight back," Emily said.

"Tea?" Anna asked.

Sam nodded and sank into a chair at the table. This much kindness was almost more than he could handle. He cleared the moisture from his throat and watched Emily form the kneaded dough into a mound and drape a towel over it. Anna warmed the teapot and spooned loose tea into it. One of the things that fascinated him when they first met was her refusal to use tea bags, instead carrying a small china teapot to the college dining room every morning. It was hard to remember their idyllic beginning, how happy they were until the ultrasound and Zoe's birth. If only Anna had been able to express doubt or fear about their daughter's situation; if only he'd been able to wrap his brain around it without terror.

"What's happening with Flo?" Anna's voice was soft as sorrow.

"Bad behavior," Sam said. "Acting out even more than usual. They're going to start her on some drug to calm her down. You worked in a nursing home, didn't you, Emily? After."

"You mean after I got fired from the home care job?" Emily said. "For about six months. I hated it, partly because of those drugs."

He took a folded brochure from his pocket. "I must have read this a hundred times, but I still don't understand it. The risks are so bad—cardiac rhythm problems and heart failure, strokes and death. Why would they give her something like that?"

Emily glanced at the paper. "It's an off-label use. This med isn't recommended for elderly patients with dementia, but it's used a lot for that purpose because there's nothing better. Belligerent behavior with cognitive impairment is really hard to manage and psychotropic drugs work. Sort of."

Sam watched Anna pour boiling water into the teapot. "What else does it do?"

"All the nasties you mentioned. Sometimes it triggers a cascade of medical problems. It can also act like a sedative. Some people become lethargic." Emily hesitated. "How bad is her cognitive function?"

"Up and down," he said. "I mean, I know that's supposed to be common, but it's so variable. One day she's pretty cogent, makes sense and everything. The next day, she looks at me like she's not quite sure of my name, but she thinks she remembers that I'm an okay guy so she should be nice to me." He paused. "She can't stay there unless she takes the medicine. Should I try to move her to a different place?"

"You could try," Emily said. "But I think most facilities medicate patients to control antisocial behavior. They have to, and sometimes the meds work pretty well. There's no magic bullet for this." Her voice softened. "There might be no better option."

Anna scooted her chair closer to Sam's and put both arms around him. "I'm so sorry, Sam. I always admired your mother, how tough and fierce she is, even though she didn't have much use for me."

"She liked you," he said. "As much as she liked anyone who wasn't a blood relative or a comrade. Preferably both."

Emily poured three cups of tea. Sam inhaled the tea steam and the aroma transported him to the apartment he and Anna rented in those first deliriously happy months. He had to clear his throat again.

He stood up. "I can't do this."

"Sit down," Anna said. "Talk to me about Zoe and this boy."

Sam sat. "Jeremy? He's a good kid."

Anna made a face. "But he's so much older. And got to admit I'm concerned about his family. Prison and the commune or cult or whatever it was?"

"Come on," Sam said. "You can't hold the kid responsible for his family. Besides, is your family any saner? Emily's dad was in prison, just like Jeremy's."

"It's not only his family," Anna said. "It sounds like he's not that stable emotionally. That worries me."

Sam started to argue with her. He liked Jeremy and wanted Anna to like him too, but he didn't have the energy for it, not today. He stood up again. "It might take him a while, but Jeremy will figure it out. But right now I can't focus on anything except my mother. She's declining pretty fast. Is that normal?"

"Nothing is normal with this disease," Emily said. "I'm so sorry."

Anna stood too and hugged him. "Let me know if I can do anything, okay?"

"Me too," Emily added. "One of the hardest things about this disease is that it doesn't progress in an orderly manner. Some days there's profound memory loss. Other days, people remember a lot. Including how much they've lost and will lose."

"I'm not sure which of those is worse," Sam said.

Chapter Twenty-One

Salvaging his academic status took Jeremy almost a week of persuasive talking and solemn promises to work all summer. Then a week of lab work and papers before he could finally spare a day to volunteer at the university permaculture garden. He waited in the shade of the shed looking across the garden section labeled "Teas, Herbs and Medicinals." Penny royal and oregano, spearmint and lemon balm, marigolds and clover grew in profusion.

The weather was warm for early May, and sweat-loving gnats swarmed around his face and neck. Plants rarely bit or stung—one of the reasons he liked them more than critters, sometimes more than people. Not more than Zoe, of course, which made him forgot about the itchy bumps on the back of his neck.

A tall woman in a staff tee and rubber boots joined him. "Alice," she said. "I'm garden leader today."

"Jeremy. It's my first time here."

"Welcome. You got any experience growing vegetables or herbs?"

He nodded. "My family grew most of our food."

"On a farm?" Alice asked.

"No. In the city. In Springfield." Jeremy ignored her skeptical look. He'd practically grown up in the greenhouse and spent his summers seeding and weeding, pruning and harvesting. His family might have been screwed up, but they turned their city lot into an organic garden, composting before it was sexy. Of course they did it because their religion required it. He didn't have much use for most of their beliefs, but they got it right about food.

"So, I know the difference between a plant and a weed. Especially tea." He pointed at the spearmint. "Our specialty. My family used to run a teahouse."

"Great. You can start weeding in the tea bed. Any questions?"

"Yeah. Why all the clover? You can't eat that."

"Actually, the flowers *are* edible, but we plant it because it's a strong nitrogen fixer. Do you know what that is?"

He tried not to feel insulted. "I'm a botany major. And what about comfrey? For the tea?"

Alice grinned. "Nope, because it's a dynamic accumulator. You know, the deep roots access nutrients and store them in plant tissue. And we harvest the greens for mulch, especially on fruit trees."

He nodded, though he'd never heard of dynamic accumulators. "One more thing. I think I get the concept of permaculture. It's a great idea—sustainable gardens, organic methods and all. But will it have any effect on all the plant species that are becoming extinct?"

"Well, it won't bring them back, unless you agree with that guy who wants to clone them. Which sort of defeats the basic idea of following nature. But farming within biodiversity principles should slow—maybe even stop—the species loss." She laughed and her ponytail swung back and forth. "That is, if you simultaneously reverse urban sprawl and rein in corporate agribusiness."

Jeremy grinned. "Right."

Alice turned to leave. "Have fun. We break in forty minutes for tea."

"Compost tea?"

She laughed again.

"Like I said. Tea's my specialty," Jeremy said.

Jeremy squatted by the spearmint and watched Alice walk along the curved path. Her blond ponytail swung sideways with each step and the curve of her calves was lovely in the sunshine. He'd never seen Zoe in shorts, or a skirt, maybe because her legs were so scrawny. At least, she called them scrawny.

He'd like to see for himself. He closed his eyes to the image of Zoe's legs and breathed in the familiar smell of spearmint. When he was a boy, there were often batches hanging over the dining room table to dry. Francie had liked to rub the leaves between her wet fingers and dab it behind their ears. Goddess perfume, she called it. Tim would push her hand away and wrinkle his nose, but Jeremy loved it. Later, after they lost the house and the yard and their only tea came from the food coop, he longed for the aroma of fresh spearmint.

Stop being sentimental, he told himself, and reached for the weeds.

∼ↄ℮↻

Forty minutes later, a bell rang and he stood up, relishing the familiar ache behind his shoulder blades. He followed two other volunteers through Toro blueberry bushes, along quince and persimmons, toward the dining commons. The doorway was draped with a banner that read *Diversity = Resilience*.

"Spearmint, lemon verbena, or H2O," Alice said, pointing at three large mason jars in a metal bucket of ice. He poured spearmint tea into a mug with the university seal mostly rubbed off and sat on a folding chair by the open window. The breeze carried a sweet scent, honeysuckle maybe, or fruit blossoms. He let his eyes close. One of these weeks he'd catch up with assignments. And sleep.

"How'd it go, Jeremy?" Alice sat down next to him, and gestured to a dark-skinned woman in cut-off overalls. "This is Peg."

Peg nodded and Jeremy said hello.

"I liked it," Jeremy said. "It's a great antidote to too much studying."

"How'd you get involved with the garden?" Peg asked Alice.

"I'm an SFF major. Sustainable Food and Farming," Alice said. "This is what I want to do with my life. What about you?"

Peg shrugged. "I'm a lit major, but I grew up in Springfield. I was eating dinner when the tornado hit. Our house was okay, but our neighbor's house, just across the street, was totaled. Nothing left but a cellar hole. I became, like, obsessed with catastrophic weather and the fall of civilization and that we'll all have to grow our food and make our clothes and burn candles. Thought I better start learning how."

"Wow," Alice said. "I saw the tornado clips on the news."

"I'm from Springfield too," Jeremy said. "About a mile from the tornado path."

"Is that why you're interested in permaculture?" Peg asked.

Jeremy shook his head. "I've always been into plants, since I was a little kid. Drawing them, mostly. I'm a botany major as an excuse to hang out with plants." He leaned forward. "I'm interested in species extinction, trying to stop it. I'm taking Ecosystems and Climate Change this semester."

Alice interrupted. "Isn't Professor Clarke amazing? That course changed my life. And she's part of a group studying this new tree crisis. A huge die-off, like the bees, you know?"

Jeremy shook his head. "I haven't heard about that."

"I don't know details," Alice said. "But it has to do with a pathogen killing oak trees in California and Oregon, spreading across the country and into Europe. Professor Clarke is part of a research group for the feds."

"You know, I've been thinking about changing my major," Jeremy said. "To environmental studies, to do work that makes a difference." He looked from Alice to Peg. "Species loss is like a holocaust, like plant genocide."

"Wait a minute," Alice said. "You're the one with the radio program, right? The guy who . . ." Alice's voice trailed off and she looked away.

Peg stared at him. "Who what?"

"Nothing." Jeremy stood up. "I just got—I don't know—excited. Carried away. I'm fine."

A man in a staff tee stuck his head in the doorway. "Back to the trenches," he announced.

Jeremy finished his tea, which wasn't as good as Francie's, and returned the mug to the table.

"I'm pretty much done with the tea section," he told Alice.

"Want to transplant some lettuce seedlings?" she said. "I'll show you where they are."

Tucking soil around the delicate sprouts, Jeremy thought about that night at the radio station. Did Alice actually hear the program—not very likely—or just hear about it? And what did people say about him? That he was nuts, or what? Terrific. He could be followed through life by two bizarre stories, one his dad's and one his own.

Ten minutes later, Jeremy's phone buzzed. He sat back on the pebble pathway and wiped his hands on his jeans before answering.

"Hey, Zoe. What's up?"

"It's my grandma."

He could hear the panic in Zoe's voice. How cool, he thought. Not that she was worried but that he knew her voice well enough to recognize the emotion.

"What's wrong?"

"Nothing yet, but they're starting that new drug tomorrow, so she's having a party tonight, just family and her women friends. She says she wants us to remember her before she becomes a zombie. And she especially asked you to come."

"Okay. I'll have to borrow a car," Jeremy said. "But I'll be there."

~～～

When Zoe and Jeremy got to Flo's room that evening, the party was already in progress. Mimi had set up a folding card table in the middle of the room, covered it with a tablecloth in Van Gogh colors, and set out wine, tortilla chips, and salsas labeled "Hot," "Hotter," "Hottest." Sam perched on the windowsill close to Flo, who held court in her reading chair by the window. She raised her wineglass to the newcomers.

"Welcome," Flo said. "Now, the party can really begin." She took a drink and blew them a winey kiss.

Jeremy hung back, but Zoe took his hand and pulled him into the middle of the room. "This is Jeremy," she announced. "And these," she said, waving her arm across the four women sitting side by side on the bed, "are my grandma's best buddies."

"I'm Mimi, and I'm so glad to meet you." Mimi sprung forward and gave him a mini-hug, the kind meant to welcome.

Jeremy looked surprised and Sam smiled to himself. He still felt overwhelmed in the presence of these women, even after knowing them his whole life. If Jeremy didn't feel that way now, he soon would. That is, if he stuck around.

Marlene waved. "I'm Marlene and we're the Girls' Club."

"We're the Sisterhood," Fanny interrupted. "And I'm Fanny."

Mimi laughed. "Give it a rest, guys. These kids don't care about our group's name."

Claire stood and shook Jeremy's hand. "I'm Claire and I don't care about our name, either. But I'm happy to meet you."

Flo leaned forward and took the spoon from the "Hottest" salsa, licked it, and tapped it on her wineglass.

"Enough small talk," she said. "Tonight's party is in honor of my brain, my doomed and decaying brain, and my big mouth. Tomorrow they start drugs to shut me up."

"You have such a delicate way with words, Ma," Sam said. "Not to mention a healthy dose of paranoia. You know, the medicine *might* help."

Flo dipped her head at him, in regal acknowledgement of the possibility. "Maybe. But tonight might be my last chance to say what I think."

Mimi laughed. "You've been saying what you think every single day for the forty-five years I've known you. Probably long before that too."

"Still, this might be my intellectual swan song. And I particularly want to address these young people. They're the ones to carry on my work."

Sam rolled his eyes. "Please, Ma. No political speeches."

Flo pointed the spoon at Sam and he saw her eyes fog over for a quick moment, as if she was looking past him, and then she continued. "Just because you're an apolitical slug, doesn't that mean your daughter and her young man are also."

She turned to Jeremy. "You asked me a question a few days ago. You asked how to fight a threat that's overwhelming, when defeat and disaster seem inevitable."

Jeremy nodded. Zoe took his hand.

"Which threat?" Mimi asked. "There are so many."

"Terracide," Jeremy said. "Global warming is killing off plant species, destroying the biodiversity of Earth." He glanced at Flo but she was gazing into her wine, deep in thought.

"'I speak for the trees, for the trees have no tongues,'" quoted Zoe. "*The Lorax* was my favorite book as a kid. What's your wise advice for us, Grandma? How do we save the world?"

Flo stared into her wineglass, swirling the rich burgundy liquid into a vortex that climbed higher and higher up the sides of the glass, pulling her in like the tide. The words swirled too, all those Seuss-words she used to recite over and over with Zoe. "'The trees have no tongues,'" she whispered and the eddy pulled her in deeper and she spun the glass faster and the tide pulled harder and the wine climbed closer to the rim and then it was over the rim and onto her hand and into her lap and the glass fell to the floor and shattered.

◆

After cleaning up the broken glass and spilled wine, Flo's friends packed up the chips and salsa and sunny tablecloth and folding card table.

"Leave the wine," Flo told them. "Bet I can't drink after tomorrow. It's probably not allowed with that medicine."

"The bottle is all yours." Mimi kissed Flo goodnight.

Zoe started to disagree, then stopped herself. Why shouldn't her grandma get blotto tonight if she wanted to?

While Jeremy and Sam walked the women down to their car, carrying the table and bags, Zoe helped Flo get into her flannel nightgown and under the covers. She transferred from her chair onto the edge of the bed and leaned close, pushing Flo's flyaway hair away from her face.

"You okay, Grandma?"

Flo shrugged, then pointed to Jeremy standing in the doorway.

"Sam said he needed a cup of coffee," Jeremy said. "He'll be up soon."

Flo patted the bed, the space between her and Zoe. "Sit, Jeremy. I want to tell you something, something important."

Zoe took Jeremy's hand and squeezed, hoping her grandma wasn't going to get too weird with the guy and scare him off. Flo could be pretty intense. But then, maybe Flo and Jeremy had that in common.

"About what you asked me, before. Whatever action you take—gathering petitions or bombing the stock exchange—make sure that when the smoke clears and the rulers are still in power, you can live with what you did."

Whoa, Zoe thought. Where did that come from? Did her grandma do something she couldn't live with? She glanced at Jeremy but couldn't read his face.

Flo pushed her finger into Jeremy's chest. "What I mean is, you've got to make a life that does good work and still gives you room for, you know, for love." She patted Zoe's cheek.

"Now go home," Flo said. "I'm tired."

Chapter Twenty-Two

Jeremy thought about Flo's words all week. While he was pulling weeds at the garden, he wondered what Flo did that she couldn't live with. Or maybe what she regretted not doing? Catching up on missed assignments in the botany lab, he thought about Mary. He hadn't been able to find anything on the Internet about her arrest. Did she really blow something up? Alone in his dorm room in the evenings, he wondered how Flo was doing with the new medicine. Zoe didn't seem to know, or didn't want to talk about it during their nightly phone conversations. Mostly she made plans for his weekend visit.

Friday afternoon he took the bus to Springfield and joined Sam and Zoe for lasagna.

"This is great." Jeremy wrapped an escaping tendril of mozzarella around his finger and licked it off. "How'd you learn to cook like this?" he asked Sam.

Sam and Zoe looked at each other and laughed.

"It was one of the conditions before my mom let me move upstairs," Zoe said. She wagged her fork at Sam. "Dad had to demonstrate his ability to cook five healthy meals. Nothing store-bought or microwaved."

"Five?"

"Yeah, Mom cooks for us on Sunday and she agreed we could eat out once a week."

Jeremy laughed. "Your mother isn't, um, a control freak or anything."

"She just wanted to be sure Zoe would be well taken care of," Sam said. "In hindsight, I'm glad she did it."

Jeremy touched Zoe's hand, the one holding the fork. "So I'm curious. What were the five meals?"

Zoe shrugged. "Who remembers? That was like four years ago and we both cook now. I made this salad and everything's fresh from the farmers market."

Sam leaned closer to Jeremy and mock-whispered, "Some of us prefer a burger."

"Some of us aren't very smart." Zoe passed the salad bowl to Jeremy.

"Better eat your greens," Sam told Jeremy. "She's tough, just like her grandmother. Sure you want to hang out with such a bossy broad?"

"Dad!"

Sam laughed. "Sorry. So, how's it going making up the work you missed?"

"Okay I guess. It'll take me most of the summer though. Especially with the hours I'm spending at the permaculture garden." Jeremy put down his fork and leaned forward. "I've gone three times and really like it. Alice—she's the manager—invited me to come to the garden committee on Wednesday. She said they might hire me this summer."

"Oh," Zoe said.

Something in her voice grabbed Jeremy's attention. She wasn't happy. "What?"

"It's just that, you know, I was hoping you'd be in Springfield for the summer."

"I can't breathe in my parents' apartment," he said. "But I'll come home every weekend." He looked at Sam. "And maybe your dad would let you visit me on campus some weekend?"

Sam looked down. Zoe made a face.

Okay, maybe not. "Um," Jeremy said. "So how's Flo doing with the new medicine?"

Neither Sam nor Zoe answered right away, then they both spoke at once.

"Too soon to tell," Sam said. "It's only been a week."

"She's sleepy all the time," Zoe said. "Come on. You know that's true. She's like, not herself. A zombie."

Sam rubbed his eyes hard. "Lethargy is a common side effect. Sometimes it goes away."

"You haven't been yourself all week either," Zoe said. "What's up?"

"Nothing. I'm fine."

"*Tell* me, Papa."

Sam sighed. "Something Flo said threw me, that's all. It's nothing. Probably just the protein plaques and nerve cell tangles talking."

"What did she say?"

"That Brad, the man I always thought was my father, wasn't. That my biologic father was this guy named Charlie, who she met on a picket line in Maryland."

"Wow," Zoe said. "Did you ask her for details?"

"Of course, but you know how vague she can be. All she would add was that she was a coward. And that doesn't make sense."

Jeremy nodded, not sure if he should say anything, or even be part of this discussion.

"There's more," Sam said. "I got this guy's full name from online articles about the picketing thing. I saw his picture."

"Do you look like him?" Zoe asked.

"Hard to make out his features in those grainy old newspaper shots. But the photo did explain some things." Sam held out his hand. He stared at it, turned it over so that his fingers pointed toward the ceiling, then let his arm rest on the table. "Charlie is black."

"Wow." Zoe put her hand, two shades lighter, on his arm. "No wonder you always look tan. That's huge. So did you Google the guy, your dad?"

"My *alleged* dad," Sam said. "He was easy enough to find. He was a UAW organizer in Detroit. I found an article about his retirement party, and photos of the guy with his wife and sons and grandchildren."

"Double wow," Zoe said. "I wonder if Grandma knows where he is. I wonder what happened, you know? What went wrong."

"*If* it's true." Sam shrugged. "She could have made up the whole thing."

"I bet they had a wild romance and something tragic happened."

"We'll probably never know. But you're right about one thing. I haven't been myself all week."

"Do you want to meet him?" Zoe asked.

"Charlie? I don't know. My brain is still reeling about Brad maybe not being my dad. And about my real father being black."

Jeremy cleared his throat. Maybe he should stay out of it, because it really wasn't any of his business. But he really liked Zoe and her dad was pretty cool. He put his arm on the table, next to Sam's. Their skin was almost the same hue.

"My dad's black too," he said. "We're half and half. What's the big deal?"

"It's not the race, *per se*." Sam spoke slowly. "It's the surprise of it. And all of a sudden not being just one thing. Being two different things, opposite things."

"Black and white aren't really opposites," Zoe said. "Just different. She shrugged. "Don't you think everyone holds contrasting things, opposites even, inside our skin?"

Both men looked at her. Skeptically, she thought.

"What," she said. "You don't think having spina bifida is like that? I am able-bodied and impaired, whole and broken. You think *those* aren't opposites?"

⁓⁓

It took forever to shuffle to the bathroom because the carpet had sprouted prickly needles. Flo held onto the wall with her hand, her brain loopde-looping like an amusement park ride. She was grateful for the safety bar next to the toilet and grabbed it, stopping to rest. She looked into the toilet bowl. Did she need to throw up or did she dream that? The memory of vomiting, or maybe just the thought, made the wooziness in her middle tumble harder and start to come up her throat. No, she refused to give in to it, or to the dizziness either. She sat on the toilet seat and put her head between her knees, like she used to when she was pregnant with Sam and it worked, just like it did back then.

"Flo?" a voice called from the bedroom.

It was Mimi's voice. Flo smiled. She couldn't think the last time she saw Mimi. "In here," she called back.

"You okay?"

"Not really," Flo said. What was she doing in the bathroom, anyway? Did she need to pee? She couldn't remember, not with her head spinning like this, scrambling her thoughts.

Mimi came in and helped her stand. That's when Flo caught a glimpse of herself in the mirror. That couldn't be her face. That was an old lady covered with wrinkles and there was something very wrong about the wrinkles, besides being not hers. They were heavy, pulling her skin and flesh downward. Their weight was ripping her face off her bones like a demented rubber Halloween mask. Mimi murmured something and gripped her elbow more firmly and Flo looked away and they shuffled to the bedroom.

Her gang of women friends were waiting for her. Their smiles were stiff, like when you don't know whether to grin or wail. Flo was glad to see them, but really she'd just as soon wail. Why were they there? She'd known them for years, but did she really know them? Why were they staring at her like that? Was it the wrinkles and was her face now totally gone? Or maybe they weren't really her friends, after all. Maybe they didn't even like her. Maybe they had never loved her and now that she was weak they wanted to hurt her and take her things.

"You okay now, Flo?" Mimi's voice was soft but solid.

She nodded. "I'm fine."

Well, maybe not quite fine, not right at that moment. But she was resilient and she'd *be* fine. Flo looked at her friends, from one to the other. Mimi stood next to her, holding her elbow. Claire and Marlene sat on her bed, Fanny on the reading chair by the window next to her book, splayed across the upholstered arm, open to the same page as a week ago. Why were they here?

Mimi must have read her confusion. "Our new meeting schedule," she said.

Fanny smiled. "Saturday mornings, right here."

"The Girls' Club," Marlene added.

"How're you doing on the new medicine?" Claire asked.

Flo let go of Mimi's arm and put both hands on her chest. She wanted to scream. How do I look like I'm doing?

But she couldn't speak. Her words felt born in slow motion. Stillborn. Her tongue was thick and sluggish, her lips stupid. Was it the medicine making her so woozy or was this her now-brain? She stared at Claire, always trying to be the professional one, the nurse, the know-it-all. Claire was probably making mental notes right now about Flo's cognitive deterioration. Decay. Rot. And there wasn't a damn thing Flo could do about it. Come to think about it, Claire had always been like that. Assessing and evaluating. Always judging *her*. Well, Flo had had enough of that.

Flo reached for the hand mirror on her chest of drawers. Her right hand wouldn't move so she grabbed it with her left and pulled her arm back to throw. She managed to send the mirror wobbling toward Claire, handle over oval frame over handle over glass.

Something was happening. She couldn't figure it out. It was so odd. She heard her own breathing, raspy and much too fast. She could see her hands but couldn't feel them and then it was her whole body and she swayed back and forth and her head went spinning out of the universe and then her legs melted and she lost her balance. The wooden bedpost reached up and smashed into her chest as she collapsed onto the floor.

∽⌒⌲

Saturday mornings were usually a productive work time for Sam, while Zoe slept late and hardly anyone called. Today he couldn't concentrate on the website redesign for the pet supply store, couldn't stop thinking about how weird his mom was acting on the new medicine, couldn't stop wondering what was the true story of Brad and Charlie, couldn't stop worrying about what Zoe and her boyfriend were doing in the living room until he finally heard the squeak of her wheelchair in the hallway at 2:00 a.m.

Around and around his worries spun, but they kept circling back to Jeremy's comment about his own father's race. "What's the big deal?" Jeremy had asked.

It *was* a big deal but Sam couldn't say exactly why. Sam wasn't sure why it made him so uncomfortable. Was he a racist for not being pleased to learn this new fact about his paternity? He wondered—just for a brief moment—whether maybe this Charlie man had coerced Flo or swept her off her feet. But then he was immediately ashamed because that was wrong and he knew it. It was more than wrong. He knew better than to think things like that. Besides, Flo said she loved Charlie and her voice was tender when she said his name and that made him feel deeply sad for her.

But mostly he was pissed off. How could his mom lie to him all these years about something as important as his father and as critical as his race? Did that mean she'd lied about other things, things he should know about and now probably never would? None of it made sense. If Flo loved the guy and got pregnant, and if Charlie didn't want a kid, did she consider an abortion? It was still illegal back then, so it would have been hard to get. Scary. Risky. But not impossible, and his mother could do anything she set her mind to, back then.

Abortion. That thought led down a familiar path of regret. It brought the rush of another shame that always came when he revisited the ultrasound showing the hole in Zoe's spine. How he hadn't wanted his daughter to be born and Anna insisted this baby would be wonderful and Anna won because it was her body and she was so certain. Anna had been right and he had been abysmally wrong. How empty his life would be without Zoe.

He tried to shake the old Zoe remorse from his head and that brought him back to Flo. His mom had always seen disaster everywhere, and now it was worse than ever, and it must be genetic because apparently he was catching her downer disease.

That's what Sam was thinking when the phone rang.

"Your mom had a fall," Mimi said. "It's bad. Meet us at the ER."

On the short drive to the emergency room, Sam pictured one worst-case scenario after another. He tried to tamp down the terror that filled his chest, leaving little space for breathing. By the time he parked the car and made his way through the queues of worried family members and official red tape, Flo was settled on a stretcher surrounded by sea green curtains and connected by wires to a bank of monitors. It's just the reflection of the curtain hue that makes her skin look so sick, he told himself. Mimi leaned on the pillow, eyes closed and mouth close to Flo's ear.

"I'm here, Ma," Sam said.

Flo didn't stir. Mimi slipped her hand from Flo's and stood up, pulling Sam outside the curtained area.

"She hasn't woken up yet." Mimi took off her glasses and swiped the back of her hand across her eyes.

"Tell me what happened."

"I'm not sure. When the four of us got to her apartment today, Flo was acting strange. Loopy and agitated. Then she seemed to get angry *at* us, although I have no idea why. She threw a mirror at Claire, that's when she fell. But it wasn't exactly a fall—she seemed to collapse, slow motion. First her face fell and then her body and her arms and legs—she just crumpled. Anyway, she hit her chest as she fell and I yelled for help and the staff called 911 and here we are."

He covered his face with both hands. He'd been afraid of something like this. His mom had been so spacey on the new medicine. Why hadn't he insisted they stop it? This was his fault.

Mimi touched his arm. "It's not your fault, Sam."

"What have they done so far?"

"The nurse started the IV and did an EKG and a doctor examined her and called the cardiologist. Now we're waiting."

"What did the doctor say?"

"Something about heart failure. The EKG showed an arrhythmia." Mimi hesitated. "And she's severely dehydrated."

Sam closed his eyes. Damn that medicine. Damn his inaction.

"Have you called your family?" Mimi asked. "Zoe?"

"Not yet," he said. "I will. Anna and Emily will bring Zoe. Emily can translate the medical jargon for us."

Mimi nodded. "I'll stay if you want me to."

"Not necessary. I'm fine," Sam said. "I'll call you when I know anything more." He paused. "Thanks for everything. I'm really glad you were with her, when it happened."

After Mimi left, Sam dropped onto the metal chair. He took Flo's hand. "I'm sorry, Ma. I shouldn't have let them give you that medicine."

He closed his eyes. He wasn't good at hospitals, even with all the practice Zoe's condition had provided. Anyway, this was worlds away from the children's hospital with its bright murals and larger-than-life animal statues and generally hopeful atmosphere. This was like when his dad died.

Sam had been doing his geometry homework at the kitchen table, that same table now scorched and junked, when that phone call came. Flo was working in her home office and it was his job to answer the phone after school. His dad—well, Brad—had collapsed at work and was en route to the hospital. They met him here, at this hospital, maybe even this very same crowded cubicle with puke green curtains.

That time it was Brad who was gray-faced and hooked up to the ma-chines. Flo was in charge, insisting on better specialists and more morphine and a larger cubicle. Constantly at the nurses' station, demanding that they hurry up the neurology consult or what was that new blip on the monitor and what did they mean her husband's blood pressure and cholesterol were sky-high—his own doctor never said anything about that. His mother had been a force of nature back then. Sam let his head drop forward to rest on his mother's pillow.

"Hang in there, Ma," he whispered. "I love you."

He didn't tell her that often enough. She must know.

After Brad died, it had been just the two of them, but sometimes Flo was more parent than Sam could take. He spent high school torn between admiring her largeness in the world and cringing from it. Take Career Day his senior year, when Flo's presentation on the glorious independence of freelancing both embarrassed him and brought him some reflected glory. Flo hadn't been satisfied to just describe her work doing audio narration for films and TV programs; no, she had to wax poetic about being a feminist and being her own boss and only working on material that contributed to positive change in the world. He could still picture her up there on the small stage in the high school auditorium, her face flushed with enthusiasm and her faded Women's International Terrorist Conspiracy from Hell T-shirt only partially obscured by the rainbow scarf she wore for special occasions. Where was that scarf? A victim of the fire, most likely. His friend Kenny, sitting next to him during the assembly, elbowed him as Flo left the stage to applause and a few catcalls and whispered, "Quite the pistol, your mom."

She *was* a pistol. Had been a pistol. Sam looked at his mother's deflated face, the flesh sunken into the bones. He smoothed her hair back and tucked it behind her ear. She was a tangled mess of contradictions too. He'd never understand how one woman could contain so many worries, could see danger around every corner, and yet live so fearlessly.

Chapter Twenty-Three

Jeremy wanted to stay in town and be helpful, but Sam said there was nothing much to do. Flo had been admitted to a cardiac unit and it would take a few days to determine exactly what happened and how much she might recover. Plus, it would cause more trouble with his parents if he stayed. As it was, Francie yelled at him about spending the whole weekend with Zoe.

"Nice of you to visit," Francie said when she dropped him at the bus station. "You like that girl's family better than your own."

It didn't feel right to take the bus back to Amherst Sunday afternoon, as if nothing had happened, but that's what he did. He called Zoe every evening, like usual, but she sounded preoccupied. She was probably worried about her grandma, but Jeremy wished they could talk for hours, like they had before.

Tuesday evening, Zoe said goodbye after ten minutes.

"I'm so tired," she said. "I sat with Grandma from right after school until Papa came with pizza for dinner. I talked to her, but she didn't seem to hear me. Then I did my homework while he talked with her. At her, really, because she didn't talk back. We just got home and I've still got a biology lab to write up."

He offered to help with the lab report but she sounded annoyed, said a quick gotta-go and hung up. When the phone rang again right away, he thought that Zoe was calling to apologize, but it wasn't her name displayed, some number with an area code he didn't recognize.

"Jeremy?" a woman's voice asked. "It's Mary. Mary Matheson."

"Mary," he said. "Wow. Are you okay? Where are you?"

"Oregon. I've been better. I got your number from Greenhope. Listen, you're going to hear some bad news about me, and I wanted to explain in person."

"What kind of bad?" he asked, although away from Brooklyn and Greenhope and the group, he wasn't likely to hear anything about Mary.

"It'll be in the papers," she said. "They charged me with several felonies and they've threatened terrorism enhancements. It probably would have meant spending the rest of my life in prison. At least, all of my son's childhood."

"Did you do it? What they say you did?"

Mary's voice was quiet. "Always assume the phone is tapped and don't say anything you wouldn't want the world to hear."

Jeremy's cheeks blazed. He knew that. "Sorry."

"Anyway," she continued. "I've pled guilty to lesser charges and will only serve a year."

"I don't understand," he said. "Why did they let you off?"

She didn't answer for a long moment. "I gave them some names. I *had* to, Jeremy. Just two. Carl and Sari."

Jeremy felt stunned. "I don't understand," he repeated. "How could you do that?"

"I'm a single mom. Who would raise my boy?"

Jeremy had no answer for that, but he had a question of his own. "Did you mention me?"

"No."

"Why are you calling me?"

"Just to tell you, personally, I guess," she said, her voice now spent. "I wanted to warn you to stay far away from the others."

"You were my hero," he whispered.

"I know," Mary said. "And I'm sorry. You have to be your own hero."

He mumbled something and disconnected. He wiped his face on his T-shirt and wished he could talk to Zoe. Instead, he tried to work on a long-overdue history paper, but the events leading up to Shays' Rebellion couldn't distract him from what Mary said.

∽୭ᴖᴜᴖ

The permaculture committee meeting the next morning wasn't much of a distraction either, especially after pulling an all-nighter to finish the history paper. Jeremy sat on a rolling desk chair with a wobbly wheel, facing the window overlooking the garden. From his position just outside the meeting circle, he could see the entire office. The low table under the window held seedlings in clay pots, some staked and leaning against the wall. The dozen or so students sat on mismatched chairs, elbows propped on knees, or cross-legged on the floor, all leaning into the discussion. These people were seriously intense.

Alice had explained that it was an honor to be invited to attend as a guest. And he hoped they would hire him for a few hours a week during the summer because that would really help with expenses. But he wasn't so sure about joining the group fall semester, even though he could use the credits. He was having a hard time just following this conversation which ping-ponged energetically from the benefits of a huge lavender puffball perennial called Welsh onion, to questioning the group's requirement for consensus, to consideration of the ethical slippery-slope of growing annuals.

Across the circle from Jeremy, a young man with braided hair flowing down his T-shirt was fired up about the annuals issue. "Our mission is to model permaculture to the community, to demonstrate totally sustainable farming," he said.

How would that help endangered plants? Jeremy wondered.

Sitting on the floor in front of the braided guy, a young woman leaned back, her arms entwined around his legs. She nodded in vigorous agreement. "Plants that aren't self-renewing have no role in our mission."

Behind the braided couple, the seedlings on the table began sending sprouts up along the white wall, snaking toward the windows. Jeremy blinked hard, because that was impossible, but slender stems still crawled.

"Modeling is only part of it," Alice argued. "We're also committed to growing veggies for the university dining halls. Healthy, yes, but food that students recognize and will eat."

"That's *way* down the priority list," the braided kid insisted. "Permaculture is about transforming civilization, remember? Students—people—will learn to appreciate new foods and to love them because we'll teach them to. And because otherwise we'll all starve."

Alice stood up. "This is a great discussion and we'll get back to it later. But I'm going to interrupt it now because we have a guest. Professor Clarke is one of our faculty advisors and she's here to talk to us about something critically important."

"Thanks, Alice." The professor stood in front of the windows, her coppery hair backlit. "You all know about Sudden Oak Death, right?"

Professor Clarke had lectured on the disease earlier in the semester, before Brooklyn, and Jeremy struggled to remember the details. He glanced at Alice. Didn't she, didn't anyone else, notice the climbing plants, suckers attaching to the wall, and now to the window glass as well, behind the professor?

"Until recently," Professor Clarke continued, "the spread has been slow but constant. A few years ago, APHIS set up a national reporting system, and we've been running samples as part of that." She paused and looked around the room. "In the last two months, the spread has accelerated dramatically, worldwide."

Jeremy's fingers started tingling, that familiar pulsation, that warning sting. He glanced down at the green shoots pushing through the skin of his fingertips, inching along the smooth cotton of his shorts.

"Our planet is so fucked." The braided kid looked like he was ready to cry. "This could be even worse than the honeybees."

The professor smiled. "You're right. It's important. Oaks are a keystone species, an ecosystem lynchpin. But we're working on it, and that's why I wanted to talk to you today. We've been funded for six student internships for the summer and fall. See me if you're interested in applying." She turned to Alice. "Thanks for letting me interrupt your meeting."

Working for Professor Clarke would be fantastic, but she'd probably choose grad students or seniors. Still, it couldn't hurt to look into it. Once he figured out what was happening with these vines, now crawling across his lap and wrapping around his legs. He rolled his chair slightly back, away from the others, and let his hands slide toward the floor. Maybe this was just his sleep-deprived brain playing a trick. Even so, he should probably leave before the plants grew so much that other people noticed.

Uh-oh. It might be too late for that, because the ones by the window had accelerated their growth—they now covered the glass in a thicket of vines and leaves, a dense forest of growing greens. Small white flowers, trumpet-shaped with a splash of fuchsia inside, blossomed against the glass. Jeremy recognized it then, *Nesiota elliptica* from St. Helena Island. Supposed to be extinct, but maybe the plants were fighting back, like those elephants in Cameroon Mary talked about, the elephants who attacked villages of poachers. He laughed out loud.

Faces in the circle turned to look at him, and Jeremy turned the laugh into a cough. Maybe the vegetable kingdom had something to say about Sudden Oak Death or permaculture gardens or transforming civilization. Maybe they had a different perspective, a different set of priorities. Maybe they wanted students to deal with plants in peril, with species at risk. For a moment he hoped that the plants would expand, would send their persuasive shoots into the other students at the meeting. Would weave them all together into one glorious living organism and they could talk about saving the planet and wouldn't *that* be an interesting conversation. He wished Zoe's grandma were there too—she'd love it, and she'd understand too. He knew she would.

But no. The plants weren't touching any of the other students. Just him, and he had better get out of here.

He tried to stand up, but he couldn't. The green stems—so tender when sprouting from his fingers—had thickened. Now they tethered him to the chair. The vines wound tight around the seat, twisted around the metal chair legs and his bare legs. They wove in and out of the spokes on the small wheels on his chair. They began encircling his chest, making it hard to breathe. This was new. Scary. The plants had never frightened him before. He began to pull at the vines, trying to loosen them. "*Begonia eiromischa,*" he begged. "*Nesiota elliptica. Camellia sinensis.*" But the plants continued to grow, to tighten.

"The plants," Jeremy called out. "They won't let me go. Help me."

～～✺✺～～

Jeremy had only patchy memories of the trip to the Urgent Care Clinic. He remembered Alice taking charge, saying something about a history of emotional problems that made the other permaculture students step back. He remembered saying he couldn't get up, so she pushed his chair the two blocks to Health Services. She leaned forward with the effort so that her ponytail swung wildly at the edge of his vision, in time to the clacking of the wobbly wheels on the uneven sidewalk.

A group of white coats were waiting for him at Urgent Care. Patty was there too. Right before he passed out, he looked down at his fingers, his wrists and arms. His skin was clear. The plants were gone. They left no trace.

～～✺✺～～

Once the nurses had Jeremy settled, hooked up to a monitor, and had started an IV, Patty sat at his bedside and considered the situation. Was Jeremy—such a sweet kid, if a little odd—losing his grip on reality?

She made a mental list of the possible etiology of his episodes. Hallucinations could signal a brain tumor. An infection, bacterial or viral. Drugs or toxins. Mental illness; he was the right age for onset of schizophrenia. None of these were good. She'd start with blood and urine testing and an MRI of the brain, but her gut told her this was emotional, not organic disease. He had seemed a bit evasive when they met before, but when he wasn't imagining the return—revenge?—of extinct plants, he seemed so normal and healthy. Likeable, too. Who *was* this kid?

She opened the bedside laptop, typed Jeremy Beaujolais into the search engine, and pressed Enter.

Nothing came up for his name except an honorary mention in the Central High School science fair three years earlier. No social media sites or blog postings. But someone named Francine Beaujolais had a number of hits, mostly news stories about a dozen years earlier. A quick check of university demographic data confirmed that Francine Beaujolais was Jeremy's mother. Patty read the articles chronologically—about the family's commune, the deaths of Jeremy's half-siblings, the trials and prison sentences.

Okay, so this was a kid with mega-secrets.

Patty wondered what charcoal-sketched monsters lived in the cobweb corners of this boy's imagination. Whatever happened when he was young, he would have to decipher his childhood history enough to build himself an adult home and figure out how to live there. She studied the newspaper photograph of Francine hugging her husband Sebastian at his sentencing hearing and then looked at Jeremy. His eyes were open.

"Welcome back," she said.

Seeing the nurse practitioner sitting at his bedside in the curtained cubicle, Jeremy's first thought was where was her mustard-colored sweater? His second thought was a cavernous, face-blazing embarrassment. He covered his face with both hands.

"I can't believe it happened again," he mumbled.

"How many times is this?" Patty asked.

He had to think. Once when he was a little kid, in the greenhouse. Then at the radio station, when they sent him to Patty the first time. Twice in Brooklyn, in the garden and at the demonstration. And today.

He held up his hand, fingers splayed. "Five, I think."

Oh, six. There was the birthday party and dancing with Zoe. But that was different, pleasurable, and not scary at all. And none of Patty's business.

"Tell me about the first time."

"I don't remember much," he said. "I was nine."

That wasn't true. He remembered everything: his dad in jail. The flickering candles in the greenhouse. The funeral chants. Sitting on the floor in a circle, sharing a pillow with Tim. The candle flames danced and soon the plants were dancing too and when they grew around his fingers and up his arms and around his skinny body, he felt less alone, less sad.

"Jeremy?" Patty asked. "Are you remembering something?"

"Yeah. I guess. But listen, I'm pretty tired."

Patty stood up. "Why don't you rest for a bit then. But here's what I think. These episodes are apparently happening more frequently, and they are disturbing to everyone. You, most of all. I'll order some tests to rule out potential physical causes. But I strongly suspect this is a reaction to some stress in your life, some emotional trauma."

He closed his eyes.

"I think," she continued, "that you're going to have to face whatever it is sometime and it might as well be now. I think you need to talk with someone at the counseling center and try to figure it out."

"Someone? You mean a shrink?"

"A therapist."

He rubbed his eyes, hard. He was an adult and he hadn't broken any laws, so they couldn't make him talk to anyone, could they? It was hard to imagine how talking could help. He wasn't even sure he wanted the hallucinations—or whatever they were—to go away. There was something comforting about them, like a crazy uncle you adored and were embarrassed by, all at the same time. Still, he liked talking to Patty. And he was scared.

"I'll talk to you, but no shrink."

"I'm a nurse practitioner, Jeremy. I'm not trained to do in-depth psychological work."

"That's okay, because I'm not crazy."

She didn't speak for a few minutes, and Jeremy thought she was going to refuse, insist he talk to some stiff jerk who wouldn't *get* anything.

Then she smiled. "Fair enough. I can consult with a therapist. You and I will do this together. But we can't make a habit of meeting like this, when there's a crisis. We'll talk every week. And we need to get another adult involved, to support you." She paused. "Are your parents still in Europe?"

Jeremy felt foolish. "I lied about that," he admitted. "They never were. I'm sorry, but I didn't think they could deal with this. They still can't."

"Okay. Is there someone else?"

He hesitated, then said slowly. "My . . . girlfriend's dad is cool. He might come."

"Will you call him? Tell him we're going to do some tests and ask him to come pick you up tomorrow afternoon. Take you home and keep an eye on you for a day or two?"

"I guess."

"One other thing. Are you willing to share your feelings with me, even when it's hard?"

"I'll try." He removed the newspaper clipping from his wallet and handed it to her. "I guess you can start by reading this."

Chapter Twenty-Four

While Jeremy wrestled with his demons that Wednesday morning, Sam followed the food services cart down the hospital corridor. Metal wheels clanged across the tile floor, pausing at each doorway while the kitchen worker collected dirty trays. Stylized flowers draped the walls in plastic scallops of purple and yellow. Soiled sheets and towels escaped from linen bags. The overhead page summoned Dr. Strong STAT to ICU. Heartbeats marched in muffled syncopated beeps across the rows of monitors behind the nurses' station. Flo's room was silent except for the hum from the special oxygen mask designed to prevent her lungs from collapsing during the long hesitations between breaths.

Her tray was untouched. A scum glistened on the surface of the cream of wheat. Sam sniffed the coffee; it had no smell. On his mother's admission five days earlier, he told the staff that Flo only drank tea, steeped four minutes sharp. She hated coffee, always had. She never learned to brew it either, even though Dad—no, Brad—chugged it by the gallon. He made his own, in a percolator on the stove. It smelled wonderful but tasted like burnt tires.

Sam lifted the plastic thermal cup to his lips and sipped. The coffee was tepid, weak. Scooting the metal guest chair closer to the bed, he took his mother's hand, careful not to disturb the IV or bother the bruises blooming on her arm.

The young hospitalist came through the doorway with a clipboard. Yesterday it had been a female doc who asked if he wanted to sign a DNR order. Do Not Resuscitate. Did he want "heroic" measures? What was heroic about shoving a breathing tube down her throat and attaching her to machines? Sam had told her that he needed twenty-four hours to think about it.

"Good morning." Today's doctor shook his hand, then turned to Flo. He leaned over her and spoke quietly, then lifted each eyelid gently to shine a small flashlight. No response. He tugged at her forearm; her skin stayed up in a pale tent. "She's still dehydrated," the doctor said. "No discernible neurological improvement."

"Will she wake up?"

"She might. She could even have intermittent periods of lucidity."

"Do you think she'll recover?"

The doctor shrugged, just like his colleague did yesterday. "No way to know how much she'll regain. But with her constellation of problems—heart failure and dementia—regaining significant quality of life isn't likely."

Sam grabbed onto the bedrail and held tight. The doctor's words weren't a surprise, except how much they hurt and how hard it was to think clearly. To try to understand. To unclench his voice to speak.

"Do you think the new pill caused this? She was fine before. At least her heart was. That new medicine made her too sick to eat or drink. Heart disease and arrhythmias were listed as risks."

The doctor shrugged again. They must teach that gesture in medical school, with its don't-blame-me message. "I know you want an answer, but that's impossible to know."

"What can you do to help her?"

"Let her heal. Manage the dehydration. But her heart is compromised and can't handle too much fluid."

Sam glanced at his mother motionless in the bed. Flo despised compromise. She would hate the doctor using that term without a hint of irony.

Sam was becoming familiar with the impossible balancing acts of a failing heart: give her enough fluid to maintain blood pressure, but not enough to make her lungs fill up. Enough blood-thinners to prevent clots, but not enough to cause internal bleeding.

"That's all you can do?" Sam asked.

"What would you like us to do?" The doctor sounded sincere, as if he really wanted to know.

Sam thought about it. He'd like Flo returned to the way she was before the memory loss became much more than that. And if he couldn't have his gloriously outrageous pistol of a mother back, then maybe he wanted her to die. But not here and not yet. Not without saying a proper goodbye to Zoe, to Mimi and the others.

"She's too young," he said, knowing it was whiney and irrelevant.

The doctor waited.

"How much longer will she need to stay here?" Sam asked.

"A few days, maybe a week." When she's more stable, she can go to a skilled nursing facility.

Sam couldn't ask the next question, couldn't bear the answer he already knew. There must be *something*. Something that would matter.

The doctor picked up his clipboard from the bedside table.

"Can you do anything about the bruises?" Sam pointed toward the enlarging purple splotch on her chest, over her heart, where she hit the bedpost when she collapsed.

"I can decrease her heparin." The doctor hesitated, then handed Sam the clipboard and a pen.

Sam read the swirling purple script written on the pen and sounded out the syllables: *metoprolol.* The word—must be the name of a drug—sounded soothing. Like water tumbling gently over rocks in some peaceful, summery place, not like disease and side effects and risks and dread. How was he supposed to know what Flo would want? Flo was still alive and intact in his mind, despite the terrible evidence to the contrary on the bed.

"You're sure she won't recover?"

That shrug again. Sam hated that gesture of not-knowing, not-caring all that much. "I can't be certain," the doctor said. "But it's unlikely."

Unlikely. Sam didn't like it either. But he didn't seem to have much choice. He hesitated, staring hard at the doctor, begging in his eyes. The doctor put his hand on Sam's shoulder and shook his head slightly. Sam signed. His stomach clenched and he breathed shallow breaths to keep from vomiting. He followed the white coat to the doorway and watched him walk to the next room. When he turned back to the bed, Flo's eyes were open but blank.

"Hi, Ma."

No response.

He lifted the oxygen mask slightly off her face, touched the red pressure marks from the plastic edge. They must hurt. He massaged them a little before putting the mask back. He ran his finger lightly along her cheekbone. It had only been ten days since she started the medicine and stopped eating but the weight loss had already strip-mined her face. With the excess flesh gone—she had always struggled with her weight—her face was elemental, revealing new planes and angles. "Good bones," Flo would have said, about someone else.

"Does that help?" he asked. He felt foolish speaking when she was so out of it. But the nurse had told him to talk to her. "Patients hear everything," she claimed, "even when they're like this." So sure, he could talk and his mom had always loved words. But now he wasn't sure if anything could penetrate her confusion, her illness, her faraway-ness. If anything or anyone could reach her, it would be Zoe.

"Zoe should be here soon," he told Flo. "She's coming after school. And Mimi promised to stop by."

Flo didn't respond. Maybe his words were too soft to hear with the racket of the breathing machine.

He was relieved when his cell phone rang. He didn't recognize the number on the screen but he answered it, grateful to escape for a few minutes. Maybe Flo in her coma would like eavesdropping on his conversation, like she did when she was awake.

It was Jeremy.

"I need a favor, Sam." The kid's voice was odder than usual. Soft and spacey; maybe scared. "I'm having some, some problems, and I need someone to pick me up at school. And a place to stay for a couple of days."

"What about your—"

Jeremy interrupted. "I can't ask my parents."

"What's going on?" Sam asked. Maybe it was none of his business, but if he was going to bring this boy into his house, with Zoe, then he had a right to know, didn't he?

"It's complicated," Jeremy said. "But I guess you could say it's about what happened back then, you know, with my dad and everything."

Sam sighed. He had rescued Jeremy and his brother once before, so he figured he was already involved. Plus, Zoe would never forgive him if he said no.

"All right," he said. "When?"

"They want to do some tests first. Tomorrow afternoon?"

"Zoe and I will come after school. Where will you be?"

"Health Services," Jeremy said. "Urgent care."

Terrific, Sam thought and hung up. Just terrific.

⁓

When Zoe and her dad entered the waiting room at Health Services the next afternoon, they went in different directions. Zoe wheeled right over to Jeremy, sitting alone on a yellow vinyl sofa. He didn't look sick, so she gave him a hug. Maybe it was a tentative hug, since she didn't know what had happened and was a little nervous. Her dad said that with the federal privacy laws, they'd have to wait for Jeremy to fill them in. Sam stood at the registration desk, deep in conversation with a nice-looking woman who had a stethoscope draped around her neck.

"You okay?" Zoe asked.

"Yeah." He was watching Sam and the woman too. "Thanks for coming to get me."

"No problem." Zoe pointed toward Sam and the woman. "Who's she?"

"The nurse practitioner I've seen a couple of times. Patty. She's cool."

Sam smiled at something Patty said, and she touched his arm. She handed him a business card and waited while he wrote something on a post-it note and gave it to her. She touched his arm again before turning to Jeremy and waving goodbye. Sam was smiling broadly and his face looked rosier than his usual tan.

Zoe pointed. "My dad seems to think so too."

～◦◦◦

On the drive home, the three of them rode sealed each in their envelope of silence. Jeremy debated with himself about whether or not to tell his parents he was in town. His dad wouldn't say anything, just signal his disappointment in his pathetic son by snapping more rubber bands. Francie would alternate between concern, ire and angst. No, he'd stay away from campus for two days like Patty asked, but he wasn't going home.

"Drop your bag in my office," Sam told him. "You can sleep in there. I'm going to call the hospital and check on my mom, then we'll order pizza for dinner."

Sam disappeared into his bedroom and closed the door. Zoe and Jeremy sat at either end of the living room sofa.

"So what's going on?" Zoe asked, tilting her head in that way Jeremy liked.

"I promise I'll tell you everything," he said. "But not quite yet. Is that all right?"

"I guess." She paused. "Did something happen at the permaculture farm?"

"Yeah. And that means no summer job at the farm. Alice, she's one of the managers, came by this morning, and told me. And no campus job means I can't stay in the dorm. But Alice said maybe I can join the garden committee in the fall. If Patty says I'm ready."

Zoe smiled. "Cool. So you'll be home this summer."

Home? He hadn't lived in the Sumner Avenue apartment since high school, finding summer jobs on campus instead. He loved his folks but his mom's combination of lonely and bitter was too painful on a daily basis. And with Tian home the atmosphere in the apartment would be even more charged and unpredictable. He'd better think of an alternative. For a brief moment, the idea of returning to Tim's apartment flashed across his mind, but he pushed it away. Brooklyn had its own ghosts. He looked at Zoe. Too bad he couldn't stay with her, through she looked pretty miserable at the moment too.

"I don't know what I'll do this summer," he said. That internship with Professor Clarke was probably out too. No one wanted an employee who might hallucinate a homegrown garden at any moment. Change the subject, he told himself. "I'm sorry your grandma is so sick."

Zoe covered her face with her hands. She said something but her words were muffled.

Jeremy scooted closer and put his arms around her. His hands felt foreign on her back, which radiated warmth right through her sweater. She hid her face in his neck and he could feel the dampness on his skin. They sat like that, not speaking, rocking slightly, back and forth. Was she crying? He couldn't tell. Should he say something? What could he say?

Be brave, he told himself, and wiped a tear from her cheek with his finger. She burrowed her face deeper into his neck. He wanted to kiss her, but maybe that would exploit her sorrow. Or take advantage of her feeling sorry for *his* troubles. Besides, Patty had suggested that the plants came alive at times of strong emotion and he certainly didn't need speed-growing vines complicating this moment. And anyway, Sam was in the other room and could walk in on them any minute. Better wait on the kiss.

He touched her cheek again. How smooth it was, and how perfect. Wait a minute. If Sam was half black, then Zoe was a quarter black. She was racially mixed, like him. Had she thought about that? Did it matter? For a split second he thought about their children, and wondered what they would look like, but that was really crazy and he pushed the thought away. Could Zoe even have children, with her condition?

He stroked his finger over the curve of her chin and into the damp warmth of her neck. Her carotid pulse surprised him, and he left his hand there for a moment, feeling the strong beat. He pulled an escaping curl of her hair from his mouth and pushed it behind her ear. He let his hand stay there, between her ear and her hairline, not daring to move again. His fingers were motionless but so alive.

There was something there, under his little finger. Something hard. His hand pushed against it, then tensed.

"What's that?" he asked.

"My shunt."

He'd read about shunts on the spina bifida website. But a picture on a computer screen was worlds away from something hard and foreign burrowed under this soft skin.

"It's a plastic tube that drains excess fluid from my brain," Zoe said.

"Does it hurt?"

Zoe smiled. "Only when it fails and I need an operation. But that's only happened twice."

"Where does it go?"

Zoe lifted her sweater a few inches, revealing a puckered scar on her abdomen. "It gets dumped in my belly and reabsorbed." She pulled her sweater down and rested her head on his shoulder.

Jeremy's index finger rose and fell with her pulse. He moved his little finger slightly, along the bulge of the shunt tubing. He imagined following the tubing along the curve of her neck to the place it disappeared under the collar of her sweater. Her skin would be satin and his hands would be gentle. Okay, they'd be scared and tentative. But in his imagination, he'd be brave.

The ring of his cell phone startled them both. His mother's name on the screen rattled him more.

"Hey."

"Where are you, Jeremy?"

He hesitated. "At Zoe's."

"In Springfield? You're here?"

"Yeah."

There was silence on the line. "Well, Jeremy. There's a matched set of FBI agents at our apartment to question you. Something about a firebombing in Brooklyn. And your dad is about ready to explode too. I think you'd better get over here. Now."

Chapter Twenty-Five

Even after Jeremy left the apartment, even as her heart rate slowed toward normal, Zoe's skin sizzled with the heat of his hands. She had learned about her body early in life. Her mom and Aunt Emily wanted her to understand both the healthy parts and the parts affected by her condition. She knew the names of bones and muscles, of organs and blood vessels. She knew in great detail what spina bifida did to different body systems and could recognize early symptoms of a dysfunction. But no one ever told her that the big vessels in her neck, her carotid artery and jugular vein, could miss the light touch of a finger. No one had ever mentioned that her shunt tubing could sigh with yearning, from the slightly bulging lateral ventricle all the way down to the peritoneal cavity.

She wanted to shriek in joy or spin her wheelchair in dizzy circles or . . . or talk to someone. But she didn't have the kinds of friends who talked about those feelings. Xander would roll his eyes. Her girlfriends avoided discussing boys, probably assuming that Zoe couldn't have what they were talking about. Pathetic as it might sound, the someone she most wanted to talk to was her grandmother. And now that might never be possible, ever again. Her grandma might never get to see her grow up, attend her wedding, if she ever managed to find someone to love her that much. Her grandma was probably going to die. Joy and sorrow battled inside her and she wanted to scream.

"Dad," she shouted toward his room. "Did you call the hospital?"

Sam wore his jacket and shoulder bag. "The nurse says Ma's agitated. I'm going to go over there and spend some time with her. Maybe I can calm her down."

"I'll come with you," Zoe said.

"No. She's pretty upset now. Wait until tomorrow." He leaned down and kissed the top of her head. "Order yourself some pizza. And save me some." He looked around. "Where's Jeremy?"

"His mom called. He had to go home for a bit."

Why didn't she tell him about the FBI? It wasn't like Jeremy did anything wrong.

~ஒ

The two FBI agents stood as Jeremy walked into his parents' living room. They might have spoken their names but Jeremy didn't hear. He glanced at his father, who stood with arms folded across his chest, half aggressively in the room and half escaping down the hallway.

"You don't have to talk to them," Tian said. "That's the law."

"It's okay," Jeremy said. "I've got nothing to hide."

Francie hugged Jeremy. "Do you want me to stay with you?" she whispered. Her eyes couldn't help flickering to Tian and Jeremy caught the worry there.

Jeremy shook his head. "I'm okay. You stay with Dad." Tian looked jumpy, wired, ready to spring or collapse, who knew which. If he went ballistic, he could make this interview so much worse.

Francie squeezed his arm. "Holler if you need me." She took Tian's hand and led him down the hallway.

Jeremy looked down at the scuffed pine floorboards between his feet. He tried to remember what you were supposed to do when questioned by federal agents. Just tell them your name, right? Did he need a lawyer?

These guys looked pretty tame. One thing he remembered from eleven years ago was that he shouldn't blabber. Just answer the questions. He waited.

"You're Jeremy Beaujolais?" the older agent asked.

"Yes."

"You live here?"

"My parents do. I live in a dorm at UMass."

"Do you know why we're here?"

"No, I don't," Jeremy said, which was, strictly speaking, true.

"We're investigating a firebombing in Brooklyn," the older agent said, glancing down at his spiral notebook. "April 22. We understand you were there."

"I was part of the group that marched down Court Street and occupied Borough Hall. We refused to leave and were arrested."

"We?"

"I was with some other people."

The younger agent leaned forward. "We're interested in who those people were. Who you met with before the demonstration and who you marched with."

Jeremy shrugged. "I never knew many names. I was just in Brooklyn for a few weeks, visiting my brother."

The older guy looked at his notebook again. "That would be Timothy Beaujolais?"

"Uh-huh."

"Timothy gave us a few names of people you were involved with when you stayed with him. So we already know some of your friends."

The agent handed Jeremy a page torn from his spiral notebook, the small holes ripped open. Five names were listed in neat handwriting: Greenhope Murphy. Sari Gupta. Carl Goldman. Thomas von Kregg. Mary Matheson.

Jeremy returned the paper. "Not really friends. More like acquaintances. Greenhope and I were arrested together that day. The others might have been part of the group, but I only went to a few meetings, and we introduced ourselves using first names only."

"Quite a coincidence then," the older agent said softly, "that a few days after your acquaintance Mary Matheson left town there were similar bombings of fossil fuel companies in Oregon and in Brooklyn. That smells like a conspiracy to me."

"And why," asked the younger agent with a slight smirk, "did this acquaintance Mary Matheson, who now happens to be under indictment for terrorism in Oregon, telephone you two days ago?"

"What?" Jeremy sprang to his feet. "You're tapping my phone? Is that legal?"

"Of course not," the young agent said. "Not yours."

"I don't want to talk with you any more." Jeremy walked to the apartment door and opened it. "I don't know anything about any firebombing or what Mary did or didn't do." He wanted to cry, but not in front of these smirking men. "I just care about the plants."

～∂⍴

Zoe sat at the kitchen table, watching the clock, working on the lab report, and eating pizza. She had planned to make a big salad for dinner, but imagining her dad's disappointment when he returned from the hospital, she ordered pizza instead. Was Jeremy a vegetarian, she wondered? If you loved plants, did you want to eat them?

Jeremy returned before her father.

"What did the FBI want?" she asked. "Are you in trouble? Are you okay?"

"I'm starved." He stuffed a third of a pizza slice into his mouth.

"What's going on?"

He finished chewing. "It's so complicated."

"I'm not a baby," she said. "You promised to tell me."

"I will," he said. "I want to. But there are two different things happening. There's this thing that landed me at Health Services twice in three months. And now the FBI. So I don't know where to start."

His expression was so forlorn, as if his face threatened to crumple. Zoe reached across the table and pulled a strand of cheese from his chin. "When I was little," she said, "my dad called stringy things 'lurgies.' Cheese threads and okra slime and those long slimy fibers inside bananas."

Jeremy laughed. "Please, rescue me from the lurgies." He reached for another slice.

She waited.

"Okay. So the FBI guys wanted me to rat on people I knew in Brooklyn, the people I got arrested with. They're activists against global warming. The cops think that they were involved with a firebombing on Earth Day. I think I heard the explosion when I was being arrested."

"Were they involved?"

Did he hesitate or did she imagine that?

"I don't know," he said.

"Were these the same people you heard talking about Molotov cocktails?"

"I don't know if I heard them right. Or if they did anything," he said again, this time whispering. "Maybe they just talked about it." He paused. "And then there's Mary."

"The one who called herself an eco-terrorist, right? And then was arrested for bombing something?"

"Yeah. She called me two nights ago and said she named names, of a couple of people from the Brooklyn group. Those same two people who, might have, been talking about, you know. She said she did it because she's a single mom. Her kid is nine. That's how old I was, when . . . it all happened in my family."

"What about you? Did she give them your name?"

"No. She said she didn't." He paused. "But she called me and the FBI was monitoring her phone, and now they *know* she called me."

Sam's footsteps on the outside staircase startled them both and they leaned back in their chairs. Zoe mimed a zipping gesture across her lips.

"We saved you some pizza," Zoe told her father. "How's Grandma?"

Sam took two bites before answering. "Good news and bad news. The excellent news is that she's more alert and they've been able to take out some of the tubes."

"That's great," Zoe said. "Can I call her?"

"Not quite that alert. Not yet. And the nurse said her heart rhythm problem has resolved." He shook his head. What did that mean, resolved? Gone away forever? Been banished to under the bed for a day or two? Why didn't they speak English?

"And the bad news?" Zoe asked.

"The bad news is that she won't take her medicines. Or eat. Or drink."

Zoe looked at the pizza box on the table. "What about her brain? Can she talk and think and everything?"

"I don't know. Mostly she lies there with her eyes closed and I wish I knew what's she's thinking." Was she thinking about Charlie? About his maybe-father? "In any case, there's not much more the hospital can do. She'll be discharged in a few days."

"Back to Hillside?" Zoe asked.

"Not exactly," Sam said. "To the nursing home on the top of the hill."

"Hilltop. But that's temporary, right? Just until she's better?"

"I don't know, Zoe. I don't know if she's going to get better."

⁓∙∙⁓

Sunday morning, Jeremy insisted on taking the bus back to school.

"You sure you're ready to go?" Zoe asked. She wasn't ready for him to leave.

"I'm fine," Jeremy said. "I've got my first session with Patty tomorrow morning and Tuesday is the one final exam I'm ready to take. I want to finish as much make-up work as possible before they kick me out of the dorm."

"Come on," Sam said. "I'll give you a lift to the bus station."

Zoe hugged him. "Come back next weekend," she whispered. "You promised to tell me the rest of the story."

The other reason Jeremy needed to return to school was his brother. They Skyped every Sunday evening at 8:00 and he'd left his laptop at school. It was their one dependable brotherly connection, trumping their conflicting academic interests, opinions, and temperament. Trudging up the hill to his dorm, Jeremy realized that for the first time he couldn't share everything in his life with his twin. Was there a way to disagree about most things that matter and still be close?

As he cut through the parking lot and walked around the corner to his dorm, he noticed the woman sitting on the stone steps, hunched over and hugging her knees. Wisps of pink hair escaped the brown felt cloche pulled low over her face. Uh-oh. He considered turning back, but Greenhope saw him. She stood and walked quickly toward him.

"We've got to talk," she said, taking his arm. "Privately."

"Not here." Jeremy brushed her arm away. "I'm already in enough trouble. The FBI came to my parents' apartment." He started walking into the parking lot.

She hurried to catch up with him. "They questioned me too," she said. "All of us. They've convened a grand jury and subpoenaed Carl and Sari to testify."

Jeremy stopped walking and looked at her. "You don't think Carl and Sari . . ."

"Had anything to do with the firebombing?" she finished his sentence. "I don't know. I don't *want* to know."

He didn't mention the burrito bar, or Sari's backpack, or Mary's phone call.

"I want to tell you about something, but I've got to move quickly. Is there an ATM around here? I need cash and then I'm on my way."

"In the lobby of my dorm," he said, pointing across the parking lot.

"Listen." Her voice cracked. "There's really bad shit happening, ecologically, much worse than the FBI hassling us. Moose are dying off in huge numbers, and certain kinds of fish. And I've heard there's something else, some environmental crisis, like the honeybee colony collapse disorder, but bigger. I think it has to do with trees and fungicides but the big corporations have blacked out the news reports."

"Sudden Oak Death," Jeremy said. "But I don't think there's any conspiracy."

In the lobby, she inserted her card into the ATM, then stuffed the bills into her pocket. She took a deep breath and turned to face Jeremy.

"A few of us are seriously freaked out about everything that's happening and we're going north. To get away from the investigation, and start a community. We're going to save seeds, grow our food and preserve it. A self-sufficient community that's totally off the grid."

"How?" Jeremy asked. "And where?" He couldn't decipher his emotions. Was he tempted or disdainful, impressed or scornful?

"Vermont," she whispered. "Northeast Kingdom. My parents own land there. Not under their own names, so hopefully no one can find us. My folks were part of the back-to-the-land movement up there in the seventies."

"Really? Your parents were hippies?" Maybe he and Greenhope had more in common than he thought.

"How do you think I got a name like Greenhope?"

Jeremy laughed, but Greenhope stopped him with an intense look and a hand on his cheek. "Come with me?" she asked softly.

For a split-second he was tempted. Her hand offered more than friendship. At least, he thought it did. And wouldn't it be sweet to escape the culture of greed and doom, to really *live* their beliefs? But what about Zoe, and all those plant species in peril. And there was Tim—and a Skype date in thirty minutes—and, even, his parents.

"I can't," he said. "Not right now anyway. There's too much going on here. But I'd like to keep in touch. You know, in case I change my mind in a few months or something?"

She shook her head. "No cell phones, no computers. We don't want the feds or anyone else to be able to track us down."

Jeremy stepped back. "Good luck," he said.

Watching her walk away, he wondered if he made the right choice. There was something very attractive about her plan. And what was it that Flo said, about making sure you could live with your actions, even if you didn't win? When you were stuck and confused in the middle of things, how could you possibly know how you'd feel when the smoke cleared?

He checked his watch. Time to Skype. If only he had the kind of brother he could ask about these things. If only he could ask Tim's opinion and expect a reasonable conversation about it.

Tim sat at his desk and opened his laptop. He looked forward to these conversations with Jeremy and dreaded them, both at the same time. These days, Jeremy was a minefield and Tim had to step carefully, avoiding potentially explosive topics that could detonate in their almost identical faces.

He opened the Skype program and clicked on Jeremy's photo icon, listening to the musical dialing. Then quickly he re-angled the screen so that the wall empty of posters was no longer in view. Not that he had ever invited Jeremy into his bedroom, but who knows, maybe he snooped during his Brooklyn weeks. Tim wasn't sure he could explain why he took down the X-Men posters. Or why he sometimes felt bereft with their torn remains folded in the bottom drawer of his bureau, under his high school yearbook and other relics of childhood.

Even the threat of explosion didn't lessen Tim's pleasure when Jeremy's face appeared on the screen. "Hey, bro," he said.

Jeremy smiled too, although it didn't reach beyond his mouth. "Hey."

"What's up? Trouble in paradise?"

Jeremy looked sincerely puzzled at that. "Huh?"

Tim laughed. "Mom says you're spending a lot of time with wheelchair girl. A 'hot romance,' she said."

"You called Mom? Alert the media!"

Tim made a face, but he would allow Jeremy to change the subject. His brother had never been very good with women. He was probably embarrassed about dating a cripple. "Nah. Mom called me. And you *know* she's got to be majorly worried to contact the twin who doesn't give a damn. She said you're still having those dead plant visions?"

Jeremy shrugged. His reluctance to talk was visible on every part of his face.

". . . She said the FBI followed you up there?"

"Yeah. Thanks for giving them my address. These were the local feds and they came to Mom and Dad's apartment. You can imagine how well that went down. They said you gave them names of the people in the Earth Day group. Thanks a lot, bro."

"They would have gotten them anyway," Tim said. He did have a small pang of regret about supplying the names. But his business school scholarship could be revoked so easily. Just a phone call to the dean, really. And global warming was a running joke in his classes, a pathetic left-wing conspiracy to attack the business community. "That's what you get, anyway, for getting involved with those eco-nuts."

Jeremy shook his head. "You've still got your head stuck deep in the sand, don't you? Well, this is important, an epidemic keystone species die-off. Big enough that the government is suppressing the news. Greenhope and bunch of the others are going off to . . ." Jeremy stopped abruptly and he blushed deeply.

"What?"

"It's just . . . My phone is tapped. So this computer probably is too."

"The feds probably already know everything, bro. They've got all this neat technology to keep tabs on troublemakers," Tim said. "Like your friends."

Like his brother, Tim thought. But Jeremy was silent, so Tim continued. There had to be some way to drum some sense into his thick skull. "Greenhope came over last night, asked me how to find you at UMass. I knew she was strange, but not that strange."

"Don't knock it, Tim, just because you don't see the whole picture."

"What I see, bro, is you trying to replicate the demented family we grew up in. Creating another fucking pie-in-the-sky commune opting out and growing food. That's what I see and it makes me sick."

And it did. It made Tim nauseous, because his brother was too far gone to listen to reason. He shook his head, hard, and reached for the keyboard.

"Let me try to explain it to you," Jeremy said.

"I can't." Tim pressed the hang-up icon. The screen went blank.

Chapter Twenty-Six

The cat curled up warm against Flo's feet. She wiggled her toes against his solid presence, against his jackhammer purring that vibrated through the weave of the blanket and into her thick yellow socks with no-slip patches on the soles. His respirations rose and fell and she felt every breath push through her worn-out skin and into her blood, carrying feline comfort to her comfort-hungry cells. Charlie was way too smart to die in a fire, whatever they said. Charlie would have nosed open a window and jumped to safety, or crawled through a ventilation shaft like on that television program Brad used to like, where they were always escaping certain doom to complete a mission.

She opened her eyes. She was in a bed, propped up on pillows so she could look around, but it was not her room. A bedside table with a blue plastic tub. A water pitcher and cup with a straw. She looked away. These were not her things. This room was wrong. Quiet and dim, with two beds, the other empty. Just her and the cat.

The cat was wrong too; he was black with white boots. Charlie was gray and much smaller. Charlie always slept tight against her chest, so she could feel the tremble of his purring directly into her heart.

Charlie was dead in the fire. She remembered the smoke. She remembered the "Cook with Honey" music, how the ghosts danced her around the living room and then smoke was in the honey and in her eyes and in her mouth.

She closed her eyes and floated. Her body felt airy and light, tethered to the bed only by the vibrations of the cat, each rumble in sync with her own heartbeat.

~~∽☙~~

Sam drove the winding driveway to the top of the hill. The nursing home overlooked the river, with an unobstructed view of the city to the south and conservation land to the west. When Flo was admitted Monday afternoon, her nurse told him that in a week or two the spring-swollen river would be so raucous that his mother would want to keep her window closed. He hoped Flo would be back to her cranky self by then; if she complained about the loud rush of river, he'd gladly open and close her window a thousand times.

The brick walls of the building were gloomy in the afternoon shadow. He parked the car, killed the engine and sat there, not getting out, not wanting to deal with it all. An orderly waved as he walked by on the paved pathway, pushing a gnome-like resident in a wheelchair. He felt ashamed about procrastinating and climbed out of the car, gathering Flo's clean laundry and a plastic tub of chicken soup Zoe made. "Of course she'll eat chicken soup," Zoe had insisted.

He hesitated for a few moments at the fork in the sidewalk. Waiting to sign the admission papers two days before, he'd studied the large aerial map in the nursing home hallway, so he knew that the smaller path led into the wooded river view area, to a gazebo in a clearing. Another time, he thought.

After the cacophony of the hospital, the quiet of the nursing home was startling. Soft music from the activities room replaced the beeping monitors. Food carts wouldn't click on these carpeted hallways. If only his mother would eat, drink. How long could she last without food and water? Maybe he could ask Emily about that, for her professional opinion. Or maybe that Patty, at UMass. She had been so easy to talk to. And Jeremy seemed to trust her.

He hesitated in the doorway to his mother's room. The light was dim. Flo was motionless in the first bed, the one farther from the window, her eyes closed. A large black cat slept in a puddle of sunlight near her feet.

Mimi sat at the bedside. She put her index finger to her lips and pointed at Flo's hands. "Watch," she whispered.

The bed covers were pulled up to Flo's chin, but her hands had escaped from the confinement of the fabric. Her fingers moved rhythmically along the tender loops of pink chenille. Her knuckles were swollen, the skin shiny and red, but her fingers tapped and jumped and danced over the blanket.

What was she doing? Typing, maybe? Sam heard a few faint musical notes and realized his mother was playing an imaginary piano. She always claimed she had been a serious music student as a child, but gave it up entirely over some argument with her father.

"Playing the piano? I always figured that was just another one of her tall stories," he whispered. True or not, her finger-music made him sad. He turned away and put the laundry basket and soup container on the bureau.

Mimi shrugged. "Who knows? Your mother is a multi-talented woman."

Maybe, Sam thought. But she didn't have much respect for the truth.

As if she could mind-read his unkind thoughts, Flo's hands stopped dancing and turned over, the fingers curved up and trembling. She opened her eyes.

"Hey, Sleeping Beauty," Mimi said. "How're you doing?"

Flo murmured something that might have been, "Ducky." Or not.

Mimi took a bottle from her handbag, squeezed a dollop of pale green lotion onto the palm of her hand and sniffed.

"Coriander. Your favorite." she said, rubbing the lotion into Flo's hand, over the swollen knuckles and into the empty sleeve of extra skin hanging from her forearm. Mimi looked at Sam with droopy eyes. "It's too dry in here. Irritating. I wish they wouldn't overheat these places."

"Ma likes it warm," Sam said. He walked to the window and studied the lawn in its slide downhill toward the river. The gazebo roof peak was just visible above the new leaves, a copper green that reflected the afternoon sun.

Careful not to disturb the sleeping cat, Mimi uncovered Flo's foot and gently massaged the lotion into the rough callus over her bunion.

"Ma," Sam said, turning back to face the bed. "Zoe made you chicken soup. Can I give you some?"

Flo closed her eyes and turned her face to the wall.

"Guess that's a no," he muttered.

"She hasn't eaten anything in three days," Mimi said. "Your mother is an incredibly stubborn woman." She stood up. "I've got to go. Wednesday is yoga. Is anyone else coming to visit?"

"Anna's bringing Zoe, after school."

"Good." Mimi held out the coriander lotion toward Sam. "Maybe you could do the other side?"

He stared at the bottle. His mother had never been a physical person, at least not with him. Plenty of bedtime hugs and kisses when he was little, but soon words replaced touch in their connection. He knew she loved him, but it was cerebral rather than visceral. Still, he could do this.

"Sure." He accepted the bottle.

After Mimi left, Sam took her seat at the bedside. "I'm here, Ma," he whispered. There was no response. He wanted something, some kind of acknowledgement, of connection. Even a goodbye, if that's what it had to be.

He squeezed some lotion into his palm and rubbed his hands together, the way he'd seen Mimi do it. He sniffed the odd scent that had been his mother's trademark fragrance as long as he could remember. How strange that each of the important women in his life had a personal perfume. Flo's lotion was almost pungent. Anna liked to dab a drop of scented oil called *Rain* behind her ears, though he never really understood how rain smelled. Zoe used an almond shampoo. He wondered about Patty; how would she smell?

He took Flo's hand between his. How slight it was, how insubstantial. He massaged the lotion onto each finger, then between them, around each nail, and across the lattice of knobby veins, coffee-splotch age spots, and hospital needle bruises on the back of her hand. When had his mother become this old?

Flo opened her eyes and squinted at him. "Who're you?"

He caught his breath, totally unprepared for that sucker punch. Oh, he knew that happened with dementia, but not *his* mother. Did she really not know him? He took her hand, rubbed his thumb across a swollen knuckle.

"I'm Sam. Your son, Sam."

She stared at him then, her eyes clearing as she examined his features. Then she smiled.

"You look like your daddy," she stopped, then added, "Who's your daddy?"

Sam tried to control his voice. "You tell me. I always thought Brad was my father, but now you say it's someone I've never heard of." Sam sounded like a cranky six-year-old, but he couldn't stop himself. "Is my dad really some guy named Charlie?"

Flo closed her eyes. "I never said that."

"You did, Ma. You said my father was a guy named Charlie."

"You heard wrong," Flo said. "Charlie's my cat."

⌇

In the two days following his first session with Patty, Jeremy replayed their conversation many times in his head. He hadn't known what to expect and was surprised that there was no couch, no shrink-talk, and especially no pity. They sat on comfortable chairs, half-facing each other, separated by a small round table with a lamp and a box of tissues. The tissues put him off a bit; did people cry a lot in therapy sessions? But

Patty just asked questions, simple ones really, and he talked. The more he talked, the more he wanted to tell her, the more the words overflowed from somewhere in the center of his chest and out of his mouth, leaving no loss, no ache, no emptiness in their place. When the hour was up— how fast it flew by—he had a question for her.

"Do you think I'm nuts?" he said. "Is that why I'm having these . . . episodes?"

"Hallucinations," she said. "No. I don't think you're nuts. You went through some intense experiences as a child. Memories you tried not to think about, that you successfully buried. Sometimes a new stress can bring back old worries."

"Like my dad coming home?"

She nodded. "Could be."

"But why hallucinations?"

"I'm not sure. Maybe because it's complicated and your brain is trying to make sense of it?"

He still didn't understand. "But why the plants? That has nothing to do with my dad."

"Why do you think?"

He shook his head. He had no clue.

Patty stood up. "We'll talk more next time."

Wednesday afternoon, walking back from the library to his dorm, he was still thinking about her question. What *did* he think? He half-wished for a flashbulb epiphany moment, but half-wanted it all to just disappear and leave him alone.

He stopped in the dorm lobby for his mail. There was a thick envelop from Alice with a book, the syllabus for the sustainability studies seminar in the fall, and a handwritten note. *Start with this book*, she wrote. *It's about the concept of plentitude, a kinder, gentler approach to the ecological decline crisis.*

Crisis, he thought. That reminded him of the oak epidemic and Professor Clarke talking about it as the plants twined around his body, and Greenhope had mentioned it too. He should be reading about it, and putting in his application. He still had course assignments to make up too, and with no summer job on campus he had to be out of his dorm room by Saturday. Three days until he had to move back to Springfield and share the apartment with Francie and Tian.

~~~

Zoe pushed her chair down the nursing home hallway ahead of her mom and Emily. She slowed at a doorway and pointed. "That's the guest kitchen, Mom."

"Thanks," Anna said, putting her bag on the kitchen counter. "I'll meet you in Flo's room in a few minutes."

Zoe and Emily paused in the doorway to the room. Flo's eyes were closed and Sam sat on the bedside chair, hunched over so that his head rested on the pillow next to his mother. How could they sleep with that smell? Zoe turned away from the pungent odor and buried her face in Emily's sweater.

"She peed herself," Zoe whispered.

Emily squeezed Zoe's shoulder. "I'm so sorry," she said. "It's common."

"I don't get it," Zoe said. Didn't Alzheimer's usually go on forever? Xander's grandfather had it for like ten years before he died. "Why is this happening so fast?"

Emily shook her head. "There are different kinds of dementia. And it seems the medicine made things worse for Flo. Why don't you go help your mom make tea? I'll find someone to clean her up."

Zoe was grateful to leave the smell, happy to crowd with her mother in the small kitchen space where the kettle was singing. "Why make tea?" she asked. "I thought Grandma isn't eating or drinking anything?"

"Tea helps. Helps me, anyway." Anna poured the boiling water over the tea leaves in the heated pot and covered it with a patchwork cozy. "Maybe Flo's special blend will entice her. We can take this to her room now."

Zoe usually rolled her eyes at her mom's old-timey tea tradition, but today it seemed less stupid. She accepted the canvas bag from her mother and balanced it on her lap. She didn't move.

"We can't go yet," she said. "Grandma had an accident and Emily is looking for her nurse."

Anna's lip trembled. "Flo would hate this. Hate all of it. I just hope that her mind is too far gone to realize what's happening."

Sam and Emily joined them in the tiny kitchen. "They asked us to wait," Sam said. "While they change, you know, clean her up."

"I'm sorry, Sam."

"This morning she didn't know me. Asked me my name." His eyes filled and he sniffled. "Then she denied it, denied ever saying anything about a man named Charlie being my dad. Zoe asked me if I want to meet this guy." He grabbed a tissue from the counter and blew his nose. "I have no idea."

"Oh, Sam," Emily said. "You've been such a good son to her and . . ."

"Dad," Zoe interrupted. "What's a Stalinist?"

"Where did *that* come from?" asked Sam.

Zoe wasn't sure where, except that she couldn't stand all the sadness. She had to change the subject or explode. "Because you always say that Grandma is one. I'm just curious."

"She wasn't really a Stalinist. At least not for decades. She hasn't even been in the Party for years." He smiled. "She says they booted her out."

"Why'd they do that?" Zoe asked.

"I don't know. Maybe she told Mimi the story." He laughed a small laugh. "Probably her big mouth. She always sounded proud of being kicked out. Or it could've been pure bravado. It was sometimes hard to tell with your grandmother. Anyway, I used the term loosely to describe how rigid she could be in her views. How ungenerous, when you disagreed with her."

"She *was* harsh, when she didn't approve." Anna touched his hand. "I'll bet it was sometimes hard to be her son."

"Stop talking about her like she's dead!" Zoe pushed out of the room, running her wheel over Sam's foot. Her comment had backfired, seriously. She left the ruckus behind her. The adults talking all at once, squeezing through the bottleneck of the doorway, about how they didn't mean it, Sweetie, and the ding of Anna's phone timer, that the tea was steeped.

In the hallway, Flo's nurse walked toward them. "You can come back in now."

They reconfigured themselves around the bedside. Zoe backed her chair into the narrow space between the bed and the wall. Emily perched on the second empty bed and Sam sat at Flo's feet. Anna took the bedside chair and set up the teapot on the bedside table.

Zoe sniffed. "Smells good."

"Your favorite," Anna told Flo. "I took it from Sam's apartment." Anna arranged five teacups on the bedside table. She poured the tea and a small cloud of cinnamon steam surrounded them.

Flo breathed deeply. Steam. Tea. Her tea. Sam. Cloud. Smoke? No, steam. Cat. Charlie.

"Look," Zoe said. "She's smiling." She brushed Flo's flyaway hair away from her ear and whispered, "You look beautiful, Grandma."

Flo didn't open her eyes and her voice was cracked and worn, but Zoe heard her clearly. "Nuts," Flo said.

The nurse stuck her head into the room. "Smells wonderful in here. Do you folks need anything?"

"I have a question," Zoe said, her heart thumping loud in her chest. So many questions. So many things didn't make sense. Like that sometimes her grandmother was totally gone, and other times she seemed to understand things, and even answer. And, was she really starving herself to *death*?

The nurse walked into the room and sat on the empty bed, facing Zoe. "Shoot."

"Is it, like, time to start a deathbed vigil?" Zoe asked. "You know, should we be here all the time?"

Sam touched his index finger to his lips, then pointed to Flo. The nurse said that maybe she could still hear them. He wasn't ready for this. "Come on, Zoe. You read too many novels."

The nurse looked right at Zoe when she spoke. "Your grandmother stopped eating and drinking a week ago. Her lucid moments are getting fewer. So, yes. It's time."

Chapter Twenty-Seven

It rained hard on Saturday and the early bus from Amherst got a late start. As they approached the Springfield exit, Jeremy decided it was late enough to call Zoe.

She answered right away. "Hey," she said. "You home?"

"Almost," he said. "I'm going to hang out with my dad a little." How strange that sounded. "Do you want to take a walk in the park this afternoon? If the rain stops?"

That sounded stupid. Did you ask a girl who couldn't walk to take a walk in the park? Go for a roll, maybe? That sounded worse. Why couldn't he get this right?

"I'd like to, Jer. But I'm going to sit with Flo after her women's group leaves. I don't know when I'll be home. Tomorrow morning, maybe?"

Jer? He liked that. A nickname. Better than *Jerry*, like Carl insisted on calling him. Carl. He didn't want to think about Carl and Sari. He hadn't done anything wrong, except overhear two words in a burrito bar. "Sure. How is she?"

Zoe paused before saying, "She's dying. We're keeping her company."

Jeremy hesitated. "I could come sit with you too."

"That'd be great," Zoe said. "Mid-afternoon?"

It was almost ten by the time Jeremy lugged his wet duffle bag up the stairs to his parents' apartment and dropped it on the dusty entry floor. As he dug in his pocket for the apartment key, the door opened and Tian stepped into the hallway. He quickly pulled the door closed behind him.

"They're back." Tian's voice was a harsh whisper. "Those feds." He grabbed the duffle and swung it into Jeremy's arms. "Get out of here quick, Son. I'll tell them it was kids selling Girl Scout cookies or something."

Jeremy studied his father's face, contorted with something. Worry? Anger? He couldn't tell which or something entirely else. How weird— how sad—to not be able to read his own dad.

The apartment door opened again and the two agents stood framed in the doorway.

"Girl Scouts cookies, huh?" The short guy smirked.

Jeremy glanced at Tian, trying to gauge his dad's temper. Didn't seem too bad, but it was sometimes hard to tell. When Tim and Jeremy came home the weekend Tian was released, Tim had suggested that the number of rubber bands on their dad's wrist might be a stress level indicator. Jeremy could see four now, three tan and one red, but he didn't know how bad that was.

"Where's Mom?" he asked.

"Sleeping. She worked last night."

Jeremy shouldered in front of his father so that he stood facing the older agent. He'd been more reasonable last time, concentrating on writing in that spiral notebook.

"What do you want now?" Jeremy asked.

"We've got more questions. This time we need answers." The guy sounded disappointed, as if Jeremy had personally let him down.

"And this time," the younger agent said, taking Jeremy's arm, "we're taking you downtown."

"You can't do that," Tian said. "Do you have an arrest warrant? Are you charging him with something?"

"We could, if you like, Mr. Jailhouse Lawyer. Accessory, maybe. Or conspiracy?" The young agent jabbed his finger inches from Tian's face. "We don't need a warrant. He was about to run away, so we can bring him in for questioning."

Tian shook his head. "That's not the law. But if you take him, I'm coming too."

"Interfering with us is a violation of your parole, Mr. Williams."

"I know my rights," Tian said. "And none of this is legal."

"You're on parole and you got no rights." The agent jerked Jeremy's arm and pulled him toward the stairs.

Jeremy looked back at his father, slumped against the doorframe. That couldn't be true, could it? A person didn't lose all their rights just because they were convicted of a crime.

Tian picked up Jeremy's duffle bag. "Don't say anything without a lawyer," he called to Jeremy. "Anything. I'll be there as soon as I can."

⁓᷒ᷔ

Jeremy wasn't sure if he was relieved or disappointed at the ordinary room tucked at the end of a long corridor in a high rise Main Street office building. No metal detector or one-way mirror or handcuffs. Just a standard issue metal desk with a shoe-sized dent in the side and dust bunnies in the corner. He was pointed to a chair and left alone.

His chair must have had a short leg. It wobbled each time he changed position. The silence made Jeremy nervous. He wiggled back and forth on the chair, making it tap on the gray linoleum floor. What were they waiting for?

"So?" he asked the closed door. "Why am I here?"

Nothing.

Twenty minutes or two hours later, the two agents entered and took seats facing Jeremy.

"We're not happy with you," the older guy said, and he sounded disappointed. "You withheld information last time. For one thing, you didn't tell us who your daddy is."

"You didn't ask about him," Jeremy said. He had promised himself to say nothing until his father found a lawyer, but that could take forever, and he had nothing to hide.

The agent leaned forward, leaning both elbows on his knees. "You didn't think it was relevant that your father just got out of prison?"

"Why? He has nothing to do with this."

The older man slapped his notebook on the desktop in disgust. "Is there anything you'd like to share about your friends in Brooklyn?"

Jeremy shook his head.

"You might be interested to know that Sari Gupta and Carl Goldman have been subpoenaed to the grand jury looking into that firebombing. They'll certainly be indicted and they'll no doubt be convicted. With terrorism enhancements, they could face very long sentences."

"And," the young guy interrupted, "if you're an accessory, so could you. If you cooperate, we won't have to subpoena you."

"I'm not part of any of this," Jeremy said. "I keep telling you that."

The young agent stood up and walked close to Jeremy's chair. He looked down at him. "Do you understand that lying to a federal agent is a serious crime?"

Jeremy nodded. Had he said anything that wasn't true?

"You still claim that you haven't seen any of the Brooklyn group?" the agent asked. "Not even Greenhope Murphy?"

Jeremy stared at his wet shoes, still wet from his walk from the bus stop. He wiggled his toes, wondering if they were wrinkled prunes.

"Look," the young guy said, squatting so that his face was close to Jeremy's. "We know she visited you at UMass and we want to talk with her. If you tell us where we can find her, you can go home."

How could they know about UMass? They weren't following him, were they? He shook his head. "How?"

"Amateurs. Remember that ATM on campus? Geez. So, where is the green lady heading?"

They *were* amateurs and Jeremy didn't know if that was good because they were innocent, or bad because being innocent might not matter to these people. Still, he didn't know where Greenhope was going, not really, not exactly.

"I don't know where she's going," Jeremy said. "She didn't tell me." We're not that amateurish, he thought. At least, Greenhope wasn't.

The older agent shrugged and put his notebook under his arm. "Then I'm afraid you're in big trouble." He opened the door for his partner, and they both left the room.

Alone, Jeremy wished he hadn't said anything. He hadn't actually lied about anything, had he? He looked down at his hands. If ever there was a time he needed the plant delusions to rescue him, it was now. He tried to summon the tingling in his fingertips. He wiggled his fingers, urging the pinch of shoots pushing through muscle and skin. He beckoned green vines, urging them to twine around his arms, encircle his heart, protect him from these men and their accusations. He yearned for red blossoms covering his body, shielding his face, taking him away from these men and this place. But nothing happened.

~~~

"Just act normal, everyone?" Claire instructed the group. "She's still our Flo."

Mimi wiped the raindrops off her glasses and pushed ahead of the others in the quiet hallway. "There's nothing normal about this. It's horrible." Maybe this had been a bad idea, for the women's group to meet this morning. Probably the last time before Flo left them. Mimi didn't think she could bear Claire ending one more declarative sentence with a question. She couldn't stand one more go-round of their recurring discussion about a name for their group. Marlene would suggest the Girls' Club and Fanny would counter with Sisterhood. Claire would reply that it was too much like the Hadassah and she herself would mutter Geezer-hood. Around and around in circles they talked and it didn't matter. The only thing that mattered was that her best friend in the world was dying.

There had been other deaths in their forty-five years together. Sarah's breast cancer was the first and it shocked them because she was so young and they still thought they'd live forever. When Sandy killed herself, they didn't know whether to mourn or feel guilty that they hadn't realized how bad it was, hadn't been able to help her. And of course Joanna, her beloved Joanna, but that was so quick, with no time to say goodbye, no time to say anything at all.

Standing in the doorway of Flo's room, all these losses returned and they merged together in the overheated air of the nursing home, each memory magnifying the sorrow of losing Flo. Mimi's throat ached, the pressure of unshed tears pushed deep into her sinuses and her brain and her ears until her skull wanted to burst.

"Mocha delight for you," Marlene said, holding a take-out cup with Coffee Hut printed on the cardboard. "And one for Flo."

Wordless, Mimi grasped both cups and took the seat closest to Flo's head.

"What a sweet kitty," Fanny cooed, sitting on the foot of the bed and petting the sleeping black cat. "You know how much Flo loves kitties, don't you, big guy?"

And how much Flo hates baby talk, Mimi thought, but she stopped herself from making an unkind comment. Everyone was doing their best, Marlene picking up their favorite hot drinks and Fanny talking silly. At least Claire hadn't brought her stethoscope and gone all medical on them. Mimi would just lose it if Claire did that.

And none of it made any difference. In the center of their circle, Flo just lay there, motionless. Her chest barely moving. Her flesh a deflated balloon, like someone opened a vital valve and let the air out.

Mimi had called Sam's cell early that morning, asking if it was okay for the group to come for a visit. "It's our usual meeting, you know. Sat-urday morning at 10:00."

"That's fine," Sam had said. His voice sounded thin on the phone. "I could use a break."

"Are you okay?" she'd asked. She and Joanna hadn't had children. Sam was as close to a son as she had. "Is there anything I can do?"

"No," Sam answered. "And no. But thanks."

She'd try to comfort Sam later. Now, Mimi tried to soothe herself. She searched her friend's face for any sign of life but saw nothing. "Oh, Flo," she whispered. "I'm going to miss you so much."

"A toast to Flo." Marlene stood at the foot of the bed, decaf skinny latté held high. "Forty-five years of sisterhood. Of fighting patriarchy, together."

Mimi wondered if Marlene's drink was made with skim or whole milk, but why did she care? They were all going to die, no matter if they ate double fat ice cream or fat-free frozen yogurt. She blew her nose on a wadded up tissue from her jeans pocket and gave herself a swift mental kick in the rear. Enough.

"Yes. To sisterhood," Fanny echoed, nodding meaningfully at each of them.

"To my best friend in the world," Mimi said. "I love you, Flo." Mimi raised her mocha delight and leaned forward to bump cardboard cups with Marlene.

Fanny flourished a nip bottle of peppermint schnapps and poured a generous dollop into her drink and Mimi's. "Anyone else?" she asked.

Claire pursed her lips and shook her head, murmuring something about before noon, but Marlene held her cup out for a splash.

"Can you hear us, Flo?" Claire asked. "We're here with you. We love you."

"To Flo!" The four women touched their cups high over Flo's quiet form.

"To our Flo," Mimi repeated and they drank.

∽≈≈∾

Jeremy hadn't shown up by ten and her calls kept going to voice mail. Zoe redialed his number, didn't leave another message.

"What's wrong?" Sam asked.

"Jeremy said he'd be here, hours ago."

"He probably got involved with something. His family, or schoolwork." Sam squirted lotion into the palm of his hand and rubbed it into Flo's foot. "This is almost empty. Do you know where she buys this?"

Zoe looked at her father. "I don't think we'll need . . ."

"Don't say it," Sam said. He massaged the callus on his mother's heel.

Zoe wheeled away from the bed. "Be back soon," she said. "I'm going to call Jeremy's parents."

It took Zoe a few minutes to find a phone number for Francie, but she answered on the first ring.

"Hello?" Francie's voice sounded worn.

"This is Zoe. Is Jeremy there?"

"No," Francie said. "His father and a lawyer are downtown, hopefully bringing him home."

"What happened?"

"The FBI brought him in for questioning," Francie said. "I'll tell him you called."

"Thanks," Zoe said. Clearly Jeremy's mom didn't want to tell her anything.

"It'll be okay," Francie said before she hung up.

∽∾∽

Shortly after midnight, Jeremy and Tian stood awkwardly in the living room.

"Thanks, Dad." Jeremy said. "I was really glad to see you."

Jeremy remembered his surge of relief when Tian walked into the interrogation room downtown and put his arm around his shoulders. Funny how a parent—even a not-so-great parent, even a mostly-gone parent—could offer such comfort. But his relief had been tempered with anxiety about what this new Tian might do.

Tian chuckled. "You didn't look glad. You looked terrified."

"I was worried that you'd get pissed off."

"I'm not that guy any more," Tian said. "At least, I'm trying not to be. Sorry it took me so long to get you out of there. Couldn't reach my lawyer and it took a while to find someone else."

"I didn't really need a lawyer, you know. They weren't charging me or anything."

"Just trying to intimidate you. That's why you need a lawyer."

Jeremy nodded.

After several long seconds, Tian asked. "You home for good, Son?"

Jeremy almost smiled at that. He still hated being called "Son," but Tian wasn't likely to mix him up with his brother, not after all this trouble.

"Maybe for the summer. If that's okay." Jeremy picked up his duffle and started down the hallway to his room.

"I don't think I can sleep yet," Tian called after him. "I'm making coffee. You want some?"

Jeremy stopped walking. He had no experience spending time with Tian—just the two of them, two adults, father and son—without Francie orchestrating things. What would they even talk about?

First things first. "Don't call me 'Son,' okay? I have a name."

Tian shrugged. "No problem. Jeremy. *Now* do you want coffee?"

"Yeah. Sure. But I've got to make a phone call first."

He dumped the duffle on his bed and checked his messages, then dialed Zoe's phone. While it rang, he looked around the room he once shared with Tim, walls plastered with their shared heritage of X-Men posters. He wasn't at all sure how he felt about waking up every morning staring at Wolverine.

"You okay?" Zoe asked. "I was worried."

"Yeah. Just got home."

"What happened?"

"Nothing, really."

"Being taken downtown by the FBI isn't nothing."

"Nothing happened. I'll tell you all the details tomorrow, okay?"

"Okay. 10:30 at the park. At the ball field."

Tian was pouring the coffee when Jeremy returned to the kitchen. They sat across from each other at the round table.

"You called that girl?" Tian asked.

"Zoe. Her grandma's dying."

"You like her."

"Yeah." Jeremy shifted in his chair. Had they already run out of things to talk about? This was going to be a long summer. Though hopefully he'd find a job. Work plus finishing two incompletes and seeing Zoe a lot wouldn't leave too much time at home.

"What are you going to do this summer?" Tian asked.

Jeremy grinned. His dad could always read his mind when he was a kid, mostly when he had mischief in mind. "Get a job, I guess."

"Maybe there's something at the medical center."

"I'll ask Mom." Jeremy sipped the coffee. "Geez, this is strong. When did you start drinking coffee anyway?"

"In prison real men don't drink tea."

"They don't add milk either?"

Tian grinned. "Nope. But you can if you want."

"Sugar okay?"

"All you want," Tian said, pushing the bowl closer to Jeremy.

The coffee was still too hot to drink. Jeremy blew across the surface. That probably wasn't done in prison either.

"What was it like there?" Jeremy asked.

"You saw some of it, when you visited. Nasty."

"Yeah."

"The good part was, there was plenty of time to think. The bad part was, there was plenty of time to think."

More silence as they sipped the coffee. Singed tongues were easier than words, Jeremy figured. Finally, Tian pushed his cup away.

"Listen, Son. Jeremy. I've been chewing on what you said the other day. About what we all lost. I've never told you that I'm sorry. But I am. Sorry. About that night."

Jeremy closed his eyes and he was back to the snowy Solstice. They parked the van by the side entrance to Forest Park and walked single file to the dingle buried deep in the woods. They all wore white. He and Tim were nine, old enough to wear the bleached muslin robes over their fleece and long johns and walk with the adults along the path. Tim pushed him out of the way and walked ahead, even though Jeremy was a few minutes older and should have been first. Abby and Terrence were babies, bundled up in triple-layer pajama sleepers and blankets and carried by their moms.

At the sacred place, Tian let them light the bonfire that they helped build earlier that afternoon. The moms nursed their babies to sleep in the small clearing, but he and Tim got to stay up. They played the heart-beat rhythm on the clay darbuka drums and Murphy's recorder notes danced between drumbeats. Everyone chanted and Adele danced, her big belly hidden in robes until the end, when Tian parted her robes and offered the baby to the Goddess, just like each of the other children in the family had been offered, even the ones whose parents moved out and took them to live away.

Later, when the adults started drinking the libation and dancing crazy and wild, Francie settled Jeremy and Tim in their nest of sleeping bags and tarps and blankets at the edge of the circle, where they'd be warm and could watch until they fell asleep. Tim snuck a couple of swallows of the libation and nodded off right away, but Jeremy watched, cocooned warm and safe in his sleeping bag.

The snow drifted down and sizzled on the hot rocks ringing the fire pit. The sparkly smoke rose into the sky making new clouds with the snow. His whole family danced a swirling, whirling joyous parade around the bonfire, taking turns on the drums and the recorder and the dancing stone. Jeremy floated in and out of sleep, dreams merging with memories. Much later, when the party was quiet, he heard Abby and

Terrence babbling to each other and thought about checking on them, or did he dream that part?

Tian shook his shoulder. "You daydreaming? You need more coffee?"

"Sorry, Dad. I was just remembering. The night Abby and Terrence went missing. Do you ever think about it?"

Tian's hand went to his wrist. He fingered the red rubber band, but didn't snap it. He was silent for so long Jeremy wondered if he heard the question. Of course he heard, but that didn't mean he would answer it.

"Every day," Tian finally whispered. "I think about those babies every single day."

Chapter Twenty-Eight

In Jeremy's first childhood memory, at age five or six, he stepped outside with his mom and Tim after a spring rain and sniffed the earthy air.

"What's that smell?" he had asked.

"Petrichor," Francie told him. "It's a mix of bacterial secretion with plant oil. Rain after a long dry spell releases it into the air."

"Yuck!" Tim held his nose. "I don't want to breathe bug oil."

Jeremy loved the smell and he loved the sound of the word peh-tra-chore and he loved that his mom had worked in Forest Park and knew about plants and nature. Jeremy's first homeschool project was studying petrichor, how the oil protected the plants and kept them from germinating until conditions were right for their growth.

~≈⌐

"Don't you love that smell?" he asked Zoe the next morning. The rain had stopped and the park sparkled. "It's called petrichor. Peh-tra-chore." He sang the syllables in time to his footsteps. "Peh-tra-chore."

They were walking—well, Zoe was rolling, but the details really didn't matter—along the main road looping around the playing fields.

He couldn't stop smiling, which could have been the perfect weather or could have been Zoe. He took her hand.

Zoe giggled. "I need them both." She demonstrated what happened when she pushed her chair one-handed.

"Guess I've got you going in circles," Jeremy said. He was amazed; he'd never talked like that to a girl. Had never imagined he could flirt like people in the movies.

She laughed. "Not exactly. But listen, I want to know what's going on with you. Last time, the lurgies saved you, but there are no strings of cheese or banana here. So talk."

The last thing in the world he wanted at that moment was to think about hard stuff. He wanted to sit on a park bench and kiss Zoe until it got dark. He wanted to feel carefree and happy and silly. The serious look on her face made it clear that she had other ideas.

"First," he said, "tell me what's happening with your grandmother."

"She's dying. After our walk, I'm going back to sit with her."

"Can I come with you?"

"Sure, but don't try to change the subject. Why don't you start with the FBI visit," she prompted, "and then move on to Mary-the-terrorist and your friends with the Molotov cocktails. After that, you can fill me in about whatever it was that got you sent to the hospital."

"Health Services," he said. "Not hospital."

"Okay," she said. "Health Services."

"First of all, they're not really my friends. I mean, I knew them for a few weeks in Brooklyn and we worked together planning Earth Day. But they never told me anything about Molotov cocktails and I didn't even like them much." He looked at Zoe. Did she really care about this? "In some ways, I care about them more now that they're in trouble, if that makes any sense."

"That's because you're a good person," she said. "What did the FBI want?"

He described the agents and their questions, and their return visit the day before. "I think they were just fishing, trying to intimidate me, to get me to say something bad about Sari and Carl."

"You didn't, right?"

He shook his head. "I don't know much."

Zoe frowned. "You know what you *heard*."

"I'm not even sure about that any more." He pushed the mental picture of Sari's backpack and the bottles further into the secret part of his brain, where he stored the images he couldn't look at. "I keep thinking about Mary telling the feds about people. That feels so wrong." He shook his head again. Mary's son was nine. What would happen to him?

Zoe nodded. "What about Health Services? What's with that?"

How to explain the episodes? How to be truthful without sending Zoe running for the hills, or wherever a sixteen-year-old girl from western Massachusetts would run to escape a wannabe boyfriend regularly imagining plants growing out of his body?

"It's hard to describe," he began. "I've had a couple of these . . . episodes where plants seem to be growing out of my hands." He wiggled his fingers at her.

"Wow," Zoe slowed down. "That's pretty intense. Are they, like, hallucinations?"

"I guess so. Tomorrow I have another meeting with Patty—she's the nurse practitioner at Health Services." He looked at Zoe. "It's not that big a deal."

"Sounds like a pretty big deal to me. And scary."

He didn't want her sympathy and would rather talk about anything other than his plant delusions. But he had to know. "Does it scare *you*?"

"Doesn't bother me," Zoe said. "I've got some challenges too, in case you haven't noticed."

"One more thing about the Brooklyn people," he said, glad to change the subject. "They got me started reading books about climate change and species loss, how to fight back. Like this one book, it's like their bible or something. It's pretty amazing and I can't stop thinking about it. It's both terrible and totally right."

"What does it say?"

"That civilization is destroying the planet. They argue for ending corporations and industry and the consumer culture and the greed of the rich. They want no more fossil fuels or production of plastics and other crap. To return to a much simpler lifestyle."

Zoe stopped rolling. "But without technology, a lot of people would die."

"The Green Book people would say that a lot of people are dying now, every day, all around the world."

She put both hands on her hips and frowned at him. "That's easy for you to say, Jeremy. But *I* would die. Without plastic tubing and high-tech devices and medicines, it would be a race to see if hydrocephalus or kidney failure got me first. Did you think about that, Mr. Save-the-world?"

Zoe spun her wheelchair around and wheeled away toward the park entrance. Her hair streamed behind her, and he remembered how her hair flew around when she danced, how it curled around his fingers as if it belonged there.

What just happened? He watched her dash down the sidewalk. Should he run after her? Had he ruined everything?

"Zoe," he called. "Come back."

"Leave me alone."

Why couldn't he get this stuff right? He tried to console himself; at least now he had something to discuss with Patty the next day besides vegetable matter growing out of his fingertips.

~~∽~~

The gazebo was exactly the way Sam imagined it. The copper green roof rose to a central peak like a circus tent. Between wooden upright beams, the room was open on all sides to the hillside, the woods and river. Shrubs growing just outside sent branches twisting around the beams and climbing to the ceiling with the fuzz of tender new leaves along their length.

He sat on the bench facing the water and thought about Charlie. Would the truth make a difference? He'd always known that his mother told lies. Exaggerated, if you were inclined to soften the language. But somewhere the truth existed: either Brad was his biologic father or Charlie was. He told himself not to care. Brad did all those dad-things and Sam loved him. Why should it matter whose sperm it was?

Sometimes there's a moment when a person changes their mind about something, after teetering on the precipice of a realization or an acceptance. After days or weeks of not knowing, a time comes when we tip over the edge into knowing. That's what the moment felt like to Sam, when he knew that Charlie was his father.

A mockingbird's chatter broke the silence and something—an acorn, maybe—fell onto the metal roof with a loud snap. It rolled and bounced and skittered down the slope and then stopped. He wondered if anyone ever cleaned out the gutters, if this structure had gutters. After a few minutes of sitting in the fresh green cocoon, his breathing returned to normal. He could think straight about his mother and knew he would soon lose her.

Ten minutes later he stood up to leave and the movement must have startled a bird, which sprung from the intertwined branches climbing the gazebo walls. It flew in a circle inside the small enclosure, spiraling up and around as if disoriented. At the copper peak, its gray wings fluttered hard, then rippled down like a parachute. In the next instant, the bird turned and flew through the window opening. Sam watched it soar away, dark against the open sky. It was time to return to Flo.

In his mother's room, Mimi sat by the window and the nurse leaned over the bed, listening and touching and measuring and writing numbers on her clipboard, then turned to Sam.

"See how irregular her breathing has become?" the nurse asked. "Those longer spells of apnea, of not breathing, usually mean the patient is beginning to leave us."

"How long?"

"Could be hours, or days. It's impossible to say." She looked at Sam's face and then added, "Probably not today."

"Can she still hear me?" Sam asked.

"I believe so." She turned Flo onto her side, as if preventing bedsores was still critical, then put her hand on Sam's shoulder and squeezed. "Do you need anything?"

He shook his head, unable to speak without spilling over.

The nurse paused in the doorway. "Sometimes," she said, "dying people are waiting for something. Permission. Or forgiveness. Talk to her."

Sam joined Mimi at the window.

"I've been thinking," he said, "about some of Ma's stories. Wondering what's actually true. Like, do you know why she was kicked out of the Communist Party?"

"Not really. It was before she moved up here. Actually I'm not sure if she was booted out, or if she resigned in protest of someone else being purged from the group. She would never tell me the complete story, but it had something to do with interracial dating. She ranted on and on about how misguided the Party was."

"I thought the Party approved of interracial relationships," Sam said.

"Until Black Power. In the late sixties, many groups reversed their position. In particular, black men dating white women was a no-no. It was seen as devaluing black women and undermining race solidarity."

"I don't get it," Sam said. "Why should that get my mom kicked out? Unless."

"Unless she was involved with a Black guy," Mimi said. "It's possible. By the time I met Flo, she was pregnant with you and married to Brad. Of course, she could have resigned as a political statement."

"Being kicked out is more dramatic." He tried to smile. "Ma and her stories. She always had a flexible approach to the truth."

"She *has* imagination," Mimi corrected him, standing up. "We'll probably never know the whole story. I'm going home for a while. I'll be back this evening."

He nodded. "Thanks."

"Talk to her, Sam," Mimi said as she left.

Talk to her. Easy for them to say. When it came to conversation with his mother, Sam always spent a lot more time listening than talking. He pulled the guest chair close to the bed and took her hand. Forgiveness or permission, the nurse had said.

"I'm here, Ma. I love you." He hesitated. "And, if there's anything you want forgiveness for, which I very much doubt, consider yourself forgiven." No, that sounded snotty. "Really," he added, feeling foolish.

The black cat jumped onto the bed. He gazed at Sam for a moment, looking dubious, before curling up against the twin chenille hills of Flo's feet.

"Okay," he told his mother. "I forgive you for being outrageous when I was old enough to be embarrassed by you. For being permissive, when I desperately wanted some rules. For demonstrating that a person didn't have to toe the line, when all I wanted was to find my own line, so I could figure out how not to step over it." His words became whispers and the whispers became wisps of memories and the memories became a kind of peace.

He put his head on her pillow, close to hers. With his free hand, he played a silent lullaby on the pink chenille spread over the small mound of her hip, thinking of a tune she tried to teach him as a boy. He had refused to play the piano, but now he could hear the song in his memory. She moved her head a little, as if she was listening, as if she could hear the melody he would not play.

Permission, he thought. Flo in her life never needed permission from anyone. At least, not in Sam's lifetime. But then, she had never before been in a situation like this. Dire and final.

"It's okay for you to go, Ma," he whispered, then closed his eyes. "Whenever you're ready. I love you."

Twenty minutes later Zoe and Anna found them sleeping that way, heads sharing the pillow, Sam's face burrowing in her hair. His hand rested on his mother's shoulder. The cat slept across Flo's feet.

Zoe wheeled over to scratch behind his ears. "Hey, Boots," she crooned.

At the sound of her voice, Sam's eyes opened and he blinked, then sat up.

"Anything new?" Anna asked.

He shook his head.

"You need a break?"

He shook his head again, then started weeping.

Zoe quickly pushed to his side and hugged him. "Oh, Papa. I'm sorry we left you here alone."

"I'm fine," he said. "It's just harder than I expected."

Anna patted the top of his head. "A failure of imagination on your part, Sam. What do you expect when your mother is dying?"

He visibly cringed at that word, then looked at Zoe. "I thought you were hanging out with Jeremy."

"Yeah, that didn't go so well. He's a jerk," she said, grabbing Anna's canvas bag and pushing her wheelchair out of the room. "My turn to make tea."

Anna sat at the foot of the bed. "I'm so sorry, Sam. How can I help?"

Sam shook his head. How could anyone help? He felt small and alone. He felt cold and couldn't imagine being warm again. If only he and Anna were still together, and he could slip into their bed, be warmed by her skin and the down comforter she used all year round. Until Flo got so sick, he didn't realize how lonesome he was.

~●~

Jeremy couldn't decide what to do with himself. He had planned to spend the day with Zoe. He pictured himself the perfect boyfriend, taking her for a walk to distract her from her grandmother's dying, and then supporting her at the bedside. He liked that image of himself, as the helper instead of the needy one. But somehow—and he wasn't quite sure exactly why or how—all that changed in a few sentences.

He stretched out on his bed and studied the posters on the walls. The odd thing was that he didn't feel much for them beyond a faint nostalgia for a long-ago childhood memory. If he was going to spend the summer in this room, he didn't want to look at Wolverine and Storm and the gang every day. Tim might be upset with him, but Tim lived in Brooklyn so he didn't get to decide.

Carefully, Jeremy pulled the tape from the edges, trying not to tear chunks of paint from the wall. First the group photo, then Cyclops, Storm and the others. Finally, his favorite poster of Wolverine, the one with the rip across his left leg. He made a pile on his bed, then folded the papers in half, in half again and again and again. He carried the mess into the kitchen and shoved it deep into the blue recycling bucket.

When he returned to the room, a text message flashed on his phone. *Can't Skype today*, it read. *Studying for my big econ final.*

Jeremy didn't quite believe him, not after their uncomfortable conversation last week. *Okay*, he texted back. *Good luck with the exam.*

When he stretched out on the bed this time, the bare walls were comforting, like a clean slate. He couldn't remember why he felt such a kinship with those characters in the first place, why the posters mattered so much. Maybe he could talk about that with Patty the next morning. And about Zoe's reaction to a perfectly reasonable intellectual discussion. He felt silly making a mental list of things to discuss with Patty. Silly, but good.

The bedroom door swung open and Tian stuck his head in.

"I thought you were spending the day with that girl."

Jeremy shrugged. "I thought so too. Seems I pissed her off."

"How'd you do that?"

Jeremy glanced at the emotional barometer of his father's wrist, searching for an explanation of the uncharacteristic paternal concern, but there were the same few rubber bands. "I was telling her about this book I've been reading. The authors claim that the only way to reverse global warming and species destruction is to get rid of corporations and big industries and return to a simpler lifestyle."

"Makes sense she'd be angry, given her situation."

Jeremy looked at him.

"I mean, those ideas probably didn't go down too well with your girl," Tian continued, "what with her needing medicines and such for her condition. Right?"

Jeremy was sidetracked for just a moment by Tian's "your girl" comment, then realized how dense he had been, that even Tian would get that about Zoe, when he didn't have a clue. What was wrong with him?

"Yeah," he said. "She got pretty huffy about it."

"Sure she did," Tian said. "She wants her boyfriend to always be thinking about her well-being. So what're you going to do about it?"

Jeremy shrugged. "I dunno."

"Well," Tian said. "I'm clearly no Father Knows Best, but seems to me that you'd better go talk to her."

"Yeah," Jeremy said. "I guess. Tomorrow." Yes, tomorrow. He'd show up at the nursing home and help Zoe with her grandmother, whatever that meant.

Tian nodded. On his way out of the room, he gestured at the bare walls. "Redecorating, I see. Looks good."

Chapter Twenty-Nine

Sam rubbed the sleep from his eyes. It had been a long night. Flo didn't have a roommate and her nurse brought him a blanket and pillow so he could stretch out on the empty bed. Not that it was good sleep, with nurses coming in every couple of hours to check on Flo, change her position, moisten her lips with those lemony swabs. About midnight he persuaded Zoe to go home with Anna, promising that she could come back this morning and skip school.

"Nothing much happens Monday mornings anyway," Zoe had said. And then she'd said something else, something that surprised him, something that Sam had thought about and dreamt about all night, nonstop since the words left his daughter's mouth. "What are you going to do about your father?" Zoe had asked. "About Charlie?"

The thing was this: no matter how many stories his mother had made up over the years, no matter how vehemently she denied it, no matter how he felt or didn't feel about the man who raised him, Sam now simply *knew* that Charlie was his biological father. And that fact changed him, made him different from the guy he was before he knew. He tried to think about the man Charlie, who he was and what his kids were like. Did he even know he had a son named Sam?

What would his life have been like if his birth parents stayed together and they were a family? How would he be different if he grew up as a bi-racial kid, instead of being white? Or passing for white, actually. Assuming that he was white. Who was he, really? Had his whole life been a lie?

He kept thinking about Zoe's statement that everyone holds opposites inside their skin. And he kept asking himself her question: how could he understand his opposites and what was he going to do about Charlie?

~~~

Tim walked out of his morning final exam. He didn't feel good about dissing Jeremy the day before, canceling their weekly Skype visit. He stared at his phone for a few seconds and then touched the icon of Jeremy's face, so similar to his own but somehow more fragile. Or probably he was just imagining that.

"Hey, Tim," Jeremy answered. "How was your exam?"

Tim felt a pang of guilt. Why was his brother so damn nice? "Not too bad. What're you up to?"

"I'm on the bus back to UMass, to meet with this nurse practitioner, she's like a counselor."

"That's good, I guess." Was it? Of course, Jeremy was seriously screwed up about his dying plants. But he'd probably expose those old stories about their family. Tim hated thinking about those days. Luckily, Jeremy and his nurse practitioner were three hours away, and not likely to get in his face.

But brotherly concern wasn't the whole story about why he called. He'd had another visit from the two cops and promised to pass on information to Jeremy.

"Listen, bro. Sorry to be the bearer of bad news," Tim said. "But I thought you'd want to know the latest. Your two buddies refused to testify in front of the grand jury. They're in jail until they sing."

"Shoot," Jeremy said. "That's awful."

Was it? Tim wasn't sure. Did those guys really firebomb the office of some company, just because they didn't like their product? He could just imagine what his professors in the business school would say about *that*. Tim wanted no part of Jeremy's buddies or their politics.

Jeremy's voice broke into his thoughts. "Gotta go. I'm getting a text from school, something about a job offer."

"Okay," Tim said. "Just wanted to tell you I'm coming home for a few days. Bye."

～～

The text wasn't really from his school, though Alice did work at UMass. And it wasn't technically a job offer either, but it could possibly turn into one, if Jeremy was really lucky. He wasn't sure why he was grateful for an excuse to get off the phone with Tim, but he was. And why was Tim coming home?

How R U doing? Alice wrote. *Can we talk?*

What's up? he answered.

U feeling better? Becuz 2 summer jobs came thru.

He couldn't believe she'd hire him after the show he put on at the meeting. *Seriously?* he wrote.

Would need a letter from your doc.

I'll ask her today.

When can U meet?

Noon?

OK. Garden office.

His head spinning, Jeremy put his phone in his pocket. There was way too much going on. He really wanted to get back to Springfield and Zoe. But he needed a job, either at the garden or with Professor Clarke's research. In any case, walking into the permaculture office, the room where the extinct plants last came to him, *that* would be seriously weird.

～～

Waiting for Jeremy to show for his ten o'clock appointment, Patty tried to concentrate on her other patients. But compared to hallucinations and dead babies in remote parks, chlamydia and birth control options were a bit ho-hum. When she was told that Jeremy was waiting for her in an exam room, her heart rate accelerated and she realized she was anxious. If she were to be completely honest with herself, she'd admit that was partly because of his friend Sam.

But she wasn't ready to be quite that honest yet.

"How was your week?" she asked Jeremy.

"A lot going on." He told her about completing the assignments in three of his classes, leaving only two incompletes. Packing up his books and papers and clothes and schlepping it all to his parents' apartment in a major rainstorm.

"Are you still staying at Sam and Zoe's?" There, she said his name and felt her cheeks blaze as she spoke.

Jeremy gave her a surprised look. "No, I've been home with my parents. Sam and Zoe have enough to deal with right now, with Zoe's grandma dying."

"That's Sam's mother?"

Jeremy nodded. "And my dad has been . . . Well, I don't know exactly what he's been, except that he's different."

"Different how?"

"Acting more like a dad. You know, like he's concerned about me." He laughed. "Too much, sometimes. He's obsessed with these FBI agents who keep bugging me. Says they'll keep hassling me until I give them what they want."

"Which is?"

"Names, I guess. Information I don't have."

"And that's good, about your dad?"

"Yeah, I think so. Not about his FBI obsession, but that he's different." He shook his head. "But the thing I want to talk about is the hallucinations. Because Alice—she's the manager at the permaculture garden, the one who . . ."

"I remember Alice," Patty said. "She's the one who drove you here in a wheeled desk chair."

Jeremy rolled his eyes. "Yeah. She said there might be a summer job for me, if you tell them I'm stable enough to work."

"Are you?" Patty asked.

"You tell me." He shrugged. "Because I have no idea. Since I don't know what these episodes are, or why I get them."

"Let's talk about that. Your tests—the CT scan and the blood work—were all normal."

"So I can't blame everything on a brain tumor, huh?"

"Nope."

"I've been thinking." Jeremy spoke slowly, not sure what he wanted to say. "I'm not so sure that the, episodes, or whatever you want to call them, are so awful."

"What do you mean?"

"Just that having plants grow out of my body—or my mind, I guess—it's as if my imagination rescues them from extinction and brings them back to life. Sometimes there are even flowers and they're so pretty that I can't stand it." He hesitated. "Maybe these make-believe plants are an essential part of me, like drawing and caring about extinct species and being generally kind of a nerd. They could be a gift, not a disease, a gift from the plants because I know their names. Maybe I don't need to get rid of them, just have to learn how to control when it happens. And not be scared."

"What would that mean?"

"I don't know. And maybe I'm all wrong." This was nuts; didn't he want to get rid of these . . . these episodes? "Anyway, would you write me that note?"

"Is that what you want to do this summer?" Patty asked. "Come back to campus and work in the permaculture garden?"

Good question. That's what he *had* wanted, a few weeks ago.

"Or maybe on a research project one of my profs is running. I'm not sure," he said. "But if you write the note, I have the option."

She pulled a prescription pad from her pocket and scribbled a few lines. She ripped the page off, and handed it to him.

"I think you are stable enough to work," Alice said. "But at some point you are going to have to deal with these extinct plants growing from your body. There's a reason for these delusions."

"Maybe they're just illusions instead of delusions," Jeremy said. "And not so bad?"

"Joking about it is fine," Patty said. "But it would help you to learn some strategies, for when it happens again. And, at some point I think you should really go deeper. Talk with someone who has more psych training than me."

"I don't know," Jeremy said. "Maybe."

~~∂꩜~~

The rest of the session flew by. When Jeremy stopped for a sandwich en route to meet Alice, he was still thinking about the possibility that plants sprouting from his fingertips didn't mean he was sick or demented. Brushing crumbs from his jacket, he knocked on the permaculture office door and walked inside. Alice was on the phone at the corner desk. She put a finger to her lips and then pointed to the chairs.

They were still set up in a haphazard circle. Jeremy tried not to remember those mismatched seats filled with people, more students on the floor leaning against backpacks and jackets. He sat on a metal folding chair, perched on the edge of the seat, facing the garden. The low table was empty, all the seedlings now planted outside. There were no vines, no small white flowers with an inner splash of fuchsia blossoming against the glass. He sighed and checked his watch. The next bus for Springfield left in forty minutes.

"Sorry to keep you waiting," Alice said, dragging a chair to face him.

He handed her Patty's note. "No problem. Here's the letter you asked for. She thinks I'm okay to work. But I'm not sure if . . ."

Alice held up her hand. "I can't promise anything, you know. I'll bring this to the Permaculture Garden Board but I've gotta tell you that two Board members were here. That day." She shrugged. "They're probably pretty nervous about you."

"That's okay," he said, leaning forward. "Tell me about the jobs for Professor Clarke."

"I don't know all the details," Alice said. "And there's something odd about the project, some kind of power struggle in Washington about it. This is big—the *ramorum* organism has the potential to kill off more than oaks—redwoods and rhododendron and other related species—as well as impact wildlife and worsen soil erosion. But it seems like a huge nursery corporation tried to hide the disease and spread infected plants all over the place and they've hired lobbyists to convince Congress to freeze the funds. Until they succeed, there are three jobs working here this summer, working with leaf and bark samples from all over the eastern US"

"Wow," Jeremy said. "Guess we need an Assange or Snowden for the plant world."

Alice stood up. "Eventually, the truth will come out," she said. "You can't keep that kind of thing secret forever. And then we'll have to figure out how to respond. In the meantime, I'll take your letter to the Board meeting next week and you should let Professor Clarke know you're interested. I'm rooting for you, whichever job you decide to apply for."

Jeremy stood up too. "I appreciate it," he said. "But I don't know what I want. I'm thinking maybe it would be better to wait until fall, for me to work here."

"Oh?" Alice held the door for him.

"I might get a job in Springfield this summer. My girlfriend is there." He still blushed every time he spoke that word. "And my dad is home now, after being away for ten years."

"Away?"

"He was in prison."

He ignored Alice's stunned expression and waved goodbye. He had never said those words aloud, except to people who already knew, and it felt surprisingly liberating. Well, two-thirds terrifying and one-third liberating.

~⌑~

Flo's room was already crowded when Jeremy arrived. Sam sat on the bedside chair, his fingers looked dark against the pink chenille bedspread. He held Flo's hand, pale with the blue vessels snaking like vines under her skin.

Three women sat side by side on the empty bed by the window. See no evil, hear no evil, speak no evil, Jeremy thought, his brain trying to defuse the tension of the moment. He nodded to Sam and waved to the three women—Zoe's mother Anna, and her aunt or cousin, whatever Emily was. The older woman was Mimi, Flo's best friend. He remembered her from the night before they gave Flo the new medicine, when Zoe brought him to her grandmother's goodbye-to-herself party. Flo had been right about that, after all.

And there was Zoe. Her wheelchair was backed into the narrow space between Flo's bed and the wall. Leaning forward, Zoe rested one shoulder on the bedspread next to her grandmother, her head sharing the pillow. Both women's eyes were closed.

Jeremy stood next to her. If Zoe was sleeping, he didn't want to wake her up. But if she wasn't sleeping, she might be pissed off if he ignored her. How did guys negotiate this stuff? He touched her shoulder.

She opened her eyes. She didn't look surprised to see him and she didn't seem pissed off, either. She pushed herself up into a sitting position in her wheelchair and smiled at Jeremy, a slow, warm sunbeam as if their argument the day before never happened, as if she didn't go storming off down the Forest Park sidewalk looking like she never wanted to see him again.

"Hey," she said.

"Hey," he answered. "How is she?"

Zoe shook her head.

The nurse stepped into the room. "Everything okay in here?"

"She's sleeping," Sam said.

"It's a coma," Zoe corrected him.

The nurse touched her stethoscope to Flo's chest and listened. "Her heart rate is very slow and her breathing is irregular. I don't think it'll be too much longer."

Sam couldn't stand this. He couldn't sit around waiting for his mother to die. He gestured to the three women on the bed. "Let's take a short break. Give the younger generation a few minutes." He leaned over and kissed Flo, resting his lips on her sparse hair for a moment.

He looked at Zoe. This is your last chance, he thought. Say goodbye. "We'll be back in fifteen minutes, Poose. Okay?"

"Poose?" Jeremy asked, when they were alone with Flo.

"Baby nickname. I'll explain some other day." She took Jeremy's hand. "Grandma looks so alone."

"So get close to her," Jeremy said. "Hug her."

Zoe transferred out of her wheelchair and onto the bed. Flo was positioned on her right side and Zoe snuggled close behind her, spooning her grandmother's diminished frame. She breathed with Flo, matching breath for breath. When Flo stopped, Zoe held her breath and counted—one-one thousand, two-one thousand—until Flo gulped another ragged mouthful.

Boots abandoned Flo's feet and curled up against her chest, filling the hollow space next to her bruised ribs. His purr was a roar in the silent room.

Jeremy stroked the cat's back, watching the sparks of static electricity dance between skin and fur. He eased onto the bed at Zoe's feet.

Later, he couldn't be sure if he *made* things begin or just recognized the signs earlier. It started with the familiar tingling in his fingertips and the tremble germinating deep in his flesh. Tender sprouts grew around his muscle fibers and blood vessels, getting ready to burst out. They poked through the skin with a hot pinch of pain and his hands were spring-growing twigs, swelling and pulsing. The shoots opened—they unfurled and stretched into branches and leaves and the beginnings of buds, weaving in and out through his fingers and twining tight around his wrists and then sprinting across the space to Zoe and Flo. He had a brief flash of worry—could his plants harm other people?—but he immediately knew that wasn't the case. As the leaves grew thicker and the buds swelled, Jeremy directed the vines, with just the slightest mental nudge, to knit a green embrace around the three of them.

He glanced at Zoe. She was hugging Flo, speaking softly into her ear. She couldn't see the vines, could she? What would she think of him now?

And then the buds swelled and burst into flower and he stopped worrying about what anyone else thought. The blooms were large and spiky and deep red—red, of course, because Flo loved the color red. He knew this plant. It was *Blutaparon rigidum*, from the Galápagos Islands, only extinct a few years. The heavy blossoms covered the three of them and it was perfect and lush and comforting. More Latin names came spilling from his mouth into the warm air above the bed. "*Neisosperma brownii*," he whispered. "*Campomanesia lundiana*." There were more flowers too—different flowers from his favorite extinct species all growing together in one extended family of green—the rusty red lace of *Vanvoorstia bennettiana* and the ruby-gulleted white trumpets of *Nesiota elliptica*. His brain was the loom and their bodies the warp and the plants the weft, their supple stems weaving in and out around three waists and thirty fingers and six soft shoulders.

For a short moment, oak branches appeared with red oozing lesions on the bark. There were brittle leaves and crinkled brown around the edges. No! He would not let that happen, oak trees would *not* join this pageant of extinction. He banished the image and they were gone. Sibilant Latin names sang above them, music to accompany the shroud of scarlet and white and rusty blooms and shiny green leaves. "*Argyroxiphium virescens*," he chanted. "*Thismia americana*."

When he finished speaking names, Zoe opened her eyes. "That was beautiful. Thank you," she said. Then he thought her heard her say, "I love you" before burrowing her face into her grandmother's hair.

He rested his cheek against Zoe's sweater. He wasn't clear about what Zoe saw or if he heard her right, but he couldn't remember ever feeling this peaceful, this unafraid.

"The plants," Zoe whispered. "Are they here?"

He whispered too. "Yes."

"Maybe they're your mutant superpower," Zoe said. Her breath sent ripples into the red petals of a *Blutaparon* blossom entwined in the gray nest of Flo's hair.

His thoughts returned to leaves and branches and he wove a basket of plants living and plants gone, big enough for the three of them. Padded with clouds, swinging from stars, rocking with some half heard melody, a kinship of white trumpets and clover. There was comfort in the motion and the music and the Latin names. The calm might disappear any minute in a slammed door or angry voice. It might be psychotic or marauding brain cells gone amuck, but for now, for this moment, the world was aligned and it all made sense and was better than good.

Chapter Thirty

Zoe was the one who insisted they sit shiva.

"You know what Flo would say about that, don't you?" Sam had commented.

Zoe laughed. "Do I ever! But this won't be a religious thing. No prayers or ripped clothing or covered mirrors. Nothing solemn at all. Just remembering her and telling stories."

Balancing a plate of cookies on her lap, Zoe wheeled to the threshold of the living room and hesitated. Mimi and the other old ladies huddled on the sofa with one of grandma's old photo albums. Her dad sat with Anna and Emily and Pippa and Gabe in front of the bay window. Where should she put the cookies?

Gabe didn't wait for her decision. He scooped up the plate and stuffed a cookie in his mouth. "I'm starved."

His mother finessed the tray from his control and set it on the coffee table. "Behave yourself," Pippa said.

"Flo would have said he was behaving totally appropriately," Mimi said, looking up from the photo album. "What's that quote she loved, about well-behaved women rarely making history?"

"Well, Gabe's a kid, not a woman. Besides, Flo romanticized bad behavior, among other things," Fanny muttered, reaching for a cookie.

Claire laughed. "Our Flo was full of contradictions. She loved the idea of Party discipline but she refused to toe the line."

"*Any* line," Marlene said with a laugh.

"Speaking of lines," Mimi said, pointing to a photo. "Remember this picket? Boycott grapes or something, I think. Flo gave an amazing speech at that rally about needing dancing in her revolution."

"Thought she was Emma Goldman," Fanny muttered.

Mimi elbowed her. "Stop being such an old prune. You miss her just as much as the rest of us."

"I do," Fanny admitted. "She was spectacular. And so damn annoying."

The four women laughed. "One of a kind."

Mimi closed the photo album. "Flo had a dozen of these," she asked Sam. "Where are the rest?"

"The fire," Sam said. "The only reason this one is here is that I've been scanning her photos into a digital file, one album at a time." He called into the hallway. "Jeremy, are you done?" He turned back to the women. "He's finishing up the slide show."

Jeremy set the laptop on the bookcase. Anna moved furniture so everyone could see—the four older women squished together on the sofa, Anna, Emily, and Pippa on chairs in front of the window, and Gabe on the floor, leaning against his mother's knees.

Jeremy pulled a footstool next to Zoe's wheelchair. He wiped a tear from her cheek and tried to think of what to say, how to comfort her. Then his phone buzzed in his pocket. He read the text from Alice and clicked on the link she sent.

"Look at this." He handed the phone to Zoe. A headline on the front page of the *Times* posed The End of the Oak Tree?

They both scanned the story. "Sounds really bad," Zoe said.

"For forest diversity, for the whole ecosystem."

Zoe touched his lips and pointed to her father, standing next to the computer.

"These images are in more or less chronological order," Sam said. "But I have very few photos of Ma before she moved to Springfield."

The group erupted into laughter at a snapshot of a pre-pubescent Flo in a school play, tied to a cardboard stake as a fan rippled red tissue paper flames.

"Flo as Joan of Arc," Mimi said. "I love it."

The group was quiet as they watched Flo play blurry field hockey, graduate high school, and march for civil rights in front of the Capitol. Then a black and white newspaper photo filled the small screen, grainy and dark. A group of African-Americans carrying picket signs stood in front of an old-style roller coaster.

"Who're they?" Marlene asked.

Sam stopped the slide show and pointed. "In high school, Mom was involved in picketing to integrate this amusement park in Maryland. Glen Echo. The guy on the left is named Charlie. My mother loved him. I'm pretty sure he's my father."

Nobody spoke. After a few moments, Sam continued. "I found Charlie online and emailed him last night. To tell him that Flo died." He let the silence deepen before adding. "I haven't heard back. But if he's willing, I'd like to meet him."

"Oh, Sam. That's so huge," Anna said.

He nodded. "I'm kind of getting used to the idea. I'm intrigued to meet this guy." He pressed Play. As the slideshow resumed, he stood behind Zoe and Jeremy, one hand on each of them. Connected that way, the three of them watched Flo's life flash across the small screen, four seconds at a time. Flo pregnant, beaming at the camera. Sam in a baby carrier on Flo's chest as she marched on the Pentagon.

"That was *our* war," Claire said.

"Flo would say that it's all the same war," Mimi corrected. "Never-ending."

Sam watched the slideshow, trying to recover his life from the old images. Ice skating as a toddler at the rink in Forest Park. A rare vacation with Flo and Brad in Florida. He smiled, remembering how much Flo hated Disney World. She called Mickey Mouse a traitor to his species.

He turned to Zoe. "You asked if I wanted to meet Charlie. That got me thinking about it. So thank you."

"Wait and thank me if it works out," Zoe said. "It could be pretty weird."

"Jeremy, here's another thing that's weird," Sam said. "I invited Patty to stop by for supper. I hope you don't mind."

"Jeremy's therapist Patty?" Zoe asked.

"Nurse practitioner, actually," Sam corrected him. "She and I have been emailing, and talking on the phone. I like her."

"Just don't talk about *me*," Jeremy said.

"Promise." Sam grinned and went to sit with Anna and Emily.

"Is that too weird?" Zoe asked. "Having Sam date your therapist?"

"I guess not. Patty's cool."

"So will you stay for supper too?"

"Can't. I promised my folks I'd be home. Tim finished his finals and is coming home for a few days. Talk about weird."

"That's great," Zoe said. She took his hand. "So what are you going to do about the oak trees? Or are you going to run off to Vermont and join that off-the-grid group?"

How did *she* know about that? He smiled to himself. "Nah. I'm going to switch my major to sustainability studies. Try to work with Professor Clarke to save the oaks." He paused before adding, "I've asked the radio station if I can have my show back."

"Really?"

He nodded.

"Flo would be proud of you," Zoe whispered.

Jeremy rested his face on her head. He breathed in the marzipan smell of her shampoo. It didn't matter if Patty talked about him to Sam because he had nothing to hide. He twirled a long curl of Zoe's hair around his finger. The faint echo of Latin names danced in his ears and green shoots shimmered beneath his skin. Dormant and waiting.